TO
CATCH A
STORM

Also by Mindy Mejia

The Dragon Keeper
Everything You Want Me to Be
Leave No Trace
Strike Me Down

TO
CATCH A
STORM

A NOVEL

MINDY MEJIA

Atlantic Monthly Press
New York

For my dad, who taught me to meet the world
with hard work, spreadsheets, integrity, and laughter,
and that god's country is found in Iowa.

Thursday

We try to connect. We try to find truth. We dream and we hope.
And underneath all of these strivings, we are haunted by
the suspicion that what we see and understand of the world
is only a tiny piece of the whole.

—Alan Lightman

Eve

Twenty thousand feet in the air, I flew between the storm and the sun. Beneath the plane, a steely blanket of nimbostratus clouds covered the Earth. I'd been making passes through this system for hours while two PhD students hunched over equipment stations, single-mindedly collecting data to complete their research. The way this massive rainstorm was progressing, we might be the only people in Iowa to see the sun today. I watched the fiery orange sunrise crest the horizon and enjoyed it on behalf of everyone in the state.

I should have been worried about the implications of this supercell. A cold front was moving in from the north, which spelled imminent disaster for life on the ground, but it hadn't touched me yet. At this altitude, whether I was skipping over cirrus wisps or circling the mouth of a cyclone, there was nothing but calm. Here, I was above the weather.

"Dr. Roth?" One of my students approached the cockpit. "There's a strange readout from the airport station. Can you take a look?"

"Sure. I've already obtained landing clearance. Why don't you start taking us down?"

He slid into the copilot chair, clearly thrilled by the chance to log more air time, and I lingered for an extra minute, making sure he readied our descent correctly. The plane was my baby, a $3.2 million mobile air lab. Every instrument and panel lining the wings and cabin was custom designed to study atmospheric physics: sonic anemometers, cloud particle imagers, and electromagnetic lightning sensors. There was no storm this plane couldn't dissect. When Matthew asked me what I was going to call her, claiming it was unlucky to fly a plane with no name, I didn't hesitate.

"Joan."

His face had clouded for an instant before getting the joke. "Jett?"

I'd patted the sleek underbelly of the aircraft. "She's not afraid of a little noise."

In the years since Joan's christening, I'd flown her everywhere from Tornado Alley to the Rockies, soaring over the continent long after drones assumed most of the weather reconnaissance in the field. They could call me old school; I didn't care. I wouldn't give up this view for anything.

I checked the readouts from one of the ground monitoring stations at the Iowa City Municipal Airport. "CO_2, a thermal pocket, approximately eight hundred meters south. It appears to be standard combustion."

"A fire?" Pawan, my other student, moved to verify the reading. "In this cell?"

It didn't seem probable that any kind of fire could survive this storm, but instruments didn't lie. Had something happened at one of the hangars or the terminal building? We checked other nearby stations and Pawan pointed out a corroborating pattern in his own

4

data when a sudden jolt of turbulence almost knocked me out of my seat. We'd descended into the system now. Rain pelted the windows and our visibility dropped to zero, making it instrument-only navigation from here on out.

"Keep it steady," I called to the cockpit, making my way back to the controls, but another violent shift in airflow caught Pawan off guard and he slammed into me, sending both of us into a cabinet and tumbling to the narrow strip of floor.

"Dr. Roth?" Panic lanced the pilot's voice. The instrument panels shook, rattling hurricane-proof glass above our heads. Pawan scrambled up, apologizing as he staggered to avoid collapsing on me a second time. I thumbed him toward one of the seats outfitted with a five-point safety harness and ran through the jerking plane to the cockpit. Strapping in, I took back the controls as we broke through the bottom of the cloud layer, the rolling subdivisions and snaking line of the Iowa River less than two thousand feet below.

The student mumbled apologies into his headset as I lined up our approach. His research on ice crystal formation was excellent, but he was no storm chaser. He wouldn't have made it ten minutes during the expedition to Argentina last summer, where barbed hail, shaped like medieval torture devices, nearly chewed up the plane with us inside it.

I radioed the airport and received the air traffic controller's familiar confirmation. She sounded normal. Gail had worked at the airport for decades and not much rattled her as long as she had a steady supply of coffee and Marlboros, but maybe she didn't know. Maybe the weather station had picked up something the building's smoke alarms hadn't.

"Everything okay down there, Gail?"

"Living the dream, Dr. Roth. Living the American dream. Arrival area's clear for landing."

As I deployed the landing gear, the student next to me inhaled sharply and pointed south.

"There."

A plume of pure black eclipsed the hazy gray morning, narrow at its base and expanding and dispersing as it rose. It wasn't coming from the airport. It billowed behind the woods beyond the runway.

"A ground disturbance," I said as the plane touched down, wheels skidding on the rain-slicked runway. "You can exclude it from your data set."

But the anomaly lingered in my mind as I taxied toward the hangar. Not the pressure-tossed multimillion-dollar airplane or the student who'd floundered thousands of feet above the ground. The black cloud. Everything about it felt wrong, unnatural. It didn't belong in my sky.

As the students downloaded data and performed postflight maintenance, I unlocked one of the hangar cabinets and grabbed my phone. Cellular devices interfered with navigation, and I'd stopped allowing phones onboard altogether after I caught several students texting midflight.

Three messages filled the screen, all from my father-in-law, Earl.

You landed?
Come home when you land.
The police are here.

* * *

Two Iowa City police cruisers were parked in front of our remodeled Victorian when I pulled into the driveway. Normally, my eyes lifted every time I came home, finding the cupola above the master bedroom and the widow's walk cutting across the roof, where weather instruments lined up like crows along a telephone wire. Today, I didn't linger. I jabbed the garage door opener and sped past the house to the detached garage, not pausing until the door lifted and I registered the empty space inside. Earl's van was there, but Matthew's Tesla wasn't. It should have been parked next to his charging station, the "Bob" license plate greeting me like it always did.

"Ross?" I'd guessed, totally confused when he'd bought the custom plates.

Matthew had shaken his head, grinning. "Dylan. He's not afraid to go electric."

Matthew loved his Tesla almost as much as I loved my plane, and he insisted on driving anytime we went somewhere as a family. But where would he have gone now, leaving his father alone with the police? I parked and ran through the downpour toward the back door, where a uniformed officer met me on the porch.

"Where's Earl? Is he all right?"

"He's inside, ma'am. He's fine."

The officer gestured for me to go in first. Earl sat by the kitchen table, his matted hair and hunched shoulders drifting to one side of his wheelchair. A massive stroke had robbed most of his vocal ability, but his good hand lifted when he saw me.

I dropped to a squat next to his chair, pressing his palm between mine. It felt cool, and his good eye looked clear as it focused on me. "Are you okay?"

He nodded. The morning news he normally watched was on in the adjacent family room, and a second police officer stood behind the couch, conferring with his partner in a low voice.

"Where's Matthew?"

The coffee maker on the kitchen counter was off. After seven years of marriage, I knew my husband's habits. He rose with the predictability and energy of the sun, bursting with outsized plans for what could be packed into the waking hours ahead of us—a ten-mile charity bike ride, a gourmet picnic on the banks of the Iowa River, a new video series for his YouTube channel—all while brewing his first caffeine of the morning. Even after the scandal this fall, after I'd told Matthew to move his things to the other end of the hall, I still woke almost every morning to the comforting whirr of the coffee grinder. Today, like his garage space, the pot was empty.

"That's why we're here, ma'am." One of the officers moved closer. "We're looking for your husband."

Earl nodded at the table, where a Post-it note lay next to his iPad, scrawled with Matthew's handwriting.

Checking data on the grant before submission deadline. Back by 9.

It was 9:21. I texted Matthew from the airport after I'd gotten Earl's messages, but he hadn't replied.

"Do you know what time he left this morning?" the officer asked.

I stood up, trying to process the note. "No. I had a flight scheduled for six and was at the hangar by a little after five."

I told them what I could as my mind raced, trying to understand why Matthew would've gone to the university this morning.

8

He wasn't teaching this semester, and though he still oversaw one of his major grant projects, he always made sure to work around my schedule. Earl had lived with us for almost two years since his stroke, and we never left him alone. He could manage small transitions between his bed and the toilet with his walker, but someone had to be nearby to supervise and assist if needed.

I'd told both Matthew and Earl at dinner last night about my flight plan and that I planned to head straight to campus afterward. This was the last week of classes in the semester, and every hour was tightly scheduled. Squeezing the flight in this morning had been a challenge. Matthew knew I'd be gone all day. Why would he leave his father?

The officers asked more questions, some mundane, some bizarre, as the morning news played in the background. They wanted to know the last time I'd seen Matthew, how long he'd driven his Tesla, and whether we'd had any break-ins recently. I gave choppy, distracted replies as I called and texted Matthew. Where are you? The police are here.

"Why are you looking for him? What happened?"

They didn't answer immediately and a sick feeling began spreading in the pit of my stomach. Earl grunted, twisting in his chair.

"What is it?"

He jabbed a finger at the television.

A fireball erupted on the screen, brilliant oranges and reds coughing thick black smoke into the sky. It was so bright I couldn't see what was burning at first, just the fire itself, which filled the entire living room wall. Matthew had bought this TV. It was enormous, high definition, the kind of screen that made it feel like you could smell the stench of combustion and feel the heat of the flames. The shot panned out, becoming less grainy, until there it was—the black cloud, the anomaly we'd identified in the storm.

The clip ended and the news cut to a reporter standing in front of the shell of a burnt-out car. Earl grunted again, quieter this time.

"Ma'am?" The officer lifted his hat toward the screen. I didn't understand until he added, "That's why we're here."

A caption underneath the reporter's face read, ELECTRIC VEHICLE BURNS IN IOWA CITY RAINSTORM, and finally the car itself came into focus, the charred outline forming a silhouette I instantly recognized. On the bumper, the letters were scorched, blackened but still legible.

The cloud descended, blurring my vision, filling my lungs. My entire body shook as I stared at the license plate on the screen.

Bob.

It was Matthew's car.

Eve

After the officers left, I kept trying to reach Matthew. All my calls went straight to voice mail. I tried not to panic each time I heard his smooth prerecorded tenor saying he was sorry he'd missed me. Where was he? Why hadn't he called immediately after the accident with his car? Every passing minute presented more questions and less time to answer them: my office hour at the university had already begun. After leaving an abrupt message for a grad student who'd been working with Matthew on his grant project, I packed Earl into the van and raced to campus.

Leave me at the house, Earl texted from the back seat.

"It's not safe for you to be alone. As soon as Matthew gets home, he can pick you up." I tried to sound positive, but the words lacked conviction, drowning in the drum of rain against the van. We didn't know when Matthew would come home. We had a daunting lack of data.

The line outside my office door was double the size I expected. Marine biology, computer science, and anxious premed majors sat along the wall, phones in hand, as if camping out for tickets to a concert none of them wanted to attend. The first students in line jumped to their feet when I appeared, but one glance at the wheel-chair I was muscling through the hallway halted their backpacks in midshrug.

"Two minutes, please," I called as we wheeled past. "And I promise to bear enough potential energy to convert all your queries into comfort."

A few of them looked sick. I understood how they felt.

I wanted to run straight to the biology building and find my best friend, Natalia Flores. Natalia would invite Earl into her office with a smile and a wave of manicured fingernails, entertaining him with stories about nights in Santa Cruz de la Sierra. And as soon as classes were over, she'd show up at the house with a bottle of cab sauv, a sectioned map of Iowa City, and a detailed plan to find Matthew. But Natalia wasn't on campus—or even in the state. She was finishing a semester abroad in Costa Rica with a troupe of biochemistry students, and I had no guide for what to do next. Should I start calling hospitals?

Swallowing another wave of anxiety, I pushed Earl to the ad-ministrative office and the maze of hand-me-down desks belonging to the TAs.

Because I was the only physics professor at the University of Iowa who wore lipstick and Stella McCartney platform sneakers, most of the teaching assistants fell into one of two categories: they either thought I was cool and went overboard in displays of knowl-edge and work ethic, or they snubbed me for my *serious* male col-leagues who spent their careers submerged in thought experiments about the milliseconds after the big bang. My work in atmospheric physics, predicting the trajectory and severity of storms and the meteorological effects of climate change on our pedestrian little planet, was—to some—merely cute.

Normally I didn't care about TA opinions, but today I needed a fan. Pawan had gone straight to campus from the airfield, and I found him hunched over his desk analyzing the data he'd collected from our flight. He'd studied under me for three years now and had attended every backyard Hawkeye preparty Matthew had thrown, dressed religiously in black and gold. The two had spent hours drinking beer and talking sports—or whatever men did to prepare themselves to watch football games—and when Matthew bought the Tesla, Pawan had examined every inch of the machine, laughed at its name, and even helped wire solar panels for the garage.

He was also one of the only TAs brave enough to say anything to me after Matthew was suspended this fall. Everyone else on campus fell suspiciously quiet the minute I walked into a room, but Pawan had asked if there was anything he could do. I'd said no at the time. Professionally, there was nothing to do except wait. An administrative panel had been formed to investigate the allegations regarding Matthew's behavior and decide whether to let him continue teaching. Now, though, I needed help.

I parked the wheelchair by his desk. "Pawan Mishra, meet Earl Moore."

Pawan gave a hesitant wave. I explained, "He's Professor Moore's father. Would you mind keeping him company during my classes this morning?" Earl had his iPad and was addicted to Candy Crush, even though he closed the app and denied it whenever I caught him playing. I hoped games would be enough to distract him, at least for a few hours.

"Yes, of course." Pawan's hands worked nervously, as though rubbing nonexistent lotion into his palms. "Did Professor Moore, uh, is he . . . ?"

"We don't know where he is." It was the first time I said it out loud, and saying it somehow made it more real. Matthew was missing. The knowledge had been building during the entire walk across campus, where every quad and path teemed with memories. The arched stone doorway of the building housing Matthew's office, dark with rain. The riverbank where we'd exchanged wedding vows, empty. I needed data, not ghosts. I needed to know where Matthew was, and that need ballooned in my chest until I practically vibrated with it.

Two desks down, several TAs gathered around a computer, watching footage of a flaming car. Like a moth, I moved toward it and stared at the licking tongues of fire.

One of the students turned to me, bright with excitement. "Wouldn't it make a great case study for the biophysics lab? How a car can burn in the middle of a rainstorm."

"Oh my god." Pawan covered his mouth as the camera panned the Tesla silhouette and the license plate came into focus. The other TAs fell silent, looking from my face to Pawan's, their excitement paling as they realized this was about more than an academic experiment. Earl wheeled himself to my other side.

"Was"—Pawan swallowed, fumbling for a discreet word—"uh, anyone, in the car?"

"No."

The officers had assured us no one was inside, but they also said all the windows had been lowered, which meant the rain would have soaked the interior and made it even less likely for a fire to catch or grow.

"How did it?" I murmured. Something about the footage seemed off. "Play it again."

We watched the video twice more in silence. The clip was brief, the tail end of a spectacle captured from a distance, but I understood what felt wrong. The fire jumped, flaring erratically in different areas, as if finding pockets of gunpowder like lost change scattered in the seats.

How does a car burn in the middle of a rainstorm?

On purpose.

I don't know how I got through my office hour or the classes that followed. One part of my brain regurgitated a high-level review of Physics 101, moving mechanically from Newton to Einstein's field equations, while the rest of my mind replayed the footage on a loop, trying desperately to figure out what had happened this morning.

Combustion was the simple chemical reaction of a fuel and an oxidant. The oxidant was the easy part—air—but what fuel? It could've been an interior or exterior source and had to burn hot enough to sustain the reaction amid the deluge of cold rain. I cycled through possibility after possibility, playing out each scenario, trying to make the hypothesis fit what I'd seen in the footage and knew of the conditions of the environment and vehicle. When my students raised their hands, I stared at them blankly, seeing a black plume of smoke rise instead of fingers, hearing pops and hisses in place of words.

Matthew always said I became obsessed with questions. Whenever I got an unexpected result, either inside the lab or out, I pored through variables, possibilities, and statistical models, anything I could find that would explain the outlier. He shouldn't have minded. It was why I became interested in him in the first place.

The first time I met Matthew Moore at a University of Iowa networking event for new professors, he'd been the outlier. He looked like a Ken doll in a sea of conservative button-downs with his blond, wavy hair and broad jaw, the rising star of the Chemistry Department. I expected him to drone on about his credentials and publication credits, but he spent the whole evening asking about my research and methodology. He wanted to know what it felt like to look inside a tornado, how the world changed at the edge of the troposphere. I wasn't used to male colleagues showing more interest in my work than their own and when I told him that, he grinned and pushed his hair back to reveal overlarge ears. "I was embarrassed by them as a kid, but my mother said big ears made for exceptional listeners."

"Or that's just how she tricked you into behaving."

He laughed and let his hair fall back into place. "If that's true, it didn't work."

"So you're not an exceptional listener?"

"Not if you asked my father." He leaned in closer, his voice falling beneath the noise of the crowd to a low, warm tone only I could hear. "And he's right. The truth is I only listen to the exceptional."

After the event and fueled by a three-hour open bar, we snuck into a lab in the chemistry building. I sat in front of a Bunsen burner—flame warmed, charmed, and knowing it—as Matthew swirled the contents of a beaker. As he added chemicals, the color changed from clear to purple to deepest blue. He took it off the flame and breathed my name into it, *Eve Roth*, and the substance bloomed into an iridescent ball, filling the beaker and trapping the light of the fire.

"What is it?"

"Essence of Eve."

"No, honestly." I tried to examine the bottles of chemicals, wanting answers, but he coyly moved them aside.

"A magician never tells."

That was Matthew's style: big gestures, few explanations. It should have frustrated me, but we attracted like opposite poles of a magnet. He loved making things appear and watching me put together the pieces: a surprise trip to Paris for our anniversary, a petri dish in the fridge with a question mark taped to it like a dare. When he bought the old Victorian and gutted it, he had me walk through the studs of each room and guess, based on plumbing and electrical, what each space would become. I could almost see him standing by the Tesla as it burned, waiting for me to figure out the puzzle. If I did, would it bring him home?

The black plume kept rising in front of me, an anomaly in the storm. I didn't know whether it was a signal fire or a warning.

Dozens of keyboards clacked furiously throughout the lecture hall. Rain beat against the windows. I struggled through the review questions, trying to keep my voice from breaking, and hoped my shiny platform sneakers, lipstick, and rote relativity quips were enough to keep the facade in place. Earl's face, slack and blotchy with anxiety, swam through the uneven diagrams I drew on the smart board. I hoped he wasn't hungry, or listing too far to one side, or any of the other hundred things he couldn't manage on his own. As long as he didn't need the bathroom—where he wasn't used to navigating the stalls—it would be okay. I kept telling myself that, while a larger, quieter part of my brain clenched against a rising tide of fear. Nothing about this day was okay.

My cell phone vibrated in my pocket. Long, insistent buzzes. I dismissed the class a full ten minutes early without any of my usual end-of-term encouragements and rushed out of the lecture hall as a voice mail notification popped up.

It wasn't Matthew.

The message was from the Iowa City police, asking me to come to the station as soon as possible.

Jonah

The details were slipping away. Sitting in the lobby of the Iowa City Police Department, I jotted notes. Height. Weight. Gender. Skin and hair color. Trying to boil down the fading traces of what I'd seen into the kinds of facts law enforcement would listen to.

I'd gotten here in under forty minutes, burying the speedometer on the back-country roads between Davenport and Iowa City. The speed kept my head clear, helped me focus on exactly what I'd seen. But that was two hours ago now. I'd been waiting on this bench while people shuffled in and out of the station, clouding my head with the wet-dog stink of their fears and irritations. I was losing focus. Losing the details.

I'd seen a man. Average height and build. I wrote down measurements, trying to make the numbers mean something. Winter white, bread-dough skin. Big ears sticking out from his head. Brown hair or maybe dark blond; it was either wet or greasy. The harder I focused on the image, the more it blurred. And when I tried to chase it down, to make the details stay, the drainpipe came instead, the black hole of its mouth yawing open and daring me to crawl inside.

Goddamn it.

I turned up the ambient music on my noise-canceling head-phones and hunched over, folding into myself. The guy next to me slid toward the end of the bench. Away from me. I bit down on the urge to ask him to move farther and drove the heels of my hands into my eye sockets, rocking back and forth. Synthesizer notes rose and twined into each other, filling my head. I tried to relax into them.

"Danica Chase. Angela Garcia." I didn't care who heard me mumbling. "Kit Freeman. George Marcus Morrow."

People I'd found. They were talismans, burning against the force of the others, the ones who stayed lost, who lived in the rot-ting underbelly of the drainpipe. The found were always harder to remember. I had to dig them from forgotten corners, remind myself they were real. Danica, Angela, Kit, George. I repeated their names until the drainpipe faded, and something else came into focus. A detail I hadn't remembered until now.

A ring.

Sitting up, I flipped to a new page and wrote, getting the words out before they disappeared beyond my reach. I had to make them stay.

Craggy fingers rapped my arm, a zip of mustard and impa-tience. I jerked away from the touch and the impressions clinging to it, muscling down the urge to bolt. My head retracted back into the Iowa City police station with its dirty linoleum and rain-pounded windows, this delusion of shared reality.

The guy sitting next to me lifted his palm—*easy, buddy*— and pointed to the other side of the waiting room. The shock of contact sputtered out, leaving the tang of French's mustard in the back of my mouth.

The front desk clerk shot me some narrowed side-eye while she talked to the cop behind the metal detector. Max. He filled the archway with his unironic Captain America stance and gleaming head. He'd given up the fight with a receding hairline years ago. Bald suited him, unlike the sling holding his left arm against his chest. I scanned him for other injuries, but he wasn't giving away any weaknesses. Not to me, not anymore.

Max took me back to one of the interview rooms. Hiding me from the rest of the station, like I hadn't already been sitting in the lobby half the morning. He closed the door and faced the one-way glass. When I took off my headphones, he was already talking.

"—first day back and you know what the captain said to me?"

"Welcome back?" I buried my hands in the pockets of my trench coat, pulling it tight across my shoulders, a physical reminder of where I stopped and everything else started. Most people didn't need to remember their edges, to draw the boundaries of their self on an hourly basis.

"He handed me a case"—he turned around—"and told me Kendrick's out."

"Max—"

"ICPD doesn't work with Jonah Kendrick anymore."

"I get it. I fucked up." I paced the far side of the room, keeping the table between us, not looking at the sling, like that would block the low hum of pain radiating off it and echoing inside me like a tuning fork. "But Celina is still out there. And I saw someone else this morning. A man." I dug the notebook out of my pocket and flipped to the page of details. Male. White.

Blond? I closed my eyes, willing the image back.

Max sighed and there was a long silence. Trace emotions infringed on my concentration, frustration mostly, mixed with pain, anger, and a hint of warmth—the cocktail I'd made of our friendship—but Max knew me well enough to keep his feelings in check. Maybe for my benefit, maybe for his. When he finally spoke, his energy was even, in control, a monolith with a bad arm.

"In a dream."

Sweat dripped down my spine from the effort of holding the image in focus. It was a unique combination of attention and re-laxation, and I hadn't been relaxed in four months. "Yeah. I don't know how he's connected to Celina but—"

"Sometimes it's just a dream."

"I know. But this is real, and it's the first lead we've had since Belgrave."

A whip of emotion at the name. There and gone, but Max's reaction was so sudden it fractured my focus. The image of the blond man wavered.

"Have you been drinking? Off your meds? Are you still sleep-ing in bathtubs?"

I opened my eyes. Sweat-soaked dirty blond hair melted into the sheen of Max's shaved head. I rubbed the heels of my hands into my temples, waiting for the rest of the interview room to return as the words sunk in. It wasn't what he said; it was how he said it, like any cop in any city getting some crackpot tip, not a man talking to a friend he'd known twenty years. Not like Max.

"At least I can sleep," I tried to joke.

Nothing. Not even a hint of a smile. He went for the door and I cut him off, blocking the way out. "What is this?"

"I told you. ICPD doesn't work with Jonah Kendrick."

"I'm sorry, okay? You have no idea how sorry I am, but don't throw this shit at me. I tried calling you this morning—"

"I blocked your number."

I hadn't heard him right. I couldn't have. I didn't know I was moving backward until my boots hit the door.

I hadn't seen Max in six weeks, not since his wife Shelley tossed me out of his hospital room. She was right to do it; she should have kicked me out of their lives years ago, but this wasn't about us. This was a lead and Max never turned down a lead.

"I need this job, Jonah." He spoke to the floor as the fluorescent lights glared off his head. "I've got a family to support. A mortgage. Bills."

"Will you look at this?" I ripped the paper out of my notebook with the description of the man and the ring. "All I need is a name, and I'll be gone."

The interview room door opened, pushing me toward Max. I stumbled into his sling, and a shock of pain ripped through him, echoing in me. He winced but drew himself up when Jon Larsen, ICPD captain of field operations, appeared in the doorway. Larsen was more slab than man, with a ruddy face and a crew cut, the kind of cop who clocked every threat in the room before uttering a word. He looked past me like I didn't exist.

"Everything under control?"

Max jerked his head once. "I'm showing him the door."

"Good." Larsen didn't leave. His gaze narrowed on Max's sling and the sudden whiteness of his face. Larsen was Max's direct superior, but I could feel his concern, his protectiveness. He was the type of person Max needed in his life, someone who would watch his back, someone who was the opposite of me.

They talked about the forecast for a minute and how the department planned to handle the storm. Finally, Larsen acknowledged my existence, and his energy cooled to the temperature of the coming freeze.

"Summerlin doesn't go hunting anymore. Understand?"

Max looked anywhere but at me.

"I've got a tip. About Celina's case."

"We're still processing your last tip." Larsen's energy turned hostile, boring into me. I hunched against the sheer force of it. "I'll let you know when we're open for another one."

Another investigator popped up behind Larsen. "Summerlin, the wife of your new case is in the lobby."

Max pulled me out of the room, past the growing blockade of blue. "On it. Thanks."

Without my headphones, voices swarmed in on all sides. Looks. Whispers. Swirls of suspicion and sneering. As Max dragged me through the hallways, nausea began to build in my gut and my heart raced, pounding against a sudden constriction in my chest. I was off my meds today. I needed to be, to keep the image of the dream clear and recall as many details as I could. But I was naked without the medication, my head a fucking sieve chucked into the middle of the ocean. Sinking, drowning. I couldn't keep the water out.

"Max." I tried to shake his grip, but he'd always been stronger than me. "I can't do this."

I stumbled into a desk, where two officers glared from either side of a wet-haired woman in handcuffs. She sniffed, and the misery and depression clotting that single noise made sweat break out on my forehead. I fumbled with my jacket, hands shaking, desperate for the headphones.

"No." Max got a better hold on my elbow. "Keep the note. If I find it under my windshield wiper, I'll trash it."

"Max, I—" We reached the lobby, and the shaking moved up my arms into my entire body, turning violent, taking over. Emotions swelled and mobbed together, shoving me under their waves. I fell against the desk, and the attendant jerked away from her keyboard with an electric jolt of fear.

Max was still talking but I couldn't make out the words. Everything bled together, white noise on black noise on galloping stabs of heartbeats that grew louder and louder. I was going under. Sweat poured down my face, and I clenched down on the urge to vomit. I needed my headphones, but any movement now was a gamble. As I started sliding off the desk, a cushioned pressure enclosed my ears and the noise stopped. There was a beat of silence before slow-rising ambient chords surrounded me.

I opened my eyes as Max stepped back, his good hand falling to his side. He looked as ball-shriveling ragged as I felt. I wanted to say something—to tell him I understood, that I wouldn't shit all over his life anymore, that he deserved a better friend than I was capable of being, but before I could, he turned away. He was already done with me.

Slowly, the lobby came back into focus. Everyone on the benches stared and at least one person recorded the episode on their phone. Two people waited on the other side of the desk, a woman pushing the wheelchair of a silver-haired man who slumped to one side. A blast of fear rose off them, pure and undiluted. Lowering the hood of her raincoat, the woman measured me with cautious, catlike eyes. The old man's expression sagged like it had been fed halfway into a taffy-pulling machine.

Without warning, the dream returned: A man. White. Blond. Sweat-soaked and trapped. The people at the desk weren't afraid of me. They were afraid for him, the man in the dream.

I pushed myself up. Cold sweat dripped down my neck and spine. As the woman spoke to the front desk attendant, I slipped the note from my pocket into the hand of the man in the wheelchair.

Max

It was a hell of a first day back.

On the way to my desk with the family of my newest case in tow, the eyes of the whole station followed me, furtive glances taking stock. They wouldn't meet my eyes, but they were watching. My arm hurt like a motherfucker. I'd thrown Jonah out on his ass in front of all of them—I made a parade out of it and probably ripped some stitches in the process—and I already knew it wasn't enough. It might never be enough. I could serve on the ICPD for another twenty years and to some of these officers I'd still be Max Summerlin, the guy with a psychic best friend.

"Thanks for coming in so quickly."

I picked up the garbage can by my desk and dropped it with a crash next to Ciseski's, a fellow investigator who spent most his free time jawing in front of the vending machines. *Did'ja hear?* he fished for anyone who would listen. *Did'ja hear how Summerlin really got shot?*

Turning away from the stares, ignoring the shocks of pain stabbing through my arm, I focused on the interview at hand. The woman pushed the wheelchair into the spot where the garbage can had been and sat in the closest chair. She was in her late thirties, white, well-kept, with short, sleek hair the color of lit mahogany and an expensive outfit that could've come straight out of a magazine. I put the man in the wheelchair around eighty. He had a broad, sunken build and wore stained sweats and a Hawkeye hoodie. He'd been rooting around in his pocket for something since I met them in the waiting room but came up empty-handed.

"Have you found Matthew?" the woman asked. "His phone goes straight to voice mail and the voice mailbox is full."

I hadn't even gotten to the station this morning when I landed this case. Larsen texted me a link to the local news story as I was parking, and the assignment was waiting in my inbox as soon as I booted up my computer. I'd been back on active duty for all of three hours, but after dealing with Jonah, I was grateful for the distraction.

A burned-up Tesla on the south side. No witnesses. It wasn't my first car fire. I'd seen plenty of stunts in this college town, most of them fueled by alcohol, drugs, and choices made in the no-man's-land between legal adulthood and fully developed brains. At first glance the incident looked like theft with destruction of property, but the car's owner was nowhere to be found, and someone had managed to set fire to his Model S in the middle of a frigid December rain. That wasn't a stunt; that was determination.

I had to consider the freeway, too. Iowa City sat right on I-80, the transcontinental belt connecting San Francisco to New York. One of the last cases I worked before going out on disability was a fertilizer truck full of Miracle-Gro and opioids. Four million dollars' worth of drugs packed neatly between bags of nitrogen. We might be a postcard skyline blooming between hills of corn, a UNESCO city of literature, but trash blew in off the interstate every day.

"We haven't located Mr. Moore yet, but there was a phone in the car that burned in the fire. Probably his, if you haven't been able to reach him." I sat down across from the missing man's wife and opened a fresh page in my notebook. The paper helped me focus, kept my mind on the case I was working and not the one that sent me out on six weeks of disability with a gunshot wound. "When was the last time you saw him, Mrs. Moore?"

"Roth."

"Ms. Roth, then. When did you last—" The old man grunted and picked up his iPad, jabbing out a message and flashing it at me with more authority than a slumping person in a wheelchair should possess. "Fine. *Dr.* Roth."

She squeezed the old man's arm, giving him a ghost of a smile. "Last night. I left this morning before either Matthew or Earl was awake."

"You're Matthew Moore's father? And you live at the same address?"

The man started typing again as the woman explained. "Helen, Matthew's mother, passed away a few years ago and Earl had a stroke shortly afterward. He's been putting up with us ever since."

The elder Mr. Moore shoved his iPad across my desk.

What are you doing to find my son?

"We'll do everything we can to locate him. Typically, we wouldn't be concerned about a competent adult's whereabouts when he's been gone less than a day, but we treat any citizen as a missing person when circumstances indicate their safety may be at risk."

Dr. Roth leaned over the briefcase in her lap. "Did anyone see the fire start? Do you think Matthew was there when it happened?"

"I'm waiting on the report from the fire department. Let's stick with last night for a minute. Did you notice Matthew acting unusual? Did he seem off in any way?"

They both claimed he'd been quiet at dinner but otherwise normal. He'd left a note for them this morning that he was going to work on some project at the university.

"On campus?"

She gave the name of his building. The Tesla hadn't been anywhere near campus, though. It had burned up in Ryerson's Woods Park, a patch of forest tucked between the fairgrounds and a highway on the south side of town. The park was about as far as you could get from the University of Iowa and still be in city jurisdiction. When I told them that, the wife went quiet, looking down at her hands with an expression I couldn't read.

"I didn't realize . . ."

"Either of you know what he'd be doing out there?"

The old man grunted a negative. The wife didn't answer.

"Is Ryerson's Woods significant to Matthew?"

"He proposed to me there." She lifted her hand, flashing a platinum band with two diamonds hugging a large geometric blue stone.

"Pretty. That a sapphire?"

She nodded. "He made it. He said I should have a ring to match my eyes." Those eyes scanned the top of my desk, darting everywhere, landing on nothing. I didn't have the first clue how someone could make a sapphire. I'd proposed to Shelley with a thousand-dollar solitaire on sale at Greenberg's at the Coral Ridge Mall.

"Do you go back to that park a lot?"

"Not for years. We've both been busy with"—she glanced at her father-in-law and quickly away—"research."

"And this grant he was supposed to be working on, that was part of his research?"

She confirmed, and I had her list as many details as she knew: the project name, sponsor, colleagues, anyone who might have seen Matthew between last night and when his car turned into a bonfire.

"Does he gamble? Have any financial problems?"

"No, we've always been secure, financially." She had some money set aside from her father's life insurance and said Matthew inherited some investments from a close family friend.

"Does he have any enemies?"

They shifted a glance at each other, but neither volunteered any names. I waited until she was done writing down the grant stuff before ripping the Band-Aid all the way off.

"What about Kara Johnson?"

It hadn't taken more than two minutes this morning to find out Matthew Moore—wherever he was—was dirty. One quick Google search turned up ten articles about the disgraced University of Iowa chemistry professor. The story first broke in August, complete with video of Moore exiting an undergrad's apartment in the middle of the night. The footage wasn't explicit, but it showed the two of them wrapped around each other tight enough to suggest the rest. The *Press-Citizen* seethed exploitation outrage and the university immediately placed Moore on administrative leave pending the results of an investigation. When I called the university, they would only confirm the investigation was ongoing.

At the mention of the student's name, Eve Roth's back straightened and a tremor vibrated through her body. "I don't know Kara Johnson."

"But your husband did."

I waited her out, cocking an eyebrow until she became uncomfortable enough to elaborate. "Matthew said it wasn't an inappropriate relationship, that he was simply offering comfort to a student who was going through a hard time."

I noted the disclaimer: *Matthew said.*

"Are they still in contact?"

"No, not that I know of." But she didn't seem sure about that. I leaned back in my chair, considering Dr. Eve Roth, as Ciseski went to take his second morning pass at the vending machine.

After fifteen years on the force and five years of dream chasing with Jonah before that, I'd learned there were two truths in every story. I'd gotten good at putting the first kind in the computer, disjointed facts that told you nothing beyond the necessary fields of an incident report. Those truths led to arrests, records, and verdicts. The second kind was harder to know. It hid underneath the surface of things, clotting up motives and memories, the kind of truth that didn't have a time line or any witnesses to verify it. Like Jonah.

It was hard to describe the friendship I had with Jonah, the purpose we'd carved in each other, or the reason I'd left work six weeks ago with two working arms, gone out with my increasingly unhinged friend, and returned with a gunshot wound. I'd filled out the disability claim with clipped sentences, all of them accurate and none of them even touching the truth of that day. I told the truth that would fit on the form.

The story of Matthew Moore, at least the one I could enter in his missing person case file, was becoming clearer. A man with a history of "not inappropriate" relationships with women outside his marriage told his father and wife he was going to work this morning and went to a remote park instead, where his car got torched in the middle of a downpour.

There was a chance, when I first picked up the case, that Matthew Moore might have reported the car stolen, that he hadn't been involved in what happened out at Ryerson's Woods. But I'd had this case for hours now, past the window for a Tesla owner to storm into the station in a space-Karen rage. He'd lied about where he was going, maybe to cheat on his wife again, and something went sideways with the sidepiece. Or maybe the wife had had enough.

Underneath the designer briefcase and styled hair, beneath the story of the worried spouse and caring daughter-in-law could be another truth entirely: a woman with a strong motive.

"Dr. Roth, when I checked the university directory, it said your research interests include atmospheric and environmental physics."

"That's correct."

"Seems like you'd know how to burn something up in the middle of a forty-degree downpour."

She exhaled, long and steady, and stared at that rock on her hand. "It's a question of thermodynamics, the heat of the fire versus the cold of the water. Generally, the water will either absorb enough heat or suffocate the fire to put it out, but that didn't happen here, at least not before the combustion consumed all available fuel."

"Come again?"

"There must have been an accelerant." She seemed to be talking more to herself than me.

"What kind of accelerant?" My inbox notification flashed. The crime scene report on the vehicle had come in.

She shook her head and blinked, looking up. "That's what I hoped you could tell us."

I flipped my notebook shut, giving them the usual assurances that I'd let them know about any developments. After walking them out, I pulled up the crime scene report. No surprise, the technicians determined it was arson. Someone had filled part of the interior and area surrounding Matthew Moore's car with an unidentified substance—an accelerant—that turned the vehicle into an eighty-thousand-dollar pile of scrap metal, at the same park where Eve Roth's cheating husband had proposed to her.

It wasn't a truth that fit in the report, not yet, but I was just getting started.

Eve

The Ryerson's Woods parking lot was flooded. Rain pummeled my jacket hood as I stood next to the van. Snowbanks, piled high from the plows, encircled the lot, leaving the water with nowhere to drain. The sewers were blocked with packed snow. The rain was trapped, drowning a world that couldn't absorb it.

I don't know what I expected to find here—police tape, a barricade, officers scouring the area for some trace of Matthew—but there was nothing. Except for us, the lot was empty. An oblong scorch mark marred the pavement in one spot, and even that was rapidly disappearing beneath the storm.

"Don't get out."

Earl grunted from the back seat.

"I'm serious. I'll be right back."

I waded to the mark and scraped the best sample I could. It was black, sooty, and smelled faintly of garlic. There was something familiar about it, but I couldn't place what. Capping the specimen vial, I paced the edges of the rising water, searching for more evidence, anything the police might have missed. My hands shook, not from the cold or the rain. They trembled with absence, the inability to grab on to something and hold fast.

What had Matthew been doing here? His grant research focused on trace contaminants in pharmaceuticals. It was possible he'd been collecting biological samples but unlikely. Even during a rainstorm, nothing bloomed or grew in Iowa in December. Bare tree limbs hung dark and sodden at the edge of the woods.

I slogged back to the place where the Tesla had burned and pulled more vials out of my pocket. I would take a dozen samples. A hundred. There could be trace particles in the residue, something to study. Something was always better than nothing, and if the police wouldn't look, I would, for as long as it took to find Matthew.

On the way home, Earl texted from the back of the van. Was it hard being at the station?

"It doesn't feel like they're doing anything." I'd hoped Investigator Summerlin had located Matthew or at least gathered enough data to form a working hypothesis. Instead, he'd spent the whole time questioning us, as though witness testimony wasn't the least reliable and most subjective source of information. Why weren't they checking CCTV cameras or combing the area? I should've asked him more, pressed him harder to do his job.

I meant on account of your dad.

We hit a pool of standing water and hydroplaned. I gripped the wheel, getting the vehicle under control before admitting, "It was harder than I thought it would be."

I'd only been inside a police station once before today, and all I remembered of the first time was sitting in a chair trying to contain my wriggling little brother while my mother talked to men in brown hats and uniforms. I was nine. I'd stared at the door they'd walked through, hoping beyond hope that my father was back there and when they came out he'd be with them, smiling and tilting one palm the way he always did to invite me to walk the fields with him. Before the monster came and took him away.

That morning my mom had stood at the window staring at the green sky, while the weather radio played in the background. I'd thought the color was funny, pointing it out to my brother, who wouldn't have cared if the sky were striped purple and pink. But when the wind ripped the sheets off the clothesline and the radio said the word "tornado" I didn't think it was funny anymore.

Mom took us around back to the root cellar as the wind turned our clothes into sails that tried to lift us from the ground. We huddled in the cellar, squeezing my brother between us as he held his ears and screamed.

The tornado drowned him out, shrieking louder and scarier than anything I'd heard. The whole room vibrated, shaking dirt out of the walls onto our heads. And when the house shook and crashed above us, I thought how awful my dad was going to feel that we died without him. How terrible it would be for him if the monster took us. It never occurred to me that he could be the one taken.

Afterward, we found his tractor lying on its side halfway down an embankment. His lunch pail was discovered by a search party two miles away, in the upper branches of an unscathed white ash tree. The police came out to the house a few times, talking to Mom and patting her shoulder before they left, as if we wanted sympathy instead of information. As if we could be made whole again, one platitude at a time.

The Iowa City police station was probably different than the county sheriff's office. Thirty years of technology and social evolution separated the two buildings, but I couldn't have identified a single difference. All I'd known then was that my father had disappeared. Now, another police station, another person gone. But I wasn't nine years old this time, and Matthew hadn't disappeared. He was out there somewhere, and Earl and I were going to find him.

The house was dark when we got back. No messages on the landline. My cereal bowl was still in the sink, an almond milk ring congealing at the bottom. I checked the garage, the guest bedroom, the basement, Matthew's closet in the master bedroom, and even the cupola to see if he'd left me a note taped to my computer monitor—some hint of why he'd gone to the woods this morning, but there was nothing. The investigator said his phone had burned in the car, so there was no point trying to call him. I went back downstairs.

Earl still sat at the front door, looking through the glass with his hands limp and open in his lap, and my heart twisted. I'd spent countless hours watching for my dad, squinting at the horizon for any hint of movement. Was it worse to be a child waiting for a missing parent or the parent waiting for news of his child?

I'd always loved the relationship between Matthew and Earl, had even felt jealous of their easy, unspoken bond, until I commented on it one day after our wedding and Matthew had scoffed.

"Nothing I did as a kid was ever right. He said I was too loud, too greedy. He never understood why I wanted more for my life than what he'd given me."

"That can't be true." Earl was a taciturn man, but he spoke every word with deliberation and care. I couldn't imagine him berating his young son.

Matthew told me he spent more time at Sam and Bella's house—their doting, childless neighbors—than his own, especially as a teenager. "My dad has never said he was proud of me, not when I graduated college, not when I landed the associate professor job. He never approved of a single choice I made, until I met you."

I flushed, caught off guard. "Me?"

The corner of his mouth turned up, creasing into the laugh lines I adored as he stroked a finger along my jaw. "The day after they met you, they called and we must've talked for a half an hour. That is, Mom and I talked. Dad didn't say a word until right before we hung up. And then all he said was, 'She's the one. Don't screw it up.'"

I blushed harder, embarrassed even as my heart filled with sudden emotion for my new father-in-law. Over the years it became our private joke. If we argued over which restaurant to go to, I'd say, "Hey, don't screw this up." Whenever Matthew saw the amount of storm damage I'd inflicted on the plane, I'd wrap my arms around his waist and grin. "I'm the one, remember?"

I watched Matthew and Earl more closely after that, noting every time Earl clapped his son on the shoulder or nodded to something Matthew said. Maybe he didn't use the words Matthew wanted to hear, but the love was there—measurable and real. I felt it every time Earl talked to me about cloud formations. He'd squint at billows of stratocumulus drifting through the sky. "Cotton candy day." Whistle at long, snaking lines of stratus. "Witches' fingers. They good?"

"Always," I agreed.

Now, the nimbostratus clouds were a gray and oppressive silhouette to Earl's listing form as he stared silently into the rain. I crossed the foyer and squatted next to the wheelchair, touching the papery skin of his bad arm. His jaw trembled and he started blinking rapidly. Shuffling the iPad around in his lap, he managed to lean it toward me.

Did Matthew cheat on you?

I pulled back. Earl had seen the news stories. He knew Matthew wasn't teaching this semester, but I had no idea what kind of conversations the two of them had. Earl and I had never spoken a word about it to each other, until now.

I'd first heard the name Kara Johnson from Matthew himself, before the fall semester began. He'd told me he was meeting a student for coffee and I never questioned it. Matthew regularly orchestrated chemistry happy hours, pop-up experiments, and lab contests. He invited hundreds of students and faculty to our backyard barbecues every weekend during football season. He loved being immersed in campus life and thrived on the constant interaction. Kara Johnson had been just another appointment on his endless list of engagements. I hadn't thought twice about her until the cell phone video surfaced, airing on the local news.

The video showed Matthew emerging from her apartment, disheveled and shrugging into his coat. Kara—an undergrad with tattoos snaking up her shoulder and neck—had touched his face and murmured something before pulling him into an embrace.

"Eve, it's not what it looks like."

"You said you were meeting her at a coffee shop."

"No, I said we were having coffee, and that's what we did. We had coffee and talked."

He told me exactly what I repeated to the investigator today, that the girl was going through a rough time and he was trying to help her. He swore nothing inappropriate happened, but he couldn't break her trust by telling me more. The wife in me wanted to believe him, had trusted so deeply in the life and family we'd built, but I was shocked. Shocked that Matthew would refuse to explain something like this. I told him to move his things into the guest bedroom.

Had my husband cheated on me? Had he screwed up in the worst way possible? I wanted to say no to Earl's question. I wanted to say it so badly, but the truth came out instead.

"I don't know." Three months later, and I still didn't know. I swallowed and forced myself to meet my father-in-law's stare.

"Matthew's been sleeping down the hall since August. On Thursday nights, after you go to bed, we've been meeting with a therapist. I suppose I need to tell her we won't make the Zoom today."

Earl's mouth tensed and his eyes flared. He squeezed my hand.

"I know he loves me, though. That's the thing. I feel it every day. He would do anything for us, wouldn't he?"

Earl looked around the foyer and I knew he saw the same things I did: the ramps Matthew built after Earl moved in, the coat hooks placed low enough for Earl to hang his own jacket, the old-fashioned umbrella stand he'd bought at an antique store for me. This entire house was evidence of Matthew's care. The first time he took me up to the widow's walk, he stood behind me and turned me in every direction, taking in the entire 360-degree view. "It's yours, Eve," he'd whispered in my ear, "the whole sky."

I couldn't reconcile the man on the cell phone video embracing his student with the one who'd given me this house, this family, and an unobstructed view of the whole sky. Kara Johnson was a question I hadn't been able to answer for months. But it didn't matter right now. Not when Matthew was missing.

"I'm worried the police aren't looking."

Earl let go of my hand and typed.

I'll check hospitals.

We set up in the dining room, Earl using a relay service to call emergency rooms, while I checked our cell phone records and credit cards. Matthew hadn't bought anything since we ordered pizza a few days ago, and the last few calls he made were to the home health aid agency and Earl's physical therapy clinic. As I hung up with the clinic, my phone buzzed with an incoming call.

"Hello?"

"Hi, um, Dr. Roth?"

"Yes." I didn't have the number programmed, but it was local. One of the hospitals? My pulse thudded.

"This is Erik Sorenson, from the chemistry lab. You called earlier."

I'd almost forgotten. Erik was one of the grad students working on Matthew's grant project. I quickly explained the situation. "What time did Matthew leave the lab? Were you there with him this morning?"

There was a pause on the other end, and for a second I thought the call had disconnected. I checked my bars and walked into the sunroom, where the reception was better. "Are you there?"

Erik cleared his throat. "I haven't worked with Professor Moore all semester."

"Who's assigned to his grant research then?"

"No one." He paused again. "Professor Moore's grants were all redistributed. He hasn't been on campus since . . ." He stammered and trailed off.

"Was he doing supplemental research off campus?" That could explain why he'd been at the park. "It's for the Pfizer grant."

"We don't have a Pfizer grant."

I sank into a chair. Everything in me went numb.

Jonah

I knocked on the door of the Victorian and retreated to the edge of the porch. House calls weren't my favorite part of the job, but my only lead wheeled into this house thirty minutes ago. I had to follow it.

It had taken longer than usual to decompress after the police station. I'd stumbled back to my Lancer Evolution X, collapsed into the custom racing seat that hugged me from head to hip, grabbed the emergency Xanax bottle in the console, and breathed. In. Out. In. Slowing my breath, erasing every slash of anger, worry, depression, and contempt, the swill of emotion trapped in that building. Faces swarmed in front of me, ones I knew I hadn't seen inside. Lost faces. Dead faces, their features distorted and pale, noses and mouths drifting away from each other and sliding into bloated compost. I pushed them down, buried them one by one as I chanted names in time with my breath. Danica. Angela. In. Out. Kit. George.

Eventually, my heart rate slowed and the nausea curdled into vague, sour discomfort. I wanted to find some winding county highway and drop the needle to 120. Beside the pills, driving was the one thing guaranteed to clear my head, calm my nervous system, and stir some urge to eat again. But I couldn't leave. Not until they did.

It took an hour, an hour of slow-rolling ambient chords before they appeared. The woman's plaid raincoat, the listing form in the wheelchair. I was too far away to see if he had my note or hear whether he'd read or even understood it. The parking lot was the wrong place to approach them, not in the rain, so close to Larsen and the rest of the station. I waited while she loaded the man into an accessible van and tailed them.

They drove to a remote park on the south side of town. Also not a great interview spot. Better to walk into traffic than be a single man in a trench coat approaching a woman at a park. I idled in the trailer park across the highway until the van pulled out again. That's when they came here, to a house that looked like a horse and buggy could come rolling up any minute along the row of boulevard trees.

I knocked a second time, until a shadow moved behind lead glass.

The woman opened the door. I'd already seen her at the police station, but I didn't remember much about the lobby beyond sweat-slicked nausea and my pulse shooting like a bullet train through a black tunnel.

She didn't speak at first. She held a phone halfway to her face, looking disoriented. Wide, intelligent eyes scanned me, her mouth pursed, all her features holding together in comforting, irrefutable reality. I felt her quick wave of hope as she glanced behind me, clearly expecting more than a man in a black trench coat making a puddle on her porch, and the brightness of the emotion, the sudden shot of light that radiated off her would've blinded me if I hadn't taken the pill.

She surveyed the Lancer Evolution parked on the street and squared her shoulders in the frame of the door, erecting a not-so-subtle barricade. The hope evaporated.

"Yes?"

"You're looking for someone. I can help." I'd said the same words to dozens of grieving, floundering families over the years.

"Excuse me?"

"My name is Jonah Kendrick and I'm a private investigator."

She sized me up again, slower this time. I kept my hands in my pockets, gripping my headphones and notebook.

"Who am I looking for?" She closed the door a fraction of an inch.

That was the question. I'd tried the internet in front of her house, looking for a name to go with the man I'd seen. Usually Max did this part. I dreamed the person and he identified them, using all his databases and law enforcement resources. I checked the news and the blotter, hoping for a missing person report to pop up, but nothing hit in my quick, clumsy search.

Before I could answer, a clatter echoed through the house and her face tightened. She was about to slam her fancy door in my face.

I pointed through the wall toward the source of the noise. "You're looking for his son."

She let me into her entryway, shooting a suspicious glance behind her as she stalked through a hallway and disappeared. Talking drifted from the back of the house, her voice mostly, cut with some lower, more labored tones in between.

I took several deep breaths. The Xanax was still working, giving everything around me a lighter, flatter effect, but pranayama never hurt.

Stores, public places, and government buildings like the police station were the most difficult. That many people crowded together became an explosion of conflict and emotion, but the locations themselves were inherently impersonal. Houses were the opposite—trip wired land mines, every object saturated with a lifetime of sentiment, regret, and frustration. I never entered other people's houses if I could help it, because it was impossible not to absorb something of their occupants. But I'd made this decision. To walk inside. To link their search to mine.

The entryway was tall and bright, a clean and ordered space I immediately appreciated. An ornate mirror hung on one wall and a line of antique hooks underneath it held the plaid raincoat she wore earlier. The closet was closed, and the doors were painted with numbers, equations of every size and shape, swirling black symbols and letters that meant things I would never understand.

She reappeared, surprised I'd stayed where she left me. People always assumed, from shows like *CSI* and *Sherlock*, that investigators were criminally nosy. And I was, or I would be if they had laws about invading people's minds without the consent of either party.

"Are you some kind of ambulance chaser for missing persons? Did you hear about Matthew at the police station?"

Matthew. Half a name already. "No."

"The news, then?"

I hesitated. Hadn't the old man shown her my note? "I saw a report and did some preliminary research."

She sighed. "I really don't have time for this. You can show yourself out."

"Wait." I took a half step toward her, but it was enough to make her stiffen. Looking down and keeping my hands inside my pockets, I explained. "I need to ask you a few questions. I'm working on a case I think is related to Matthew's, for another client. I'm not looking for money or anything from you, except information. If I can solve my client's case, I might be able to help Matthew as well."

She stood completely still for a moment, legs braced, arms crossed, head tilted to one side to better sieve the words for bullshit. Then she lifted her phone in front of her face.

"Did you catch all that?"

"What?" I took another half step, but she raised one finger. A warning.

"Let me see him," came a voice from the phone, and the woman swiveled the screen, bringing the caller into view. I couldn't see much of her from across the room.

"Hmmm. I like him," the small voice said with a hint of a Spanish accent. "Kind of a malnourished Jon Snow."

The woman sighed. "I called you for help, Natalia."

"But he's cute."

"So was Ted Bundy." The woman turned the screen back to face herself.

"I'm standing right here," I felt compelled to point out. Neither woman cared.

"Jonah Kendrick." The caller said it slowly, like she was typing my name into a search engine.

"Here." I crossed the entryway, extending my PI license. The kitchen came into view at the end of the hallway, along with the old man sitting at the table. A tide of his frustration and suspicion rolled over me, but it was buffered by the pill. Tolerable. I kept my face passive and nonthreatening. Was he suspicious about the note? He wheeled himself down the hallway, backing up the woman.

"Who's your client?" she asked.

"Does it matter?"

She was obviously used to getting explanations. She propped one hand on her hip, measuring me. Something about her gaze landed deep, a gut check beneath the pit of my stomach. One of the things I'd gotten used to in my half-lucid life was seeing people in dreams before meeting them in the world. When I eventually saw the face in public, I'd get déjà vu, whether they were dead or alive. I expected that sick sense of inevitability. This was different. I'd never met this woman before today, and I couldn't remember dreaming about that reddish cap of hair or her clinical gaze, but I recognized her. Tall, polished, naturally in control. She was important, the kind of importance that seeped into the nerves and signaled the start of something either life-changingly great or completely fucking awful. The two were very close.

The caller piped up. "Hear him out, I guess. You don't have anything to lose right now."

The woman raised a finger again, like I was a stray dog, before retreating down the hall to the kitchen to finish her phone call. The man in the wheelchair jerked his head, and I followed him into the sunroom where a couch faced a bank of windows. A long table held beakers and test tubes filled with different kinds of leaves.

Without the woman nearby, the space was surprisingly restful. The first few minutes in a new environment were usually the hardest. Once I acclimated, I could ride the mood of a place without serious incident, unless I picked up the wrong object or walked into the wrong room. Which was why I kept my hands in my pockets and steered clear of personal areas—bedrooms, bathrooms, the places misery went to hide.

Art and photographs covered the walls in here. One photo was a wedding shot—the woman laughed in a sleek white dress between two rows of trees, their boughs dripping with strings of lights. The man standing next to her, in an unbuttoned tux and posing like a catalog model, was him: the man I'd dreamed about this morning.

He did have blond hair.

I took a photo of the picture, almost texting it to Max before I remembered he'd blocked my number. The old man watched me. Half his face sagged, and the other half pinched. It wasn't the faces from my nightmares, their features disconnected from each other, rotting echoes breaking apart, but it wasn't the bright symmetry of his daughter-in-law either. He was a man caught between worlds, suspended above the drainpipe. Like me. I took a yoga breath and moved over to him, crouching well clear of his wheels.

"You got my note?"

He grunted. *No.*

"I gave it to you at the station this morning. It was about Matthew."

Confusion leaked through his scowl, the chemical fog of prescriptions, and it wasn't all mine. He lifted his hand as if he expected the folded piece of paper to appear.

I wanted to drill him with questions about his son and how he might be connected to Celina, but decency won out in the end. I waved off the old man's confusion, trying to soothe the rankled energy.

"Don't worry about it."

The note was probably under someone's shoe on the police station floor or chucked in the garbage. It didn't matter. The description wasn't important now that I had an actual photo of the guy. I could interview the wife as soon as she got off the phone.

But the man still chewed on my question. Not knowing frustrated him. His hair hung in clumps, dove gray and only slightly receding. Liver spots dotted the splotchy skin on his forehead. He'd spent most of his life in the sun. His eyes were a subtle, glowing green and out of nowhere I heard my grandmother's voice—not whispering from the dead because that shit doesn't happen, but a memory—commenting on some guy we'd passed on the street when I was a child, my hand tucked firmly in hers as we made our way to the convenience store. Her no-nonsense, gritty declaration. "Now that man is a looker."

This man had been, too. My grandmother's voice echoed and changed, shifting in pitch until it became someone else's completely, a voice that didn't live in my head but his. This voice was softer and teasing, someone who enjoyed poking at a gruff exterior. She'd known his retorts were all bark and no bite. Not for her anyway. He'd saved his bite for the towheaded kid who always blew things up and left his damn experiments everywhere. Matthew.

I sucked in a breath. These weren't my memories; I didn't have any right to them. I stood up and pulled my coat tight, redrawing the boundaries of myself. We both needed noise, distraction. "You want to watch television?"

His good eye narrowed.

I picked up a remote from the couch, and the wedge of plastic and circuits hummed. He watched a lot of TV. I got a flash of pinwheels, bright and garish, spun by eager hands.

"Do they still play *Wheel of Fortune?*"

He grunted. *Yes.*

I flipped channels until I found it. Holy shit. They were the same people—the host and assistant completely unchanged since I'd watched the show twenty-some years ago. They either had the best plastic surgeons in the business or vampires were real.

The longer we watched, the more it felt like I'd stepped back in time and my grandmother was still alive, marching her coupons into the corner store and commenting on the beauty of men who passed her on the street. There was comfort in the uncertainty, the possibility of the impossible. As we decided who to root for in the next round, the wife appeared.

"What are you doing?"

Eve

"I have to go." I watched from the end of the hall as Earl and the alleged investigator disappeared into the sunroom, but Natalia Flores wasn't the type of friend who accepted a brush-off. Even I recognized the curses that sailed out of her mouth in Spanish.

"You need to tell me everything. Now."

"There's a stranger in my house."

"Apparently there's more than one."

I heaved out a shaky sigh and leaned against the marble island in the kitchen. I'd skyped Natalia the minute I got off the phone with the grad student. Matthew had lied to me. He'd made Earl and me believe for months that he was working on the Pfizer grant, that he hadn't trusted anyone else to take over this particular project. He'd told our therapist the grant gave him purpose and helped him find his way forward through the scandal.

And it was all a lie.

There was no grant project. Where had Matthew been going?

"Did you have any idea before today?"

"No." After the incident with Kara Johnson, I'd been irrationally worried every time Matthew left the house, but he texted constantly, sending pictures from the grocery store—*What's your position on mango salsa?*—and even a few from the university when I'd asked how things were going. "He sent at least four different pictures from the mass spectrometry lab. That's four data points out of approximately twelve to fifteen dates when he told us he was working."

"Eve." I could hear the exasperation in Natalia's voice. "Your marriage isn't an experiment."

"Every marriage is an experiment." And mine felt like it was blowing up in my face. How could so much have changed in the space of a few hours? I'd been flying over the world this morning, in control, sure of the life waiting for me on the ground. Now I was sure of nothing, least of all the word of a private investigator who showed up out of nowhere on my doorstep.

Jonah Kendrick. He appeared more in control of himself than he had been at the police station. He wasn't shaking anymore, but he still looked abnormally pale; in another century I would have said consumptive.

"He doesn't have a website." Rapid, scratchy clicks transmitted over the Skype connection as Natalia searched on her computer. "His name comes up a few times in random articles. Oh, here's one." She paused to read. "He's cited as assisting with the recovery of a runaway teenager named Danica Chase in Peoria. And here's another that names him as a private investigator who helped, ugh, identify the remains of a missing woman outside Dubuque."

I had no frame of reference for a private investigator beyond old Humphrey Bogart movies, and this man was no Bogart. He was too tall, too quiet. He didn't have a hat. And I didn't remember Bogart collapsing from anything less than a gunshot wound.

"Hear him out," Natalia said. "He's not asking for money, and you get to look at cute Jon Snow for a while."

I had no idea what I would've done without Natalia the past few months. She'd helped me pick out a couples therapist and called every week from Costa Rica to check in, but she'd also made no secret of the fact that she didn't believe Matthew. She was convinced he'd cheated on me. She'd never told me outright to divorce him, but she increasingly inserted comments like this into our conversations. Introducing variables, hinting at possibilities. I'd almost started a chart.

"My husband is missing."

Natalia leaned closer to the camera. "Have they checked with . . . ?"

I knew the name she wouldn't say.

"I don't know." The interview with Investigator Summerlin cycled through my head. "The questions the police were asking me . . . it sounds like they think I had something to do with it. The jealous wife."

Spanish curses filled the kitchen.

"I have to go."

"I wish I was there with you." Natalia's group wasn't flying home for another week. What could happen in seven days? I walked down the hall toward the sunroom, where an unstable man who reportedly identified corpses sat watching TV with my father-in-law. Anything. Anything could happen.

The stranger rummaged around in his coat pocket, pulled out a crumpled tissue, and handed it over. Earl took it and wiped the drool from his chin. Neither of them spoke or even looked away from the screen. The gesture was too casual, the kind of automatic intimacy between family, and it set off every warning bell in my head. I ended the call and stalked into the room.

"What are you doing?"

He jumped out of the chair and immediately backed up, his gaze landing somewhere in the empty space between me and Earl.

"He, um, wanted to watch television."

"I meant the tissue." I pointed at the crumpled wad in Earl's hand, feeling ridiculous even as I said it.

"He doesn't like the drool. It's embarrassing."

"Excuse me?"

"To him," he clarified quickly. "The spit embarrasses him. Not me. I don't care. I drool in my sleep all the time."

Earl grunted again and it sounded breathier this time, a grudging laugh, like they were talking in a language I couldn't hear.

"Come with me."

I steered him by the elbow back to the foyer, out of Earl's earshot. He came willingly but shrugged me off as soon as we reached the door and put as much space between us as possible.

"Well?"

He held up a plastic-encased picture. I hesitated.

"Her name is Celina, and she disappeared in August." He paused, waiting until I took the photograph. "She clocked out of her graveyard shift at an all-night diner less than five miles from here. Then she was gone."

It was a senior year high school photo. The girl leaned against a tree trunk with her arms folded, wearing a closed-mouth smile as if amused by the whole experience. Her hair lay in perfect, dark waves on her shoulders—no wind that day. And her eyes were relaxed, not squinting. It must have been partly cloudy, too. Altostratus, I guessed, based on the shadow pattern over the grass behind her.

I couldn't recall any stories or alerts about a missing girl, but in August I'd been swamped with prepping classes and beginning the semester. "Was she a student at UI?"

"No."

"What does she have to do with Matthew?" I handed him the photo back. He was careful to take it without touching me.

"Has Matthew spent time on any farms lately?"

"Not that I know of."

"Any other rural areas?"

"No." But even as I said it, I hesitated. How did I know where Matthew had been lately? The pictures he'd sent me—piles of mangoes and gas chromatography equipment—could have been taken anytime, sent from anywhere. I couldn't be sure of anything right now.

"Has he been associating with anyone new?"

My eyes narrowed, but he didn't backpedal. Lifting the photograph so I could see the girl's face again, he pushed. "Please, I'm trying to find her."

"I still don't understand the connection. Did this girl disappear in a car fire, too?"

"Car fire?" He looked confused. "What car fire?"

He told me when I'd first opened the door that he'd seen the report about Matthew. But if he had, he would have known about the Tesla and the fire at Ryerson's Woods. Everything in me went cold.

"Who are you?" I took a step closer and he moved back, his heels hitting the front door.

"I told you already. My name is Jonah Kendrick. I'm a private investigator."

"You didn't see any police report about Matthew. What are you doing here?" I opened the front closet and grabbed one of Matthew's old baseball bats.

"I didn't say I saw a *police* report." Jonah Kendrick raised both hands in surrender. "Look, uh . . ."

The knowledge of what he was fumbling for made my fingers clench the bat harder. "You don't even know my name, do you?"

He shook his head, hands still raised. "Maybe we should start over."

"Maybe you should get out of my house."

"He's trapped in a barn," Kendrick blurted as I lifted the bat, preparing to swing.

"What?"

"Your husband. I don't know anything about a car fire, but he's being held in a barn." He took a deep breath, trying to steady himself. "It's the same barn where Celina was taken. The people who took her have him, too."

The TV volume spiked. Earl was trying to use the remote with mixed success. "How do you know that?"

"It doesn't matter."

I didn't have the first clue where Matthew could be, but a barn was among the least likely possibilities. Whenever we vacationed or took a weekend away, it was to Chicago, New York, Paris. Urban areas full of culture, museums, and universities filled with welcoming colleagues. I was the one who went to farm country, the flat, open land where the only place to look was up. Not Matthew. And the idea that he was somehow trapped or being held hostage? That was the sort of thing that happened in movies, not Iowa. Tornadoes and blizzards were the only monsters that lived here.

"The police kicked you out of the station. They obviously don't believe you."

"The police limit themselves by what they deem credible."

A man collapsing on the front desk of the police station didn't present as particularly reliable to me, either, but I was willing to give him one last chance. "What's your source?"

"I . . . saw him. In a dream."

I lowered the bat, stunned. "What?"

"I have certain parapsychological abilities." When I didn't say anything, he elaborated. "To see things at a distance."

"No." For the love of Einstein, no. I pushed the bat into his chest. "Get out. Now."

He grabbed for the door handle, swinging it open and stumbling outside. I kept pushing until he tripped down the porch steps and fell into a pile of snow. A neighbor across the street stopped in her driveway, oblivious to the continuing downpour as she gaped.

"I don't expect you to believe me—"

"Excellent, because I don't." I glanced back at the glowering man on my sidewalk. "My name is Dr. Eve Roth. I'm a physicist. And the only way to see things at a distance is with a telescope. Don't come back."

Jonah

I roared out of Dr. Eve Roth's neighborhood. My coat soaked the car's racing seat, making me angrier by the second. When I got to the freeway I shifted into fifth gear, shooting into traffic and swerving between two semitrucks to reach an open lane where I could really hit the gas. Rain pounded the windshield and the turbocharged engine growled, vibrating through the steering wheel and into my clenched hands.

A bat. She'd shoved me out of her house with a bat.

Most people, when they found out I was psychic, went one of two directions. They either asked about lottery numbers and whether I could check on their dead labradoodle or they acted like I was contagious. New clients usually fell on the suspicious side, but I always told them the same thing. Believe me or don't believe me. I didn't care. How I got the information wasn't important. If they chose to hire me, I only got paid on success.

Max helped me come up with the pitch, which was why it sounded like him—direct, easy to digest, and good. And because of that, only a handful of clients had ever turned me down.

They never thought about what success could look like, though. They wanted a tearful reunion, close call, danger-averted success. Danicas, Angelas, Kits, and Georges. But I couldn't control the results I delivered and sometimes it was the other kind, the body-in-a-drainpipe success, their missing person too decomposed for anything but dental verification. They got something to bury. The worst possible answer was still better than no answer. I kept telling myself that, even when I dreamed about drainpipes with entire families huddled inside, clutching their horror tightly between them.

Sometimes clients didn't pay. Sometimes they ghosted me. I'd been laughed at, ostracized, cursed, and scorned. Once, when I told a guy in high school his girlfriend was cheating on him, he'd choked me against a locker. But I'd never been shooed away with a bat and dumped into a pile of slush like vermin. Who the hell did that?

Dr. Eve *Don't-Come-Back* Roth.

I couldn't get the image of her out of my head, no matter how fast I pushed the Evolution. The speedometer drifted past a hundred and other cars became metal blurs. When a pickup tried to cut in front of me, I veered to the shoulder, leaving a trail of Chevy horn blasting at my receding bumper. There was no satisfaction in it, though, none of the usual adrenaline I counted on to clear my head, and I knew why: she'd touched me.

When Eve Roth grabbed my elbow, the contact had been a lightning rod, focusing all my attention on the woman about to throw me out of her house. Her mind had a steady hum as it observed and analyzed. She was as controlled as Max but naturally so, not affecting a Zen state like Max did around me. I could sense her anxiety, the fear tightening around her like a held breath, but it was tempered by an iron grid of logic, every input in her world slotted into its place. Action and reaction. Experiment and conclusion, and her conclusion about me was visceral. I wanted to erase the taste of it, but physical contact always made people linger.

And in some black corner, part of me was scared her reaction was dead on.

Sometimes it's just a dream.

Maybe Max was right. Maybe Celina's disappearance had finally obliterated the last shreds of my sanity, and I couldn't see past the drainpipe anymore.

I pushed the gas pedal to the floor, the endless straightaway calling me into the rolling hills and gray horizons. I drove halfway to Cedar Rapids before Eve Roth's energy finally faded, and I remembered her husband's face in the wedding photo. His mouth ungagged, hands unbound, but the same man I'd seen in the barn. It was him. Matthew.

It wasn't just a dream. It was oneiros, my path to Celina.

I doubled back on the freeway and found a hotel on the outskirts of the city—a place so new the furniture was still off-gassing—and checked into a room. I'd take formaldehyde over the lingering impressions of previous guests any day.

I changed out of my wet clothes, then turned on the police scanner and taped my case file over the walls and counter of the bathroom, turning the space into a mosaic of names, dates, interview notes, and pictures. Bathrooms were always better for thinking. Hard surfaces, less room for thoughts to crack and disintegrate. Sitting in the bathtub, I took a wax crayon to the tile, outlining what I'd learned so far. I'd found some stuff online, but the rest I'd seen and felt, the knowledge resonating off some tuning fork lodged inside my body, and all of it—I reminded myself with each scrawled word—was true.

My mom had called me intuitive as a kid. It was an adjective then, before the term became a whole category of woo-wooey people. I'd always had feelings about things, gut instincts that were sometimes eerily accurate, but no one thought anything about it because I was a twin. Everyone accepted the connection between twins. Like déjà vu or karma, twins slipped unnoticed through the world's logic loophole.

It started in kindergarten when the school separated Jason and me into different classes. One day while making a paper turkey shaped like my hand, pain shot up my arm. The teacher couldn't find anything wrong but eventually sent me to the nurse to shut me up. I got there right as another teacher ran in carrying Jason, who'd fallen off the monkey bars and broken his arm.

"You're part of each other," my mom said while we waited for Jason's X-rays in the doctor's office. "It's natural for you to know things about your brother, things other people might not be able to know."

She used to ask me where Jason was when dinner was ready and, even if I hadn't seen him since breakfast, I could always tell her which friend's house he was playing at. Jason was the outgoing one, the twin who raced around the neighborhood while I sat home playing video games or throwing a stick for the dog. I never resented him for his friends. Jason dealt with people so I didn't have to.

As we grew, so did the range of my intuition. In fifth grade, a quiet girl with one long braid down her back always sat across from me on the bus. One day she wasn't at the bus stop and a friend of hers wondered what happened to her.

"She's sick," I said. "She's got red bumps all over and they hurt a lot."

"How do you know that?" another louder girl asked. "Did you talk to her? Is she your girlfriend?"

Everyone within hearing distance laughed.

"I'm a twin," I said, like that answered everything.

"You're a freak," the girl yelled, and Jason stepped in, like always, to call the girl stupid and gross, the worst words we packed in a ten-year-old vocabulary.

The next day we heard the girl had gotten chicken pox. She came back to school two weeks later, confused by the gibes that Jonah Kendrick was her boyfriend. She didn't even know who I was.

Physically, Jason and I were identical. We were both too skinny, fast as alley cats, quick to judge, and would do any chore in the house for a root beer float, no matter the season. But no one, not even our mother, called Jason intuitive. And for someone who apparently had a sixth sense, it took me almost nineteen years to realize I was different from my twin. Different from everyone, and I only found out because of Max.

I'd known Max Summerlin over half my life. In a lot of ways, we were both responsible for who the other person had become. He was the only real friend I'd had apart from Jason, and he'd tossed me out of his life. Two hours later, Eve Roth took a baseball bat to my chest and did virtually the same thing. Neither of them got it; they thought they were dealing with someone who had something to lose. Max, at least, should have known better.

I taped Celina's plastic-shrouded picture to the mirror, covering my own reflection. I could almost see her, slow spinning on her heels, taking in the walls papered with articles, disjointed notes, and the maps I'd marked up like shooting range targets. *Borderline serial killer,* she'd joked once, inspecting one of my case walls. *But in a homey way. Like a stalker with nice Pinterest boards.*

Four months. One hundred and fifteen days of cold trails and dead ends and driving to half the farms in Iowa to find fucking nothing. I would take anything at this point. I would take the worst possible answer.

I climbed back in the bathtub with my laptop while the scanner's choppy mechanical voices played in the background. The barn where Matthew Moore was being held—I'd gotten his last name googling "eve roth husband iowa?"—was the same barn where Celina had been taken after she disappeared. I knew it, the same way I knew Jason's arm had been broken in kindergarten. It was bodily knowledge, truth shooting through my veins as soon as I woke up this morning. It would have been a hell of a lot easier if his family was willing to work with me, but in the end it didn't matter. I would find Matthew Moore, and when I did, I would find Celina.

I was skimming an article about the car fire when a call on the scanner jerked me to my feet.

Young female, unresponsive.

Max

The body lay in a bathtub lined with candles. Female. White, but her skin looked more green than any other color now. Green eyes, too, although the corneas had started to cloud. I put her in her late twenties or early thirties. Probably 130 pounds before the swelling began. No ligature marks from what I could see or defensive wounds on her hands. She could have been taking a bath and fallen asleep from how she was slumped to one side, except there was no water in the tub. Just a dead woman and a hell of a smell.

I was halfway home when the request came through from patrol. As soon as I volunteered for it, Larsen called.

"It's your first day back, and no matter what your fitness-for-duty exam says I know you're still not a hundred percent."

"I'm practically at the scene already. I don't need my left arm for this."

"I'm talking about your head." Larsen didn't pull punches. He'd been monitoring me, not outright staring like everyone else, but I could tell he was keeping tabs. All day I made sure my shoulder didn't tense up with pain, that I talked enough but not too much, and every case note had the *i*'s dotted and *t*'s crossed. If I checked my back too many times, if I flinched when someone laughed unexpectedly or opened a can of soda, I recovered as quickly as I could and got back to work.

"I'm good."

"You sure?"

"Yeah."

And that was it. I could've passed this call off and focused on the Matthew Moore case, let one of the other investigators step in, but they'd been covering for me for six weeks. I wasn't giving anyone any more reasons to look sideways at me. Besides, I'd already submitted the request for court orders for the Moore case hours ago, asking for access to bank and phone records. All I could do there was wait, so instead of going home for dinner, I texted Shelley that I'd be a little longer, everything was fine, not to worry, and walked into a dead woman's apartment. To prove I was back, and I was good.

The bathroom counter was cluttered with lotions and makeup. The medicine cabinet held razors, Band-Aids, a bottle of antidepressants, and a half wheel of birth control, both prescribed to Alexis Dwyer. The last birth control pill was punched out of the foil on Tuesday, two days ago.

I paced through the apartment. It was furnished with overstuffed chairs, fuzzy blankets, plants, and framed art on the wall, the kind of rental someone had bothered to make a home. One side of the bedroom closet was cleaned out, vacuum lines still on the carpet, even, but other than that, I couldn't find anything suspicious. I was leafing through a pile of magazines when someone knocked on the front door.

"It's Alexis," the landlady said before I got the apartment door all the way open. "You don't need to check dental records."

Four foot nine and built like a decrepit pipe cleaner, she'd discovered the body when she came to collect late rent.

"What can you tell me about Alexis?" I stepped out onto the landing with her, pulling the door closed behind me to keep the smell away from the other tenants.

"Never late on rent before."

"Where'd she work?"

"Nowhere."

"She rich?" This wasn't the kind of place money lived. The building had three floors with two apartments on each floor. It was spic-and-span but old, with seventies paneling and water spots on the ceiling. It wouldn't attract the bougie types who flocked to the new flats and lofts downtown.

"She wasn't rich. He paid her bills."

"He who?"

The lady sniffed. "Lots of guys went in and out of the place at all hours, but I saw him the most. Tall, blond, older guy. Acted like he got his way too often if you ask me."

"When did you see him last?"

"Tuesday. They were fighting. I could hear it through the pipes in my unit."

"They fight a lot?"

Another sniff. "I don't tolerate that kind of ruckus in my building."

"What was the fight about? Could you tell?"

"She was louder than him was all I could hear. Kept getting louder, too, and more upset. I almost went up, but then she calmed down. He left about thirty minutes later, and I didn't see anybody after that. Figured she was avoiding me on account of the rent.

How long before I can have the cleaners come out?" She'd probably called all three industrial cleaning services in town while I'd been inside the apartment.

"We'll let you know." I thought about the empty space in the bedroom closet. "He take anything with him when he left? Suitcase, boxes, anything like that?"

"No, nothing like that."

The ME arrived and the landlady let them in, keeping an eagle eye on the proceedings. I followed them inside the apartment.

"Let me know if you think of anything else."

"There's a man in a trench coat hanging around your car in the parking lot." She turned away, already mopping the water we'd tracked in on her stairs.

An hour later, after the technicians loaded the body bag into the ambulance and drove away, Jonah stepped out of the parking lot shadows. I was exhausted. My first day back and I'd already pulled two new cases and worked a thirteen-hour shift. In the sling, my arm ached with stiffness punctuated by steady pulses of pain. The doctor had offered me opioids after surgery. I'd flatly refused.

Jonah stopped several feet away. How many times did I have to do this today? I'd already thrown him out of the station. I wanted the energy to yell, to swear. I wanted to throw a punch that wouldn't hurt me more than it hurt him. But before I could summon any of that, his choked question—"Is it her?"—washed all my anger and frustration away.

"No. It's not Celina."

His eyes narrowed, probing my head for confirmation. He didn't believe me. I guess that was fair, after this morning.

"The scanner said foul play."

"Suspected. We don't have cause of death yet."

After a beat, he breathed out a shaky sigh and nodded. The rain pounded my umbrella and soaked his head. We both stood there, neither knowing what to say next. It felt a lot like how we'd first met.

Jonah Kendrick and I were assigned to be roommates our freshman year at the University of Iowa. We weren't fast friends. I hung out with a group I knew from high school, going to frat parties and the 18+ clubs that catered to the idiocy of teenagers. From what I could tell, Jonah was always alone. He never started a single conversation in our dorm room, and when I asked about his friends, he said his twin got a baseball scholarship to a school in Louisiana. That was apparently the only friend he had.

I didn't know what to make of him. He didn't fit into any of the categories of quiet kid I knew: gamers, stoners, collectors, goths, writers, or nerds. I wondered if he was closeted and made a few awkward comments, encouraging him to come out if that was the thing, but he brushed me aside. My friends told me to ignore him, but it bothered me, living in a sixteen-by-twelve-foot room with a total stranger. We might have gone the whole year that way, me trying to engage him, him avoiding me, if it hadn't been for one thing: I was a shitty sleeper.

I'd always had insomnia. My mom said I barely slept as a baby, and I was the first one up in our house as a kid, prowling the halls and sneaking cereal at 5:00 a.m. It was the reason I chose the overnight patrol shift after the academy. If I was going to be up anyway, I might as well be working. That first year in the dorms was the hardest. I'd grown up in a sleepy summer town where the VFW closed by ten at night. Iowa City felt like New York to me. There was constant noise. If a car honked at night, I woke up. If someone shut a door down the hall, I could tell you who it was. I heard every time anyone went to the bathroom and every time the boiler clanked in the basement. I lay awake most nights, scribbling notes in the small notepads my mom always gave me so I wouldn't wake her up when I was bored. It was mostly journal stuff or things I didn't want to forget the next day, but after a month in the dorms, I found something else to write down. Jonah talked in his sleep.

He slept like the dead and sometimes snored, but halfway through fall semester he started mumbling. It was incoherent at first, nothing I could make sense of. Then I started to piece together words. And I wrote them down.

It was a creepy thing to do, no question, but when you're an insomniac you come up with games to pass the hours. Jonah's sleep talking became one of my favorite games. If he wouldn't talk to me during the day, I figured this was his way of reaching out.

One night in October, he began speaking in a completely different voice. He sounded lucid. I started to apologize for waking him up with my bed light, but his eyes were still closed, twitching underneath his eyelids, like he was watching a tennis match in his sleep. I listened and wrote, getting more confused with everything he said.

The next day I asked if he knew he sleep talked.

"Sorry if it bothers you, man." He shrugged, trying to dismiss me.

"Do you remember what you dreamed about last night?"

He didn't. I flipped to the notes I'd recorded.

"You talked almost nonstop for ten minutes around three o'clock this morning. You said, 'He's leaving the game, doesn't want to go home. A bus. The bus goes to the bar. Grease, stale popcorn. She's there. Music. A jukebox. There's a house. White, peeling paint. Across the alley.'"

He mumbled something else about not remembering and went down to dinner. I followed, badgering him with questions until a message on the cafeteria notice board caught both our attention. A kid two floors down from us had gone to the Hawkeye game the day before and never came home.

"Look at this." I ripped the paper down.

"It's probably . . ." he trailed off, staring at the grainy photocopied picture on the flyer. Something clicked behind his eyes.

"Come on."

I dragged him back to our room and dissected every word he'd said in his sleep. When I couldn't get any more details out of Jonah, I turned to the computer. It was early internet days, and we didn't have endless information at our fingertips. I found a bus map and made a list of all the lines that stopped by Kinnick Stadium, then convinced Jonah to ride each route with me and investigate every dive bar along the way. As the night wore on we figured out that not only did these places have no bouncers, but also that a few of the sketchier ones would even sell us a round. We bellied up to faux wood and Formica, gulping Budweiser and trying to act nonchalant about winning the shitty bartender lottery.

While waiting at a bus stop after one particular no-fucks-given place we vowed to revisit, he got a weird look on his face and walked away.

"Where are you going?" I followed him around the corner. When we got to a weed-choked alley, he started peering over fences and around garages.

"Dude, what is it?"

"There." He pointed to a small house with peeling paint and a single light on in one of the windows. "That's where he is."

Even in the darkness I could tell Jonah was stunned. Almost as much as I was. We walked around to the front and Jonah hung in the shadows as I knocked hard, the flint of cop already threading through my knuckles. A woman answered, looking half-drunk and rumpled. I asked for the missing student, and she opened the door wider to a cramped living room where the guy was playing video games on the couch.

"George Marcus Morrow?"

The guy froze, like he'd gotten caught smoking weed by the high school principal. I pulled the flyer out of my pocket and tossed it in his lap. "Call your parents."

Ignoring his stutters of—"Who are you? What the fuck?"—I stood over him until he picked up a phone and dialed, then turned to Jonah as an unfamiliar satisfaction ballooned inside my chest.

"Case closed."

We caught the next bus and rumbled off into the night, which looked completely different than it had ten minutes ago. There were possibilities everywhere, an entire world glinting underneath the one I knew only by sight, touch, smell, and whisper.

"Holy shit." I punched the empty seat in front of me. "You're psychic. You're fucking Nostradamus."

"Yeah, right," Jonah said, but he started to grin, too, caught up in my excitement. "I'm not predicting the apocalypse. I couldn't even remember what I'd dreamed. I thought you were making it up."

"Like I could make that shit up." I leaned across the aisle to punch him on the arm, and his smile grew wider.

I asked him if anything like this happened before, things he passed off as coincidences or intuition, and he told me about his brother and all the crazy shit he knew about his twin without ever being told.

"Jason never said anything about me talking in my sleep, though. Maybe he never heard me."

"I got you covered, man." I grinned. "Your insomniac roommate to the rescue."

And that's how it went: Jonah dreamed and I listened. We spent our free time investigating the random crap that spewed out of his sleeping mouth. He didn't talk every night, and sometimes I couldn't make out the things he mumbled, but the thrill of figuring out the clues drew us both in hard. We phoned in anonymous leads about two different runaways to the police department's public tip line, both of which proved useful as we followed the stories through the papers and the National Center for Missing and Exploited Children.

By the end of freshman year, we were inseparable. We didn't tell anyone what we were doing, Jonah because he didn't talk to anyone anyway, and me because I didn't want him to get flooded with requests for help. We figured out pretty quickly that his dreams all focused on people who were lost. It was like the world was a puzzle and his brain could sense when the pieces didn't fit where they'd been placed. If his abilities became public, the families of the nine hundred thousand missing persons in this country would never leave him alone, and since he couldn't control who he dreamed about, he couldn't choose who to help.

I was optimistic, though, about his possibilities. I was optimistic about everything then. The universe as I knew it for eighteen years had cracked open, revealing things that should've been impossible outside of superhero movies.

I bought a police scanner and while other dorm rooms pumped out the Strokes and the White Stripes, we listened to codes and calls from the Iowa City PD. Sometimes we hit crime scenes—robberies and vandalism mostly—because I was convinced Jonah could learn to pick up traces of what had happened. He never did, but we still had fun scouting the area and reconstructing the incident.

What I did teach him was how to remember his dreams. After two years in the dorms, we got a shitty apartment south of downtown, not far from the place where, twenty years later, Alexis Dwyer would die in a bathtub. I set up a voice recorder in his bedroom and we listened to it every morning over cereal. Hearing his own voice acted like a trigger and he began recalling bits and pieces of what his dream mind had seen. I helped him concentrate on one image, clearing his mind of everything else, until he could sometimes add details he hadn't articulated while unconscious. I wrote everything down while eating both our bowls of cereal and sometimes the rest of the box, depending on how long he could hold the vision. I tried to stretch the sessions out further every time, hunting his head for clues, always eager to launch our next investigation. We kept a whiteboard in the kitchen, scrawled with dream notes. If Jonah's psychic abilities were a muscle, I became his personal trainer.

I got a degree in criminal justice, which was probably inevitable in retrospect, but I'd started college with no particular direction. After graduation I convinced Jonah to open a detective agency, and we tracked down his first client together. I listened while he dialed the call and read the script we'd worked out together. "You're looking for someone. I can help."

And for twenty years we had. We found people, sometimes dead, sometimes alive and did our best to move on. I got married and had a kid. He moved into a rundown house on the bluffs of the Mississippi. As his abilities increased, he withdrew further and further from the world, but he was still my best friend, my first partner.

Then he dreamed about Celina. And everything fell apart.

I walked across the parking lot and got into my cruiser. Jonah followed. For a while, the only noise in the car was the drum of water on the roof. Neither of us seemed eager to break the silence, but I wanted to go home. Shelley was worried about my first day back. I needed to feel her arms slide around me and hold fast, to show both of us nothing happened today I couldn't handle.

"You're still listening to scanners?"

"And looking for Belgrave."

My stomach jumped. "Any luck?"

He shook his head. "I'm sorry. That's not why I'm in town."

"You shouldn't be here."

"I'm not going to make it hard. I won't come back to the station. But, this morning, I was trying to tell you"—he rubbed his forehead—"there's another person gone. Matthew Moore. His car was set on fire."

"Oh, shit." It was pointless lying to Jonah. "That's my other case."

"This guy, Matthew, he's in the same barn. Celina's barn."

Jonah's eyes were in focus, his hands steady. He looked a hell of a lot more stable than he had in the station this morning, but to connect Matthew Moore to Celina? Since she'd disappeared, his dreams had become more scattered, less reliable. I'd left Shelley and Garrett every weekend to chase the dead ends in Jonah's head, until we reached an end that almost left me dead.

He sensed my doubt. "I saw him there, Max."

"Maybe you really wanted a new lead."

"That's not it."

"You know as well as I do that sometimes it's a mash-up. Sometimes it's a replay. And sometimes it's just a dream." The rain washed everything beyond the windshield into a dark, amorphous blur. "Do you still dream about the drainpipe?"

"Fuck you."

"Yeah. Fuck both of us, but you know I'm right."

He shoved the car door open and got two steps away before stalking back and kicking the cruiser's side panel. Rain soaked the passenger door. Jonah leaned inside, dripping on the passenger seat. "Did you find the guy?"

The lights were off in the apartment building and other than us, the lot was empty. I wasn't supposed to talk to Jonah. But goddamn it, I couldn't have him stepping all over this case, too.

"Get back in."

He did, and I gave him basic details: Matthew Moore's family situation, his suspension, how the fire was set with some as-yet-unidentified substance. "The wife seemed to know a lot about it."

He straightened. "The physicist?"

"How do you know that?"

"I made a house call."

"Did you see anything out of the ordinary?"

"I mean, a roll of garbage bags, a bloody knife, and some lighter fluid, but nothing that stood out."

"Ha ha. Anything wet? Charred? Bagged up?"

"Why are you pinning this on her? What have you got?"

"I'm collecting evidence and so far, it suggests strong motive on her part. He allegedly cheated on her with a student and lied about where he was going this morning."

Jonah shook his head as I ticked off points. "I don't see Eve anywhere near this."

There was a pause while we both digested that.

"Eve, is it?" I stretched out her first name, dangling it in front of him.

"That's not it."

"Yeah, I think I see where this is going."

"Fuck off."

"Exactly what my captain wants you to do." I turned the car on and the dashboard lit up with the familiar panels and buttons, the illusion of control. "I'm serious. Stay away from this case."

"He's in the barn."

"We never found the barn, Jonah."

"Because you stopped looking."

I was halfway across the console before I caught myself, inches shy of slamming Jonah against the door. His head snapped up, waiting for the blow, expecting it. His eyes were full of things neither of us could say. The headphones around his neck trembled.

I forced myself back in my seat and strapped in with my good arm, throwing the car in reverse. "Go."

Jonah hesitated before climbing out of the car and out of my life.

Eve

Hours later, I was still furious.

"He claims he saw Matthew trapped in a barn in a dream." I whacked ladlefuls of chana masala into our bowls. "In. A. Dream."

But one look at Earl's face made me stop and breathe.

"I'm sorry." I set the pot down and dropped into a chair next to him, trying to manage the storm of emotions flooding my chest. Outside, rain continued to beat against the deck, washing away the snow that had drifted over the covered patio furniture. Only a few weeks ago, the three of us had lounged through a Sunday afternoon out there, Matthew and I poring through science journals in the fleur-de-lis wrought iron chairs while Earl watched wintering birds flit between the feeders dotting the yard. I knew I was upset about so much more than a psychic, but he was the easiest target, the one thing I'd understood how to handle today.

Earl pulled his iPad over. Helen always liked fortune-tellers.

I stirred the curry and offered him a bite. "Of course she did."

Helen was unlike any Midwestern woman I'd met. She made the most exquisite pickles, out of everything from watermelon to daikon radish, and sold them as "Lovers Ridge Culinary Creations" in mason jars tied with paisley ribbon. Her spiced apple cider won a ribbon at the Iowa State Fair. She was addicted to *New York Times* crossword puzzles and started every conversation with a hug. She and Earl spent a week in Chicago every year, seeing plays and dancing at old-time speakeasy clubs. She showed me a picture once that someone had taken of them on the dance floor. Her long, curled hair flew out behind her, and her dress billowed as she spun, caught on camera in midtwirl. Earl held her by one arm, anchoring her as she unfurled. A lock of his hair had fallen, Clark Kent style, over his forehead. They were probably near the same age as Matthew and I were now, and they looked like kids struck giddy with love.

Helen was the reason I could serve chana masala to an old-fashioned meat-and-potatoes Iowan. She'd always said that if she couldn't visit the whole world, she was determined to taste it, and if Helen tasted something, Earl did, too. On the surface they didn't make sense, his laconic manners against her bubbly charm, but after only meeting them a few times I couldn't imagine one without the other. They were the most perfect human example of a proton and an electron, equally charged opposites attracted for over forty years. Until one day, on the way home from the farmer's market, her truck collided with a combine pulling out of a field. She died in the ambulance on the way to the hospital, gone before any of us knew what had happened. Three days later, Earl left her funeral without a word, went back to their house alone, and suffered a massive stroke.

"Is it too warm?" I asked as he chewed.

He jerked his head to the side once. *No.*

I had no appetite. My mind kept cycling through the day's events—the car fire, Ryerson's Woods, Matthew's lies about the grant—looping through outlier after outlier. I wanted to tell Earl about the phone call with Matthew's grad student, but I hesitated. He'd already lost so much—his wife, his independence—and now his only child was missing. Did he want to know his son had lied on top of everything else? I wasn't even sure if it was my place to tell him. Earl and I weren't blood. We were related by marriage. What would happen to us if that marriage disintegrated? My stomach pitched and rolled as the need to be honest warred with the fear of losing my family all over again.

"I can see Helen dragging you to a fortune-teller." I forced a smile and made myself eat a bite. "Did she make you get your palm read?"

He huffed out a breath as he stared at one of his hands, flexing and relaxing the fingers, as if trying to remember the fortune drawn there, a future lost in webbed creases and broken capillaries. With effort, he reached into his hoodie pocket and pulled something out of it.

"What's that?"

The paper was damp and crumpled. When I peeled it apart, all the oxygen left my body.

Average height. Normal build. White. Dark blond (wet?) hair. He's getting weak, losing energy. He can't move, but he sees a stone. The ring he gave her in the woods, a blue stone to match her eyes. Keep her from looking up.

He's alone, trapped in a barn with old and new blood. Celina's barn.

He's afraid.

*   *   *

Earl went to the bathroom after dinner and while he negotiated the facilities, I googled Jonah Kendrick. Natalia had already emailed me the stories she'd found and beyond that there was nothing. No social media or professional sites. I tried academic databases, hoping he'd been profiled in some abnormal psychology journal, and even searched his name with Matthew's, hoping something would hit, a random picture they'd both been tagged in, but came up empty.

Somehow, Jonah Kendrick knew about Matthew's proposal.

The summer we got engaged was one of the happiest of my life. I'd published my first article in *Scientific American* and was awarded a tenfold increase in grant money to study storm severity across the Midwest. Matthew and I had taken a trip to visit my mom and she'd emailed me every day the following week to retell another anecdote about how handsome or polite or charming he'd been.

On the day he proposed, he'd packed us a picnic lunch and we walked the winding paths through Ryerson's Woods. I'd been content, full, and lazily tracking glimpses of cirrocumulus dotting the upper troposphere.

Matthew pulled me to a stop near a break in the trees. "I'm going to spend my life looking at the bottom of your chin."

"Hmm?"

"You might want to check the ground for once."

Matthew knelt beside me, wearing a giant smile and holding a small box. He opened it. A rectangular sapphire glowed inside a ring of diamonds.

"It was my grandmother's," he said, "but she had to sell the main stone during the Depression, so I made this one for you."

"You made it?"

He lifted the ring out of the box. It caught a wave of sunlight filtering through the canopy, setting the dark blue stone alive with light. "I wanted you to have a ring that matched your eyes."

Then he asked me to marry him.

I twisted the ring around my finger now, pressing the edges of the sapphire into the pad of my thumb. Matthew told the story often—he'd even held a gemstone-themed chemistry happy hour once—but it was always about making the stone and the legacy of his grandmother's ring. He never told the part about drawing my attention down from the sky, how I hadn't even noticed I was being proposed to.

But he must have. It was a simple application of Occam's razor, the scientific principle that whichever explanation required the fewest assumptions was usually the correct one. And if I had to choose between two explanations, that either a psychic magically dreamed details of my life or that Matthew shared one of our most intimate moments with this man, the choice was obvious. Painful, but obvious.

I paced the hallway outside the bathroom. The number of data points I couldn't characterize was multiplying almost faster than I could keep up. Kara Johnson. The grant that didn't exist. And now, an unstable man who knew the details of my engagement, making wild claims about Matthew being trapped in a barn.

But were they wild? Was I getting trapped in my own assumptions? A scientist's first duty was to leave biases behind and observe the data as objectively as possible. I went to the kitchen and poured myself a glass of pinot noir. Courage, perhaps. Courage because even though I knew what I needed to do, part of me was scared. I wished I was back in my air lab, Joan and I flying above the world. I wanted everything to go back to how it was before the black cloud rose on the horizon.

Half an hour later, I tucked Earl into bed and began to search. I started upstairs, in the room where Matthew had been sleeping for the past three months. It felt wrong, going through stacks of his papers and chemistry magazines, looking in the trash at receipts for takeout and groceries. I kept the ones for places I didn't remember— a Thai restaurant downtown, a donut shop in Coralville—not sure what exactly they would prove. I avoided the bed, depressed by the image of Matthew sleeping in this small, dark room, then scared because I didn't know where he would sleep tonight. *He's alone. He's afraid.* I tried to stay calm as I searched the closet and dresser, finding nothing but clothes.

The rest of the house turned up even less. Matthew had notes everywhere, chemical compounds jotted in book margins, formulas scrawled on the backs of take-out menus, but that was typical, like my closets full of rain jackets and glove compartments stuffed with handheld weather instruments. I turned every room inside out and finally, after peeking into Earl's room to make sure he was asleep, I pulled on my boots and jacket and went to the garage. The building had been a carriage house when it was first built, a two-story structure on the back of the property, but since we moved in it had always been Matthew's domain.

The bottom floor held nothing unusual—Earl's van, my car, and the empty charging station where Matthew's Tesla would normally be plugged in. All his tools and supplies were in their cabinets, his spare chemicals labeled, sealed, and lined up on ventilated shelves.

Upstairs, Matthew had set up an office on one side of the attic—an L-shaped desk bookended with a few filing cabinets. I sat down at the computer, my gaze drawn to the framed photo next to it, the only other item on the otherwise empty surface. It was from our wedding—a candid shot, not like the posed, smiling ones we hung on walls and shared with family and friends. We thought we'd snuck away through the camouflage of Helen's apple trees, but the photographer had caught us between the blossoms, my arms looped around Matthew's neck and his hand splayed across my back with one finger dipped inside my dress. It was a sweet and sexy shot, a private moment that captured more than all the public ones. Matthew loved this picture. Seeing it here in this cold and empty attic made my throat clot with an emotion I couldn't swallow or expel.

For a moment, I wavered. Maybe I'd misjudged this entire situation. Maybe I was approaching everything wrong. A good wife would be scouring the countryside right now, searching for her missing husband, not poring through his possessions for data that might not exist. What was I even trying to find?

I sat at the desk, staring at my reflection in the dark computer monitor, when a buzzing sound cut through the ping of rain, making me jump out of the chair. The buzzing stopped, then started again. I crept along the dark rafters of the long room into the shadows, as my heart pounded and the noise grew.

Tucked above one of the solar panel converters, I found it—a phone, small and cheap, one of the old flip models I hadn't seen in years.

My heart thudded louder than the rain drumming against the roof.

One new message.

I opened it, and with that one simple move, the black cloud descended, and the real storm began.

Friday

What we know is a drop.
What we don't know is an ocean.

—Isaac Newton

Max

If Matthew Moore wasn't dead, he was in serious trouble.

The court order had come through this morning and I whistled, paging through his credit report. The guy had a million-dollar past-due mortgage and was rotating another hundred thousand dollars in debt with the balance-transfer game. There were sporadic spikes over the last few years. Twenty thousand charged and paid in full. Thirty-five thousand on another card, paid up the next month. A few months ago, the balances started to stick, the money began jumping from one account to the next, and the panic set in.

Not exactly the financial security his wife talked about yesterday. Maybe she hadn't known. Or maybe she'd only found out recently.

What kind of fortysomething professors owned a million-dollar house? I'd driven by the place on my way to work this morning. It was a completely remodeled Victorian in the center of town with a wraparound porch and an honest-to-god turret on one side. Solar panels, weather vanes, and other gauges were mounted to the roof. The front steps were fitted with a wheelchair ramp, painted and trimmed to match the house—no expense spared. I could see Eve

Roth in a house like that, with her designer clothes and fancy hair, but none of it came even close to adding up to two academic salaries. Where were these two getting their money?

I pulled up the bank accounts—in Matthew's name only—and sorted through deposits.

His university paychecks had stopped coming in September, which made sense. If the university had suspended him over a student affair, they'd probably frozen his paychecks, too. But his salary wasn't the only missing income: Matthew Moore had been sending and receiving almost weekly deposits from something called Binance, for amounts that ran between two and ten thousand dollars each. I added them up from January to when they cut off in September. Over two hundred thousand dollars.

Google told me Binance was a cryptocurrency exchange. Bitcoin, Ethereum, Litecoin, Ripple. Great. My biggest financial accomplishment to date was setting up our utilities on automatic bill pay. I had no idea how cryptocurrency worked or why or even what the hell it was, but it looked like I was going to find out.

I was working through my second cup of coffee when the rest of the department started showing up. Ciseski stalked over to his desk across the aisle, shaking rain off his coat like a dog. "Your friend coming by for another tarot reading today?"

"Morning to you, too."

Ciseski and Jonah had never gotten along, but their relationship became almost violent when Ciseski had been assigned Celina's missing person case. He accused Jonah of butting in where he didn't belong, and Jonah accused Ciseski of sitting on his ass doing nothing. I'd been caught in the middle, not wanting to step on another investigator's toes but also not seeing any progress on the case while Jonah's mental state unraveled. And that's where every bad decision was born, between two conflicting priorities.

I gave up on the black hole of cryptocurrency, my head swimming with hard forks and blockchains, and clicked over to Dr. Eve Roth's credit report. The two kept separate accounts for most everything, and her credit was spotless. I hadn't seen her as the type to roll over and accept an affair, and I didn't see her putting up with a guy flailing toward bankruptcy either. No matter what Jonah claimed, Eve Roth was still at the top of my list, and nothing I'd seen this morning changed that.

"That the one in yesterday with the guy in the wheelchair?" Ciseski loitered behind my chair. I closed the window.

"Don't you have some cases?"

"More than my share." He went back to his own desk and booted up his computer. "We all had to cover for you while you were out."

"I'll try not to get shot anymore."

"Yeah, and while you're doing that—"

"Gotta go." I grabbed my coat. The medical examiner was looking at Alexis Dwyer this morning. I hadn't planned to attend, but an autopsy sounded more appealing than spending the morning working next to Ciseski.

While most people were still waking up and having their breakfasts, I stood next to a splayed body, looking through a bag of personal effects while the ME narrated the finer points of Alexis's death. "Minor abrasions on her hands and arms. Did the on-site technicians swab her fingernails?"

"Yeah."

"No obstructions in her throat or nose or signs of cranial injury. I found pulmonary emphysema and mild atherosclerosis. The combined lung weight was two thousand and thirty grams."

"That a lot?"

"Heavy lungs. She probably experienced significant breathlessness, something we often note in opiate-related deaths."

"You think this was an overdose?"

"The emphysema would support that. We'll run a blood sample for toxicology. Did she have a history of drug use?"

"Clean." Not a single arrest on file and the apartment hadn't turned up any illegal substances beyond a small bag of marijuana in a desk drawer. I spent half the night looking through her social media to find evidence of the boyfriend she'd been fighting with, but if this was an accidental overdose, there was nothing to investigate. Just another life lost to the opioid crisis. Her apartment hadn't looked like an addict's, though. She had nice things and took care of them. I made a note to pull her medical history, see if she'd been prescribed any painkillers in the last few months.

Her clothing didn't turn up much beside her phone. A Samsung Galaxy, locked, but it had some juice left in it. I picked up one of Alexis's hands and pressed her thumb to the home screen button.

"Is that necessary?"

"No privacy laws for deceased citizens." I cocked an eyebrow at the woman's inside-out ribcage. "As you should know."

I used my good hand to scroll through her messages, hoping to see a communication trail with a dealer, someone I could chase or at least log as a known associate of a dead woman, but none of her texts had the pattern of a dealer-buyer exchange. It was mostly spam sprinkled with a few people asking Alexis how she was and her responding with neutral-faced emojis or flat-out ignoring them. The photos were largely selfies taken in her apartment, alone. I paged through her apps until one of them stopped me cold.

Binance.

Unlocking it with her thumbprint, I scanned through the cryptocurrency transactions. Unlike Matthew Moore's account, this was all deposits and all the same deposit, three thousand dollars every month like clockwork. No wonder her rent payments were on time.

I flipped open my notebook and reread the landlady's description of Alexis's boyfriend: tall, blond, older, gets his way too much. My gut tensed.

A dead woman and a missing man. I didn't like where this was going.

Eve

For almost a century, scientists knew the atom was the smallest indivisible unit of matter. It was foundational knowledge, the certainty of these tiniest of bricks that built the universe and everything in it. Then, in 1897, J. J. Thomson discovered the electron and cracked open the subatomic world.

Suddenly, atoms were no longer concrete and stable but instead full of charged particles zooming at a tenth of the speed of light. We didn't understand how the world was built anymore. What was the universe now? What were we?

Thomson went on to discover that not only were atoms penetrable, but they also consisted mostly of empty space. According to rumor, he was afraid to get out of his bed the next morning. All the comforting bricks that built his world had turned into bubbles, and he was scared that if he stepped out of bed he might fall straight through the floor.

This morning I understood exactly how J. J. Thomson had felt.

It was still raining, but the world was measurably darker. A slate-colored nimbostratus layer, mottled with steely cirrus clouds, blocked any trace of sun. The temperature had held in the forties overnight, but it wasn't going to last. I'd checked the radars and models sometime around 5:00 a.m., after giving up any hope of sleep, and confirmed the calculations. Within the next six hours the stratus layer would move on, air temperatures would plummet, and the entire flooded surface of Iowa would freeze.

Around seven, Earl started moving in his bedroom.

"Need any help?" I called from the kitchen, hoping my voice didn't sound as shaky as it felt.

He answered with an emphatic grunt.

When he wheeled out of the bedroom, he stopped short at the sight of me. His thermos of iced coffee with his first pills of the morning were lined up in his spot. I circled my own mug with both hands, gravitating toward the warmth, trying not to think about Matthew making our morning coffee, Matthew performing our daily rituals.

Earl's watery gaze took in my hastily thrown together work outfit, red-rimmed eyes, and the bags underneath them. I couldn't conceal my feelings from him, and I respected him too much to lie. Whether it was my place or not, he deserved the truth. Or as much of it as I knew.

I swallowed. "We need to talk."

Last night, when I opened the flip phone hidden in the rafters of the garage, it asked for a password. Four digits. I hesitated, then typed in the code Matthew used for everything from his debit card PIN to the garage door opener—CHON, the mnemonic acronym for carbon, hydrogen, oxygen, and nitrogen, the four most common elements in every living organism.

It worked. The comfort of knowing something about my husband, being able to predict his behavior, was ripped away as fast as it arrived. This phone belonged to Matthew, and I had no idea what it was for.

I scrolled to the new message—an automatic alert about his phone account balance being low. I went back to his desk and opened an app on my own phone designed for field observations. Taking a deep, steadying breath and ignoring my pitching stomach, I started observing.

The phone was a pay-as-you-go model, not on any contracts or plans. A burner, one website called it, which for some reason made me think of the Tesla, engulfed in fire, and the black cloud rising into the storm.

No contacts or data had been programmed into the address book. There was no email or social apps, no internet history at all. The entire phone was blank except for a string of messages exchanged with a single phone number. The most recent one was listed first.

8am. RWP. cu there, lover. ;)

The message was dated yesterday morning, after I'd left for the airfield. RWP. Ryerson's Woods Park.

I dropped the phone. My hands balled into fists and tears stung my eyes at all the marriage counseling sessions, all of Matthew's patient reassurances that he'd never broken our vows. *You're the one, Eve. This is the only life I want, with you, with us. Everything I do is for us.*

I scrolled through the rest of the texts. Most were brief, only a few words back and forth, with confirmations or requests for a different time.

RWP?

😔

LRF 12:00

      can't. tomorrow 4:30?

ok don't make me wait

time to pray

      we have to be careful

make me

At the very beginning of the string was Matthew's first message.

      new phone, just for you

It was sent the day after he'd been photographed outside Kara Johnson's apartment.

I wanted to throw the burner across the room, to drop it in one of the containers of acid in the chemistry cabinet downstairs. I wanted Matthew to walk up the stairs to his office so I could push him back down and watch him fall. Natalia had told me not to believe him. The truth had been right there, in the obvious conclusion, in every sad, awkward look from every TA, staring me right in the face. Occam's razor.

I left the phone in the garage. I didn't want it anywhere near me or Earl or our house, as if it could contaminate our life by mere proximity. I spent most of the night in the cupola as rain beat against the widow's walk, charting the dates Matthew told us he was working on his grant research, and trying to match them with exchanges I'd recorded from the burner. Some fit. Others didn't. Matthew claimed he was working on the grant once or twice a week all semester, but only a handful of meetings had been scheduled on the burner. Were there other phones hidden somewhere? Other women?

After dedicating my life to pursuing data—observing, analyzing, and predicting the world around me—I was overwhelmed by the feeling that I didn't know anything anymore. I couldn't even trust my own memories. Like J. J. Thomson, the bricks of my life had disintegrated, and I was struggling not to fall straight through the floor.

I told Earl everything over our morning coffee. His face pinched tighter the longer I talked, and angry tears leaked out of his good eye, following the track of wrinkled skin down his cheek and neck. He was typing out a misspelled rant about his son when a noise outside caught both our attention. I darted to the kitchen window to see an old pickup pulling into the driveway.

Had someone picked up Matthew and given him a ride home? A surge of hope shot through me. If Matthew was back, he could explain the grant, the phone, the car fire, everything. I would drive him to the police station myself.

The man who climbed out of the truck was older, though: a tall, gray-haired figure. I didn't recognize him through the rain, not until he turned. Then confusion melted into relief.

I ran through the house and flung open the front door.

"Sam!"

A smile spread over his face.

Sam Olson was decked out in his usual coveralls and waders. An Iowan to his bones, he wore a year-round sunburn and a stubborn jaw prepared to endure both hell and high water. The first time I'd met Sam and his wife, Matthew had introduced them as his other parents. I'd assumed it was just a nice thing to say, until I got to know them and understood how true it was.

Sam and Isabella had lived next door to Earl and Helen for decades and never had kids of their own. They'd attended all of Matthew's Little League games, driving hours across the state to cheer him on. When his first chemistry set melted a hole in Helen's kitchen table, Sam had cleared out an old shed and let Matthew set up his experiments there. And when he went to prom, he brought his date to both houses for pictures. As someone who'd spent half her childhood with only one parent, growing up with four seemed like an unimaginable luxury.

But more parents meant more family to lose. Isabella had died of cancer the year after our wedding, leaving a surprise trust fund for Matthew that had allowed us to buy and remodel the Victorian. Matthew had barely come to terms with Isabella's death when we lost Helen in the car accident—a wrenching, senseless death—and Earl had suffered his stroke. Of all Matthew's parents, Sam alone remained unchanged.

He still lived an hour west of Iowa City, where the four of them had spent most of their lives together. I hated thinking about him there, with no wife beside him or best friends next door, but he claimed only an act of god could get him to move and that "big city life" would suffocate him. "Can't hardly throw a rock in Iowa City without hittin' someone," he'd joked once. We'd brought Earl out for a visit last summer, but that was six months ago. Guilt threatened to overshadow the happiness I felt at seeing him now.

"How are you?" I asked as he reached the porch.

"Heading to Davenport this morning to sell a guy a snowblower. Figured I'd say hi to these two yahoos on my way." Sam nodded behind me as he propped a boot on the porch steps. He was an ox of a man, and the years had only toughened him. "How you doing these days, Doc? Besides still being pretty as a picture."

"You haven't heard about Matthew?"

"About that student, yeah." His smile evaporated into deep creases. "Dumbest damn thing that boy's ever done."

That was newly debatable, but I didn't have time to get into it again. I told him about the fire and Matthew's disappearance, pulling the front door shut so Earl couldn't overhear. "I don't know what to do about my classes. Earl hated going to campus yesterday, but it's too late to schedule a home health aide."

Sam waved me off. "Don't say another word. I'll stay."

"Don't you need to get to Davenport?" I glanced at his pickup, where a tarp tethered the snowblower to the truck bed.

"As long as I head out by noon, I'll be fine."

"Noon. That's perfect." I couldn't help it. Gratitude propelled me toward Sam's scratchy coveralls. He chuckled at the hug, patting my back with a grizzled hand.

Inside, Sam poured himself a cup of coffee and drew up a chair next to Earl. For a moment, all I could do was watch them, a lump clotting my throat. On paper, it might not have been obvious why they were lifelong friends. Sam had been drafted into Vietnam, while Earl had received a student deferment. Earl and Helen had traveled the country, while Sam and Isabella never vacationed farther than their annual Clear Lake fishing trip. Earl was a Democrat, Sam a Republican. But none of that mattered when Sam swiveled in his chair to include me in their conversation and asked the million-dollar question.

"What happened to our boy?"

Because he was theirs. He was all they had left.

Earl's head lowered and the good side of his mouth pinched. It weighed on him—the fire, the hidden affair, even the insane idea of Matthew hurt and trapped in a barn somewhere. Every possible reality pressed against him, taking from him, making his entire body seem to shrivel. I wanted to hug him and tell them both not to worry, but how could I comfort them with anything less than the truth?

I had to find Matthew.

Eve

"Kara Johnson?"

Pawan shuffled backward toward my office door. He had a laptop balanced on top of some equipment for an end-of-course demonstration, and somewhere inside that load of supplies, glass began rattling against metal.

"Yes, the student Matthew was accused of having an affair with. Do you know her?"

I'd reviewed the evidence again during my commute: the lover's note arranging to meet at RWP, the few grant dates I'd been able to match to the phone exchanges. Maybe Kara Johnson had nothing to do with this. For all I knew, Matthew could've been seeing anyone behind my back, but Kara was the data I had. She was where I had to start.

I'd already pulled her file up in the university database. She'd enrolled as a transfer student and landed on the dean's list with classes that didn't match the typical liberal studies track. Concepts in Drawing paired with Fundamental Genetics, Neurobiology in the same semester as Art at the End of the World. I couldn't access any of her personal information—no address, phone number, or any way of contacting her beyond the standard issue university email address—and was deleting the browser session when Pawan came to collect me for our final Fluid Dynamics class of the semester.

"I don't know her."

"Have you seen her?"

"Um . . ." He looked like he'd rather fly into a supercell than continue this conversation.

Normally I would never press a TA into personal territory, but Pawan and Matthew were friends. He'd been so upset yesterday, so why was he suddenly nervous when I brought up Kara Johnson's name?

I pushed away from my desk. Pawan looked at the floor, my bookshelves, the empty hallway behind him, anywhere but at me.

"What do you know?"

The glass in his arms clinked faster, on the verge of breaking as I closed the distance between us.

"Pawan."

"Okay." He set the experiment down and pulled my office door shut. "I don't know her. I had no idea she existed until . . . well . . ." He still had trouble making eye contact. "But I saw them together."

"Last summer?"

He shook his head, clearly miserable. "A few weeks ago, at a thrift store in the ped mall. I was browsing for coats. I knew I recognized the girl behind the counter, but it wasn't until Professor Moore walked in that I placed her. He didn't see me, and the two of them went into the back room. I . . . I didn't stay long after that."

The pain was surprising, the sudden violence of it, like betrayal could be given mass and sharp, cutting force. In our therapy sessions, Matthew claimed he'd had no more contact with Kara. He said he'd realized the inappropriateness of him as a professor trying to help a student. His head hung heavy when he admitted it, his voice racked with regret, and I'd believed him. I believed every word.

Pawan gave me the name of the store and showed me where it was on his phone. "But what about the university investigation? Are you supposed to be talking to her?"

"No. Are you going to tell them?"

He shook his head. "Of course not."

"Thank you." I pulled the vials I'd collected from Ryerson's Woods Park out of my briefcase. "I have another job for you."

The ped mall covered three blocks of cobblestone-paved pedestrian streets on the east side of campus, catering to drunk undergrads by night and their visiting parents' wallets by day. Sometimes Matthew and I would walk to lunch at one of the new bistros or pubs that popped up every semester, but today I sloshed across campus alone, shivering under an umbrella and wading through dark, stagnant water at every curb.

Only a few students dotted the sidewalks. An all-campus alert had interrupted my last lecture, canceling afternoon classes ahead of the impending freeze. The alert advised students and faculty to stock up on essentials—food, water, batteries, candles—and return to their residences immediately.

While waiting at a light, I called the house.

"We're chewing on this Matthew thing," Sam said when I asked how things were going. "Trying to figure out where the kid went."

"Any luck?"

"He hasn't shown up at any hospitals. We checked as far away as Waterloo. Posted his picture on Nextdoor, too, to put the neighborhood on alert. His toothbrush is still here. Sorry, I checked. I just . . ."

"It's fine. I know."

"It's like he just walked away." His voice was gruff with concern. The TV was on in the background, and I could picture the two of them putting their heads together over coffee all morning, which sent a pang of guilt through me. Matthew and I should have done a better job keeping them connected. Earl needed his friends, especially now.

"He didn't hit his head or anything, did he? I saw a show the other day about a guy who fell off a ladder at a construction site and forgot who he was. His family, job, everything. He left work that day and disappeared. They found him three years later in Texas, driving a garbage truck."

"Put the remote down slowly, Sam, and back away."

He chuckled. "How you holding up, Doc?"

"Teaching was a good distraction. I've got one quick errand and should be home soon." I didn't mention Kara because Pawan was right: the university had specifically instructed me not to talk to or approach her while their investigation was ongoing. The fewer people who knew I was violating that directive, the better. "Are you okay staying a little longer?"

"A half hour, maybe. It's starting to look dicey out there. I can bunk overnight in Davenport when the freeze hits, but I've got to leave soon if I want to get ahead of it."

In half an hour, Earl would be alone. My time to find Kara was running out.

I glanced back as I crossed the street. Two men walked not far behind me. They weren't talking or hurrying to get out of the rain like everyone else. Their faces were shadowed by ball caps, but it felt like they were looking at me. On the other side of the street, I picked up my pace and turned the corner into the ped mall.

There were a few more people heading in and out of stores here, and I weaved my way among them, trying to put space between myself and the two men. When I turned another corner, I checked behind me again. They had stopped at a bar menu posted in a window.

The thrift store was sandwiched between another bar and an accessories boutique. The windows were filled with clothes, making it impossible to see inside, and a few racks of clearance items were set up underneath the awning. The two men hadn't appeared again yet. Maybe they were nobody. It made no sense to think they were following me, but I still ducked inside the store before they turned the corner.

The place was long and narrow, crowded with jumbled racks of clothing that smelled like old denim and cracked leather. I couldn't hear anything beyond the metallic ping of rain hitting pipes. No one manned the counter. Was the store even open? Then a murmur of voices came from a back room. My pulse picked up. Pawan had seen Matthew going into the back with Kara. What if he was here now? What if I'd walked in on them?

A sick feeling spread through my gut, but I needed to know. I crept around racks of clothing until I was a few feet from the door.

"Tonight," someone said. A woman? The voice was low and angry, making the hair on the back of my neck stand up.

"Fuck, all the way out there in this shit? It's going to be an ice rink." Another voice, slightly higher, followed by the thud of soft material striking hard. Cardboard on cement. I moved closer to the wall, counting footsteps. It sounded like at least three people, maybe more.

"He lit his car on fire. The cops are involved now. We don't have a choice."

A sudden rustling by the door sent me backward into a rack of clothes. I froze against the hangers, not daring to make a sound.

"Get your shit. One hour."

Someone said something else, but I didn't catch it. I eased the hangers back into place and backtracked as fast as I could to the middle of the store. Grabbing a random shirt, I held it up and pivoted to a mirror just as the back door opened. A guy slouched through the racks, wearing a Hawkeye baseball cap. He glanced over on his way to the counter.

"We're closing soon."

I nodded and pulled another shirt from the rack, feeling his eyes on me.

More noises came from the back, followed by a slamming door and a truck engine firing up, then a young woman appeared.

She didn't see me at first—she was flipping through pages in a notebook—but when she got to the counter, the guy jerked his head toward me. Her spine straightened. She recognized me, and we both knew it.

"Your shift's over."

The guy looked surprised. "But what about—"

"Go."

He obeyed, grabbing a backpack and making a beeline for the front door. As soon as it slammed shut, the store became uncomfortably quiet.

I hung the shirt up and moved to the counter, a dirty Formica block with an iPad chained to it. The woman slipped her notebook under a stack of papers, watching me.

She was tiny, her features spare and precise, and her tan skin and dark brown eyes spoke of a Spanish heritage I hadn't considered with a name like Kara Johnson. Despite the season, she wore a tank top with camouflage pants, and her long dark hair was swept into a simple ponytail. The tattoo I'd seen in the video of her and Matthew didn't look garish up close. It was a vine of ivy dotted with birds that climbed from her arm over her shoulder and ended in a tendril of green below her earlobe. The artwork continued up one ear lined with hoops and studs of no discernible theme. She didn't look like a typical dean's list student, but she also didn't look like someone who would be ordering people around with careless authority, and this subversion of expectations created an odd dissonance in my brain. I felt off-balance, underprepared.

"We're closed."

"This shouldn't take long."

"No." Her chin jutted out and her head tilted to the side. "It won't."

I didn't know where to start. I'd planned to come here and ask Kara Johnson point-blank about her relationship with Matthew. To be direct, honest, and request honesty in return. But the conversation I'd overheard threw all my plans out the window. They'd been talking about Matthew. Kara said Matthew lit his car on fire, that he'd done it himself. But why?

"What are you doing here?" Kara asked, emphasis on the "you."

"I wanted to introduce myself." I held out a hand that she didn't shake.

"I could call campus security."

"We're not on campus."

"Or file a harassment complaint."

"The university is committed to providing a safe space for free speech." I braced myself on the counter. "And I'd like for us to have that right now."

"A safe space for free speech?"

I nodded.

She leaned into the other side of the counter, her face too close to mine. "Then I'll say this once. Be safe and get out of here."

"I will momentarily, but in the meantime"—I pulled my phone out of my pocket and worked to keep my hand from shaking—"where's Matthew?"

"Professor Moore?" She blinked in unconvincing confusion. "I haven't seen him in months."

"I'm not blaming you. I'm not here to cause a scene. I need to know the truth."

"No." Abruptly, she pushed away from the counter and stood up. "You don't."

Given her stature, the effect shouldn't have been all that impressive, but there was something regal in her bearing, a core of strength that didn't match the fragile-looking exterior, and I was struck again by the discord embedded in this young woman. In the video, she'd clung to Matthew. And in the phone . . .

"I found his burner, the one he used to contact you."

"I don't know what you're talking about."

I lifted my own phone, swallowing as I stared at the number I'd programmed from the burner, and hit Send.

The vibration came immediately, a muffled buzz of sound against wood. The phone number Matthew had been texting was right here, beneath the counter.

A series of expressions unfolded over Kara's face. First surprise, followed by what looked like rapid mental calculations, and finally—strangest of all—resignation. Her whole body slumped, and I was trying to process what that meant when she reached underneath the counter. Instead of pulling out her phone, she produced a gun.

"What—" I dropped the phone and stepped back. My hands lifted automatically. My father had kept a rifle on the farm when I was a kid, but I'd never seen a handgun in real life, let alone had one pointed at me.

Kara picked up my phone. Shaking her head, she began scrolling and typing in commands. All the charts and data I'd recorded from last night were in my field notes app. My heart thudded in my ears as I watched her, hoping she wouldn't think to look in that application.

"What did you do to him?" I was surprised at how steady my voice sounded. Adrenaline shot through my body, helping me calculate the distance to the exits, the thickness of the walls if I had to scream.

"We have to talk."

Kara went to the entrance. As soon as her back was turned, I reached under the pile of papers on the counter and took the notebook she'd brought out of the back room with her. Slipping it in my coat pocket, I raised my hands again and turned in time to see her collide with a customer opening the front door.

I screamed.

Jonah

Ambient chords mixed with the pound of rain, the perfect cocktail to clear my head. I walked through downtown Iowa City, passing the ghosts of dive bars Max had dragged me to in college, some with the same dirty entrances, sad and unchanged, others reinvented as restaurants with scrubbed brick walls, chalkboard menus, and plants on the tables.

The pedestrian mall was almost deserted, and the few people I passed stayed blissfully trapped in their own heads. Weather had always been useful that way. Maybe it was electromagnetic whatevers in the air or maybe storms distracted people from their own cesspools of emotion. I didn't care as long as it meant I could walk down the street like a normal human. A couple people hurried under store awnings or under umbrellas. Down an alley, five or six guys scrambled into a delivery truck and pulled away. The only other person who didn't seem to mind the rain was a kid in a Hawkeye ball cap jabbing something into his phone. I got a rumble of discontent as he went past, but it broke and scattered as quickly as it came.

I hadn't dreamed last night, or if I had, the dreams weren't meant to be remembered. Enhypnion, Mom would have said. Flapping through the ivory gate.

After she learned the full extent of my intuition, my mother made it her mission to normalize me or at least find a community of freaks where I could belong. She told anyone who would listen how Abraham Lincoln had dreamt of his own assassination weeks before his death, and she took me to Virginia Beach after graduation to visit the Edgar Cayce Center, founded by the turn-of-the-century sleeping psychic. Eventually she stumbled onto ancient Greek philosophy.

The Greeks had believed there were two kinds of dreams: oneiros and enhypnion. Enhypnion were run-of-the-mill dreams, the daily compost chugging through most people's subconscious. Nothing worth bothering with after you woke up. The others, oneiros, were different. Oneiros had divine origins and were meant to be investigated.

"Your dreams come from god," she told me. Bold words from a lifelong Lutheran.

That was before the girl in the drainpipe. I hadn't yet gotten that kind of nightmare—melas oneiros, the black dream—but the more Max taught me how to remember my dreams, the more the line between my sleeping and waking life blurred. Voices chased me into the daylight hours, the stink of their fear circling me, becoming my own. When the lost people I dreamed about had been taken violently, I felt their thrashing and their bewildering pain. When they'd disappeared on their own, the hollows of their depression swallowed me whole and silent. If my dreams were from god, he was one sick bastard.

"They're a gift, Jonah," my mom insisted. "I hate seeing you suffer. I wish you didn't have the oneiros, for your own happiness, but maybe god gave you this burden because he knew you could bear it, to help others."

We argued over it for years, her benevolent grab bag theology against my refusal to acknowledge I was some instrument of the divine. The only comfort I got was in the finding, working with Max whenever a new dream came, tracking down the person and helping them find their way home.

I'd spent a while this morning on the newest oneiros, piecing together Matthew Moore's life, trying to decide which angle to follow. Missing car fire man had a glossy online presence that included a lot of clickbait chemistry headlines and showy lab experiments on YouTube, but his accounts had been silent for months. His university phone number had a permanent out-of-office message. Mother dead, no brothers or sisters, and I'd already exhausted my welcome with the father and wife. I moved on to the only other person he'd spent time with recently—Kara Johnson.

Max gave me the bare bones last night—student, clean record, no charges or complaints filed on her part over the scandal. I waded through a thousand Kara Johnson profiles online, getting nothing until I landed on a staff page at Find and Consign, a "vintage upcycler" in downtown Iowa City. With any luck, I could upcycle some information on Matthew Moore.

The second I walked into the thrift shop the world tilted. It was so sudden and absurd I didn't know if I'd slipped over the line of consciousness into a dream.

The scream came first, cutting through my headphones and hitting the ambient chords like a knife stabbing into a blanket. I barely registered the screamer—Eve Roth?—before someone else plowed into me.

Celina.

My mind stuttered. The girl shoved me into the doorframe— long, dark hair; tiny, tattooed frame; a fisted Glock and a wave of anger curling her shoulders. Not Celina. The metal slamming into my back was cold and solid. I was almost sure I was awake.

The girl said something. I didn't know what. I was still wearing my noise-canceling headphones, and my ears were full of low, spreading bass and humming synthesizer. Calming music. A playlist for meditation. I grabbed the barrel of the gun and smashed it into the wall.

She didn't drop her weapon. Using my own grip, she whipped me around and sent a kick to my groin. I felt her decision the millisecond before her leg whipped up and turned in time for the blow to connect with my hip instead. The music swelled, wrapping notes like silk threads around the force of the impact. I spun her along the wall and into the window frame hard enough to feel the crack of her skull against glass, but there was no accompanying jolt of pain.

She wasn't scared or hurt. No adrenaline or shock permeated the music. I grabbed the girl's wrist, making direct contact, and the only emotion I could pick up from this tiny, tattooed terminator was a driving pulse of determination.

Our eyes locked and her mouth moved again. I still couldn't hear anything, but a surge of purpose shot through me.

Yanking as hard as I could, I pulled her into a rack of clothes that crashed to the floor, taking both of us with it. I braced for a flash and blast, the hot, blinding pain, but when I opened my eyes, I lay on a pile of clothes, headphones knocked off and holding the Glock.

Eve was there in a flash, searching the girl's pockets. "Give me back my phone."

The girl's hands fisted, but I sat up and trained the gun on her, surfing the crest of her focus, using her own energy against her. When Eve came up with a phone, the girl shoved her into me, knocking both of us down. By the time I rolled up, she was disappearing through the back door.

I staggered up. Pain shot through my hip. Cursing, I limped into the back, clocking both sides of a long storage room full of cardboard boxes that looked like a giant, failed Jenga game before running into the alley, where a river of rainwater flooded the broken asphalt. Nothing. She was gone.

I pocketed the gun. What the hell had just happened? Eve hovered in the storage room with a metal rod from the busted clothing rack, holding it like a bat. The woman liked bats.

"Is she gone?"

I nodded, and without another word Eve turned heel and went back into the main store. I limped after her.

"You're welcome."

"For what?"

"I saved your life."

"I doubt she was going to kill me."

"She was robbing you."

Eve dropped the rod on the counter and pulled out her phone, ignoring me. Other than ruffled hair and an askew jacket, she seemed all right.

"That was Kara Johnson?"

No answer. I limped around the counter and sat on the cashier's stool, stretching out my leg. Why had I thought she was

Celina? Maybe I had dreamt about Celina last night, mixed in with the enhypnion sludge, and she'd followed me here. I shouldn't be surprised. Celina was bleeding into every waking corner of my life. I heard her in police scanners and saw her in the faces of strangers. She was the lost person my brain found everywhere.

"No." Eve's fingers flew over the phone, and her shot of panic echoed through my chest, making my pulse stutter and jump.

"What is it?" I jerked up, checking both doors.

"She wiped my phone. All of my data is gone." Eve threw the phone on the counter, a thousand-dollar device that cracked against the scarred wood.

"What did you have on there?"

"Climate logs, storm photos, all the field data I hadn't down-loaded yet. And all the information I charted last night." I had no idea what she was talking about, but it was obviously important to her. She paced, and her energy turned more emotional than anything I sensed when she was being held at gunpoint. She felt violated, out of control. "If you really were psychic, you could've shown up five minutes earlier and taken the gun before she pulled it on me."

"That's precognition. I don't have that."

"You categorize your psychosis?"

The shelves behind the counter were stuffed with a random assortment of crap. I started sifting through them. "Precognition is foresight. Being able to see the future. Seeing the past is called retrocognition."

She cocked her head as I pulled out a stack of notebooks and loose papers.

"Telepaths have mind-to-mind communication. Clairvoyants can perceive things beyond the range of the senses and draw information from objects."

"You said you see things at a distance. So you identify as clairvoyant?"

"And occasionally telepathic, if I'm close to someone. For extra fun." I flipped through the notebooks. There was something about paper. Bound paper. Ink. I focused on the contact I'd had with the girl. I'd felt determination, but it was hollow. A steel barrier surrounding a void. The paper had been an important object to her. It was all she had.

None of these papers were right. Most of the stack was just handwritten ledgers, showing an insane number of customers who bought other people's used clothes. Nothing like old sweat and laundered trauma. I tossed them aside and rounded on Eve Roth, who was shoving her phone in her pocket and getting ready to leave.

"Why would Kara Johnson wipe your phone? Why would she care about storm data and weather stuff?"

"She didn't." Reluctantly, she told me about a burner she'd found in her husband's office and the messages back and forth between Kara and Matthew. A churn of frustration and embarrassment hugged her like perfume as she admitted what a complete ass her husband was. But something was off. Why would Kara hold her lover's wife at gunpoint to cover up an affair? There was more going on here than sex.

"He was gone more than the times they arranged to meet?"

"Yes."

"How many more?"

"At least a dozen." She crossed her arms, looking away. "There could have been more women. Other phones."

I liked this guy less and less. If I didn't need him to get to Celina, it would have been tempting to let him rot in the barn forever. To watch him cycle through my dreams until he broke apart into the mire of the drainpipe.

"The burner. Where is it?"

"At home."

"We need to secure it. Now." I grabbed my headphones—still on top of the mess of clothes in the middle of the floor—and headed for the door. "If she went to this much trouble to get rid of a copy—"

"I don't have time for—"

I left before she could finish the insult.

Eve

I raced after the flapping black trench coat.

"Where are you going?"

"To get that burner before she does."

"You can't know she's going there."

Logic had no effect on him. He stalked down the pedestrian mall, hands stuffed in his coat, head down. He moved quickly, despite a slight limp, like he wanted to get away from me equally as much as he wanted to follow Kara Johnson. The rain had slowed to a mist, and the cloud cover lightened to a heather gray, but the storm was far from over. The freeze was coming.

"Why were you here?" We passed two men, not the same ones I'd seen before, but it made me look around to be sure no one was behind us. Then a suspicion made me jog faster. "Were you following me?"

"No."

"You followed me home from the police station, though."

He didn't slow down. His hair, which he hadn't bothered covering, dripped into his face and shielded most of his profile. "Aren't you following me right now?"

"That's not the same—"

"I'm looking for your husband," he interrupted. "If I can find him, I might be able to find my client. Kara Johnson obviously knows something."

"Why don't you read her mind, then?"

"It doesn't work like that. Brains aren't databases."

"It doesn't *work* at all. Clairvoyance? Telepathy? There isn't a single study that's produced replicable empirical evidence to support any of it." I'd spent a half an hour looking it up during my mostly sleepless night, and even though it didn't matter, even though I should've simply been grateful that he walked into the store when he did, I was spoiling for a fight. Matthew's lies seethed inside me with no outlet, and when I'd tried to get one single piece of reliable information, I'd had a gun pointed at me. I was done with nice.

"You can't replicate a memory," he said. "Does that make it invalid?"

"A ridiculous comparison. Everyone accepts the unidirection-ality of space-time—"

"Everyone." He smirked through a curtain of hair.

"I'm speaking of science, obtaining systematized knowledge through observation and testing." We crossed the promenade and darted through a hotel lobby into a parking garage. He unlocked the same car that had been parked in my driveway yesterday, a bright blue sedan with sleek lines and oversized tires.

"Get in if you're coming," he said before disappearing into the car. I hesitated, still mad, but the roar of his engine followed less than a breath later. He wasn't wasting time. If, in the most bizarre and unlikely of scenarios, he was actually right and Kara Johnson wanted to take the burner, I needed to get home as soon as possible. I could stop her or at least record her break-in attempt. And if, in every other plausible scenario, she wasn't trying to break into our garage, at least I'd be able to shut my front door in Jonah Kendrick's face again.

I climbed in a split second before he reversed out of the space, still groping for the seat belt as he gunned the car through the ramp toward the exit. A few people heading to their own vehicles jumped out of the way.

I texted Earl to let him know I was on the way and told him to lock the doors, just in case. It was past noon; Sam was already on his way to Davenport.

"Give me the gun."

He hesitated only a second before handing me the weapon.

I'd never held a gun before and wasn't excited to be starting now. I didn't feel powerful or macho or any of the things men puffed up with in movies. The metal was smooth and dangerously sleek, as if my finger could drift to the trigger and squeeze without thought. All the active shooter trainings I'd had to sit through at the university flashed through my mind with their repeated reminders to flee. Get the students and staff to safety. Never attempt to disarm an assailant. But Jonah Kendrick hadn't fled. He'd wrestled the gun from Kara, even as the barrel of it was pointed at his chest.

I tucked the weapon between my leg and the edge of the seat closest to the door, looking up as Kendrick flew through an intersection.

"The speed limit is twenty-five."

"I can read." His speedometer didn't fall below the fifty-mile-an-hour mark, so I refrained from telling him anything else obvious, like he was going to crash into a building and kill us both. We raced through neighborhoods where houses and stores blurred together. Twice he swerved into oncoming traffic to pass a slower vehicle. I shifted the barrel of the gun away when it fell toward me—was it loaded, was there a way to tell?—and gripped the door handle. At least he was heading in the right direction.

After a minute of nothing but the roaring engine and rain, the car still miraculously intact and not wrapped around a light pole, I asked him, "How do you know Matthew?"

"I don't. I didn't even know his name before I knocked on your door yesterday."

"You must have met him, online or in person. There's no other way you could know about the ring."

He made a noise of understanding as he took a hard left on the last main road before my neighborhood. "The blue stone to match your eyes." He glanced over, taking his attention from the street for an uncomfortable amount of time, looking at my ring finger. "Sapphire? Pretty."

"You said you didn't have the ability to see into the past. Matthew gave me that ring years ago. You can't even keep your story straight about your so-called abilities."

He sped through a light that had turned red before we even entered the intersection. "I can't see the past in and of itself. Your husband remembered proposing to you while he was in the barn. I heard his thoughts and he was thinking, for whatever reason"— Kendrick shot me some side-eye—"about you."

"But—" A set of flashing lights flared behind us.

"Oh, fuck me," he muttered, somehow surprised at this outcome. For a moment he stayed in the lane, and I had an awful vision of a car chase and police helicopters and sharpshooters, but in the next heartbeat he let off the gas and pulled swiftly to the curb, sending a cascade of icy water onto the sidewalk. The squad car parked behind us.

"Put the gun away."

"Shouldn't we tell them about it?" I glanced down. The weapon was small, but it felt enormous on the seat.

"No."

Before I could argue, another car cut onto the shoulder in front of us, boxing us in. This one was an unmarked sedan with only a single light flashing on top.

"Kara Johnson pulled this on me. I should tell them." I should have called the police the minute she fled the thrift store.

"It has more of our fingerprints on it than hers by now. Maybe you don't know the justice system very well, but victims aren't usually the ones waving guns around."

Neither officer had gotten out of their car. I picked up the weapon. "We have proof that she knows something about Matthew's disappearance. She sent him the message arranging to meet him yesterday."

"You don't have proof until we get that burner. You have a story and a gun."

"But you were there. You can, you know, corroborate." I was ninety-five percent sure that was the correct word.

He laughed—one hollow bark of sound—and for a second I thought he was laughing at my vocabulary. Then he set his hands into the ten-two position, eyes on the rearview mirror. "Sorry you didn't luck out on witnesses. They won't believe anything I say."

With a sinking feeling, I realized he was right. My witness had already been kicked out of the police station once this week, and I was the wife who'd confronted her husband's student lover. It would be my word against hers, and which one of us was more likely to pull a gun in that scenario? I should never have gone to see Kara. I trusted Pawan not to say anything, but if there was a police report, the university would find out. I could lose my job.

"It's now or never, Eve." His voice hadn't raised or changed in tone. He wasn't telling me what to do, leaving the choice to me. The officer behind us got out of his squad car.

I made a decision.

Max

"Sir, is there a situation?" the patrol officer radioed over.

"No." I rapped my fingers on the wheel, already regretting pulling over. "Proceed."

He approached Jonah's driver-side window, caution laced through his stance. I'd made him nervous. I sighed. I could still leave. I'd been on my way to the station when I passed the Lancer Evolution on the side of the road and instinct had taken over. It was muscle memory, standing between Jonah and the world, but I told myself that if he got taken in, it would become my problem anyway. Better to deal with it out here, away from Larsen and the rest of the department.

I got out. Slush soaked the patrol officer's poncho and boots every time a car sped past, so I moved to the safer side of the Evolution and waited for the passenger window to open. The person who rolled down the window, though, was Dr. Eve Roth.

I looked from her to Jonah, trying to wrap my head around finding the two of them together. Her eyes darted around the car, not landing on anything, and she was breathing like she'd run a marathon. Jonah stared straight ahead, stony, not meeting my eyes.

Last night he'd referred to her by first name. Was there some kind of relationship here? I didn't see a physicist working with a psychic detective, but I couldn't think of any other reason she'd be in Jonah's car. I'd told him to stay away from this case. Explicitly. And here he was, ferrying my main suspect around town.

"Sir?" The patrol officer spoke over the top of the hood. "He was going almost thirty miles an hour over the speed limit. He ran a light, recklessly endangered everyone else on the road, and didn't pull over right away."

"This is Jonah Kendrick."

The officer looked at the license in his hand again. He glanced between me and Jonah, the stories of the cop and his psychic best friend slowly registering, clearly unsure of the situation he'd just walked into. "Are we bringing him in?"

"Nope. In fact, we're going to give him a safe escort right out of town with the captain's compliments. Why don't you go write up the ticket as a parting gift? Something to remember us by."

After the patrol officer went back to his cruiser, Eve Roth turned to me. "He can't leave town yet. I need to get home right away."

I looked past her like she hadn't spoken. "What are you doing?"

"What I have to." Jonah's jaw was clenched.

"If you pop up on the radar for this shit again, I'm not going to be able to step in. You'll be arrested for obstruction."

"Max!" Jonah exploded, making both Eve and me flinch. "If we don't move now, there won't be any evidence left."

"What evidence?" I leaned in.

The hollows beneath his eyes were dark and bruised looking. "You work your case, and I'll work mine."

It was exactly what I'd said I wanted, for us to go our separate ways, but he knew damn well I was assigned to Matthew Moore's case. He couldn't pretend the path he'd chosen wouldn't collide directly with mine.

"Dr. Roth." I turned to Eve, who played nervously with the handle of her briefcase. "Have you found anything that could help us locate Matthew?"

"You should talk to Kara Johnson."

"Yesterday you said he wasn't in contact with her."

"I said not to my knowledge."

"But your knowledge has changed since yesterday?" I kept my voice even, calm. She gave Jonah a sidelong glance and he moved his head a fraction of an inch. *No.* She swallowed, nervous as all hell, and shook her head.

I didn't like a single thing that was happening right now. Collusion brewed between them, but Eve Roth was anxious, in a hurry, and that was as good a recipe as any for getting an honest reaction from someone. I pulled up the picture of Alexis Dwyer I'd copied off social media.

"What about her? Does Matthew know this woman?"

She was taken aback, but she studied the picture intently. "Is she a student?"

"No."

Something in her gaze flared. Anger, quickly veiled. "I don't know."

The rest of Alexis Dwyer's autopsy this morning had been uneventful. The ME found no evidence of rape, assault, or trauma, apart from a single syringe mark on her arm. One fresh mark, without any of the scar tissue that would signal habitual or past use. The ME favored ruling it an overdose, pending the toxicology report, but the real question was intent. It didn't feel accidental, with her clean record and cozy apartment, and there was no suicide note or evidence of ideation so far. The ME confirmed she'd been dead a few days, which put time of death on Tuesday, sometime after her fight with the blond boyfriend.

"Was Matthew home on Tuesday afternoon?"

"Why?"

"I'm trying to reconstruct his movements this week."

"I don't know. I was on campus all day."

"Do you know anything about Matthew trading cryptocurrency?"

She answered without hesitation. "He dabbled. I know he moved some of the investments he inherited into Bitcoin. That's how he bought the Tesla."

I wouldn't characterize two hundred thousand a year as dabbling, but before I could press her further an RV appeared down the street—an older brown-and-tan model. My bad arm tensed, throwing shocks of pain up my shoulder and crawling over my spine. Instinctively, I crouched behind the car.

The RV lumbered past. The driver was an older white lady, her hair tied back in a bandanna, wiry hands perched on the oversized wheel. A teenager slumped in the passenger seat next to her, his bored face lit up by a screen. A wave of slush from their tires crashed against the Evolution, mirroring the white noise short-circuiting inside my head.

"Max." Jonah's gaze flicked down. My good hand had snapped to my holster, tensed around the butt of the weapon.

I let go, forcing my fingers to relax, and watched the RV roll down the street. Sweat had broken out on my forehead and I pulled my hat off, rubbing a sleeve over my face.

"Are you okay?" Eve asked, and I thought of the messages on Alexis's phone. Friends checking in, making sure she was all right, and getting her neutral emoji replies. The antidepressants in her cabinet. Maybe there were suicide risks there, underneath the veneer. I could be seeing crimes that didn't exist.

The officer returned, rattling off an entire list of violations. Some couldn't have been valid, but I didn't argue and neither did Jonah. He grabbed the ticket and his license and asked if he was free to go.

I nodded to the officer, who hesitated even as another car sent a torrent of slush at him. "I'll escort them out of town."

Jonah

I took the corner to Eve Roth's block at thirty miles an hour and gunned toward the giant Victorian.

"The garage is in back." Eve pointed to the back side of their yard.

Part of me still couldn't believe she hadn't told Max the entire thing. She had the scent of a lifelong rule follower, someone who lived inside the lines. Hell, the lines were drawn for people like Dr. Eve Roth. But she'd stayed quiet. She'd followed my lead. Something had flipped inside her, and I didn't know what it was.

I pulled through the driveway to the detached building in the back. It was a dream garage, three stalls wide and two-stories tall, topped with solar panels but no windows or any way for the outside world to get in. Pick this up and put it on the bluffs of the Mississippi, away from any town or tourist overlook, and I would live in a place like this for the rest of my life.

Eve punched in a code on her phone and the doors lifted. On the back side of the building, a small, rear door stood wide open.

We glanced at each other and climbed out. The van I'd seen her drive yesterday was parked inside, but the two other stalls were empty. Eve pulled Kara's Glock out of her briefcase.

"Don't shoot me," I muttered.

"You're bait." She pushed me forward. "His office is upstairs. That's where I left the phone."

I moved to the staircase along the back wall, checking the van and the crawl spaces behind the larger machinery. The space was pristine. Epoxy floors, built-in shelves, and tools for days. A 5 HP industrial air compressor, a plasma cutter, some things I didn't even recognize. One open-faced cabinet had an elaborate air hood and rows of sealed, labeled containers. I didn't get a sense of anything being out of place, but someone had been here recently. Someone looking for something and knowing exactly where to go.

I stopped at the bottom of the stairs. Puddles dotted the steps, getting smaller as they went up. The door at the top stood open, and everything beyond it was dark. The rectangle changed, shifting until it became a different shape completely. A circle, the mouth of the drainpipe. Dripping, stagnant water echoed off the concrete and all its horror waited, breath held, inviting me inside. I froze, breaking into a cold sweat, fighting against the black dream until an elbow jabbed me in the side. The sting sent me reeling back into my own skin, and Eve's face, pale and irritated and scared, forced the drainpipe to fade into a doorway again. I shot her a dirty look, putting a finger to my lips. She nodded almost imperceptibly and tightened her grip on the gun. Her heart raced, or maybe it was mine.

I crept up and paused at the top, listening, before pushing the door all the way open. Eve rushed in behind me, flipped the lights on, and gasped.

Matthew Moore's office was destroyed.

The floor was covered in files and scattered paper. A cabinet lay facedown on its side. All the desk drawers had been pulled out, and a jagged lightning-shaped crack radiated from the corner of the desk, where a lock had been smashed open.

I stepped over the mess, checking corners, looking for anyone lurking behind the door or in the shadows of the electrical wire jungle from the solar panel equipment, but the space was empty.

"His computer's gone." Eve moved to the desk.

"Don't touch anything." I jogged down to the garage and checked the back door. The lot was deserted, and the houses on the other side of the property were dark. I grabbed some neoprene gloves from a tool bench. Upstairs, Eve was toeing some of the papers aside.

"Where was the phone?"

She didn't answer right away. The usual humming of her mind had stuttered. She was probably in shock.

I moved in front of her, closer than I wanted, and waved a gloved hand in the air. "Eve." She looked up. Her eyes were too bright, too blue, and my mind swam with the ring—the one her husband's desperate, trapped head had stuttered over in the belly of the barn. A ring to match her eyes. A ring for promises, for better or worse, sickness or health, a roulette wheel of future misery. I sucked in a breath and my hands fisted. "Think."

That jump-started her. She stepped back and blinked, and those blue eyes swept from side to side, as though reading invisible text.

"I left it on the desk, by the picture frame. There." She pointed to an empty spot and described it. A flip phone. Cheap plastic, disposable. I searched everywhere it could have fallen or been knocked accidentally, but it didn't take long to know it was gone.

Eve retreated to the edges of the room to pace. "It could have been a random burglary."

"Nope. One, there aren't random burglaries, and two, anyone targeting the house would ignore the fifty-dollar phone and grab the five-thousand-dollar plasma cutter." I'd boost the thing myself if I could get away with it.

"You're right." She continued to pace, her energy buzzing again with that hum of calculation that was weirdly soothing. "The evidence doesn't support a random crime. They came for something specific."

"Anything else missing besides the computer and phone?"

She surveyed the area again. "I don't think so. Matthew didn't keep much up here. His home office was in the guest bedroom in the house until—" She cut off, and a flush colored her energy. "I don't think anything else was taken. Maybe some papers, but only Matthew would know that."

"Why papers?" I kicked a few over. Mostly contractor receipts. Solar panel manuals and equipment warranties. Nothing valuable to anyone else. I crouched down, elbows to knees, and felt my way under the mess, trying to sense the residue of the last person here. I wasn't getting much emotion, but Kara Johnson hadn't exactly been emotional. If she wanted the phone and its incriminating texts, taking the computer and knocking over the file cabinets could be a cover.

Stage the scene. Make it look, on the surface, like a smash-and-grab.

Or it could have been someone else completely, someone connected to Alexis Dwyer. Max had shown Eve a picture of the dead woman, and he wouldn't do that for no reason. Max always had reasons, the sturdy kind that secured warrants and ended toxic friendships. Did he think Matthew Moore was somehow involved in her death? Or his disappearance was connected to it? It was an interesting angle, but I'd rather have gotten here in time to catch whoever did this instead of hearing hinted speculation on the side of the road. Fucking speed limits.

Eve picked her way among the papers as though the mess had feelings and reached for the shattered picture frame.

"Wait." I grabbed it before she could get fingerprints on it and shook the glass out of the frame. The photo reeked of soft light and happiness, things I could barely look at without squinting. I took it out of the smashed frame, trying to make as little contact with it as humanly possible, but there was more than one picture inside the frame. Two wedding photographs sandwiched a piece of paper between them.

This was what they wanted, the thing they'd been searching for. I knew it immediately, in my gut. Carefully, I unfolded it on the desk. It was a standard college rule sheet of notebook paper covered in what looked like a foreign language. Chemical symbols and polymer diagrams, scratches and lines, formulas written on top of formulas. But I recognized two words on the very edge of one margin, tiny, all capital letters that had been traced and retraced, etched into the pulp until they'd taken on their own texture.

CELINA KENDRICK.

Eve's shock ripped through her concentration, but before either of us spoke, something creaked beneath us.

Someone else was in the garage.

Eve

The noise downstairs came again, and I stopped breathing. Had Kara or whoever ransacked Matthew's office come back? Did they want something else?

I grabbed the paper with Matthew's notes on it. I didn't know what it was yet, but it was important. It proved what I'd thought impossible—that Jonah Kendrick's case was somehow connected to Matthew—and I wasn't letting any more data out of my sight. Folding it, I shoved the square under my shirt and down the side of my bra. Kendrick followed the path of the paper before looking quickly away.

We both crept to the door. There was only one way out of the office: down the stairs. Something scraped, then stopped. Whoever was down there was trying to be quiet—and not doing a very good job.

Kendrick pointed at me and then toward the stairs. I shook my head. Then he pointed at the gun and held out a hand. I sighed and shook my head again. Apparently I was going first.

I took a deep breath and ran, trying to make myself as big and loud and intimidating as possible. Something moved by the workbench and I swung the gun toward it, yelling.

Earl.

He drew up, startled, and stumbled heavily into his walker.

Jerking the barrel away, I stopped short, only to have Kendrick collide with my back. I almost fell, grabbing the railing just in time.

"Earl." I went to prop him up on his bad side, my heart still racing. "What are you doing out here? I told you to stay in and lock the doors."

He made a noise and held up a stainless steel cylinder the size of a large thermos. I took it carefully, as if there could be a bomb inside. The canister was surprisingly heavy and the contents shifted and pinged against the metal. It sounded like sand.

"What's this?"

Earl nodded at the workbench, where he must have picked the cylinder up. I hadn't noticed anything sitting there yesterday.

"Looks like those." Kendrick pointed at the chemical storage area, and he was right, except Matthew labeled everything he kept in the garage. This canister had no labels, and it was locked. I punched in the same code Matthew used for the burner—CHON, carbon, hydrogen, oxygen, and nitrogen—and it opened to reveal a half-full container of small, black pebbles.

"Lava rock?" Kendrick leaned in for a better look, but I pulled it away before he got too close.

"It could be toxic."

"Toxic lava rock."

"I don't know." I set it down and took a picture, zooming in as much as possible. It could be a mineral or a compound, unstable or completely inert; there was no way to tell without testing. It might have nothing to do with Matthew's disappearance, but it was an anomaly—unlabeled, out of place—and I couldn't ignore anomalies.

Kendrick started to say something but broke off when a car drove by, slowing down at the end of the driveway. I couldn't see the driver, but the man in the passenger seat stared at us. I felt suddenly exposed, vulnerable in a way I never had before. The threats in my life had always come from above and I'd learned how to identify them long ago, to see the funnel before it formed. But a tornado hadn't destroyed Matthew's office. A blizzard hadn't held me at gunpoint. The monsters were human now, and I had no idea how to track a threat on the ground.

I sealed the canister and bolstered Earl's arm. "Let's go inside."

The three of us sat around the kitchen table in an uncomfortable group. I'd checked all the ground floor doors and windows as soon as we got inside, making sure everything was locked. The car that drove by was probably nothing, but it reminded me of the men in the ped mall, and the same uneasiness pricked along my skin.

Earl hadn't seen anyone break into the garage. He and Sam had the TV on all morning as they made phone calls, watching the forecast and checking for news developments about Matthew. After Sam left, Earl noticed the strange car in the driveway and decided to investigate. To protect our home.

Why is he here?

Kendrick glanced at me, and I nodded. I wasn't keeping any secrets from Earl.

Briefly, Kendrick told him about Kara and the thrift store, the missing phone, and what we'd found instead. I pulled out the piece of paper and spread it on the table. Matthew always had chemistry notes lying around the house, stuffed in drawers and littered on top of the washing machine from where he'd emptied his pockets, but those were in plain sight. And this note had one significant difference.

"Celina Kendrick." I caught Kendrick's gaze and held it. "Your daughter?"

"My niece."

His behavior had seemed so strange—tailing strangers, racing to head off Kara, and whatever he'd done to get on the wrong side of the police. He'd been erratic, withdrawn yet determined at the same time. Now it all made sense. He wasn't on a job; he was searching for his family.

"Are you actually a private investigator?"

"Yes, but I haven't taken another case since Celina disappeared."

"Why didn't you tell me she was your niece?"

"People are more willing to talk to a hired detective when they think I'm just a guy doing a job. The license gives me access, credibility. I'll use anything I have to find out what happened to her."

Kendrick waited, hunched and holding his headphones like it was a struggle not to clamp them over his ears. I realized he expected me to kick him out of my house again, and that—amazingly—I didn't want to. He might still be delusional or dealing with another mental health condition, but he'd done nothing except try to help me. And this piece of paper proved that the people we were searching for were somehow connected. Matthew had known something about Celina Kendrick. The decision, once made, felt inevitable.

"What's our next move?"

Kendrick's head snapped up. He blinked, as though unsure whether to trust what he'd heard.

"If Celina and Matthew's disappearances are linked, we should look for them together. Combine our efforts."

Kendrick turned to Earl. "Is that all right with you?"

A lump formed in my throat. So many people looked at Earl and only saw the wheelchair. They spoke to the stroke, not the man, or they treated him like a hard-of-hearing child. But Kendrick met my father-in-law's eyes squarely and spoke to him with respect. It pieced something sharp and jagged back together in my heart.

Earl nodded, and I slipped my hand into his, looking across the table at the hollow man in the black coat. Our team.

We outlined everything we knew so far. Kara had arranged to meet Matthew on Thursday morning at Ryerson's Woods Park. When he got there, his Tesla was incinerated with an unidentified substance. Pawan had agreed to test the scorch mark samples, but I hadn't received any results from him yet. I told Kendrick and Earl about the conversation I'd overheard at the thrift store, how Kara claimed Matthew set the fire himself and that something had to be done tonight.

"It sounded like they'd have to drive somewhere distant. Someone complained about going 'all the way out there.'"

"What about Max's questions?" Kendrick asked. "Cryptocurrency?"

I had no idea what that was about. Matthew had some investments in Bitcoin, but I didn't have access to or even know how to use any of those accounts.

I thought about the picture Summerlin showed me, the young woman sitting in a club, dolled up and drink in hand, smiling at the camera.

"Was that Celina?"

Kendrick shook his head. "Her name was Alexis Dwyer."

"Was?" I froze at his use of past tense.

"She was found dead in her apartment on the south side of town."

When? Earl asked.

"Yesterday."

I'd wondered about other burners, other women, and now two more names had appeared. Celina Kendrick. Alexis Dwyer. One vanished, one dead. Had Matthew had affairs with them, too, or was it something worse? I'd read stories about sex trafficking, men with private islands, profiting from the vulnerable, their abuse and coercion hidden in plain sight.

There had been so many dates I couldn't match last night, times Matthew claimed he'd been working on grant research—and those were only the evenings I knew about. Summerlin wanted to know where Matthew had been on Tuesday afternoon. I asked Earl, but he wasn't sure. Days bled together for him, each so similar to the last. His home health aides came at least twice a week so Matthew could run errands. I looked at the blank calendar hanging on the wall, all the empty squares I couldn't fill in, and started to feel sick.

"What else did you find on the phone?" Kendrick went to pace the far end of the living room. "Why would Kara want it so badly?"

"RWP. LRF. Something about praying."

RWP is the park. Rest of them might be places, too.

"Maybe praying is code for a church? Or somewhere by a church?"

They dove into those leads, Earl looking up area churches on his iPad while Kendrick searched acronyms for LRF. I paced the ground floor of the house, trying to shake the idea of Matthew as a sex trafficker. I couldn't make myself believe it—not Matthew, not the man who'd built this home and family—but why had Kara pulled a gun? Why had Matthew's office been ransacked? Why did it feel like people were following me today, the back of my neck crawling with awareness? I checked the street and the cars parked along the road, feeling more paranoid by the second. The sky was getting lighter. The front yard had turned smooth and dangerously opaque.

"What about that paper?" Kendrick asked. He wanted to know what the formulas meant. Most of them were completely beyond me. It was like trying to read a book where I knew the alphabet but no words. Natalia, however, had a dozen biochemistry graduate students at her disposal. Maybe they could piece these elements and compounds together.

Snapping a picture of the paper, I sent it to my best friend with a request to keep the source confidential until we figured out what was going on. Natalia texted back immediately, promising to distribute the image—without context—and have her students put their heads together over breakfast the next morning. On an impulse, I sent the photo of the dark rocks in the canister, too. Natalia had no idea what the substance was but gave me the name of a chemistry professor who might have lab resources available. I was texting him when Kendrick began pacing next to me.

"Kara was going somewhere. A long drive. Tonight," Kendrick mumbled as he passed, rubbing both sides of his head. "Paper. The paper was important, it was all she had left."

Earl looked confused. He reached for the sheet of formulas, but Kendrick shook his head.

"No, not that. I felt something in the store, something of Kara's. It was bound, small. A diary, maybe."

The notebook. In the race to the house and all the ugly suspicions that followed, I'd forgotten about the notebook I'd stolen from the thrift store.

"This?"

I ran to my coat and pulled it out of my pocket. Kendrick's eyes lit up and we moved to the kitchen table. It was small, with heavy black covers and unlined pages. Instead of notes, it was filled with sketches. Birds, mostly, similar to the ones threaded through the tattoos on her shoulder.

The drawings were beautiful and haunting. Every time I flipped a page, the birds' eyes followed me. A dove silently screaming. A robin captured midflight in exploded view, each wing and leg detached from the whole. One page showed a hillside meadow with the skeleton of a bird half-buried among tall, waving grasses. I remembered the class I'd seen on Kara's transcript—Art at the End of the World—as we paged through the drawings. The more we saw, the worse I felt about taking it.

"There's nothing here. It's only sketches."

"It's a journal," Kendrick said, pointing to a series of numbers at the top of the page. It was reverse time: 20191016 for October 16, 2019. Kara drew one of these pictures every day. Every day another death. Every day the end of the world.

We glanced at each other and flipped to the last, most recent, drawing. The page was marked 20191206. December 6. Today.

Two brown birds huddled in the center of the page, perched on the edge of a black cliff. They leaned against each other, clinging to the edge, trying not to fall off. Both had their eyes gouged out.

"Look." Kendrick tapped the spot where their talons clung to the blackened rock. *LRF.* The letters looked like cracks between their feet, the cliff breaking underneath them.

"That's the code from the phone." Matthew could be meeting her again today, at LRF. I straightened, buzzing with the possibility of new information. "What did you find for those acronyms?"

"Nothing." Kendrick pulled up his phone search again. "Leukemia Research Foundation. Liquid rocket fuel."

"Let's hope not."

"Little Rock Field?" He paused. "Where's that?"

"It's an air force base in Arkansas."

"No." He resumed pacing. "None of these are right. It's Iowa. The barn has to be in Iowa."

"What are you talking about? This has nothing to do with a barn."

"Those birds." He jabbed at the page with today's drawing. "They're barn swallows."

"For the love of Ein—" I didn't get further before Earl's whole body jerked to the side. I rushed to help, but he wasn't hurt. Typing furiously, he shoved the iPad into my hand. I stared at it, one long beat of confusion before the words clicked.

Lovers Ridge Farm. LRF.

"Lovers Ridge?" Kendrick read over my shoulder.

"It's Earl and Helen's farm," I said. "About an hour west of here. Where Matthew grew up."

"Do you still own it?"

Earl nodded and we all fell still. It was like a veil had been pulled back, the lines of the drawing etched with sudden clarity. A pair of birds, lovers, clinging to a ridge. I stared at the black places where their eyes should have been, the crumbling rock beneath their feet, and swallowed. The farm was vacant, empty, a virtual private island on the waves of the prairie. I had no idea why Kara would go to Lovers Ridge tonight, but there was only one way to find out.

Jonah

The entire state had frozen solid.

I stood on Eve Roth's porch and stared. Ice covered everything from mailboxes to fences to the cars that had been parked outside over the last day's downpour. Roofs had grown long, glistening teeth. The road was a shadow beneath a layer of glass. To drive anywhere in this was an act of insanity. Yet somehow, in the time it took to discover a place called Lovers Ridge Farm, I'd gotten two new partners, both of them humming with the same fierce determination. The arrangement wouldn't last—Max was the only person who'd been able to tolerate me for long periods, years longer than anyone should have to—but maybe they'd put up with me long enough to find the next clue. The possibility of a real lead vibrated through me and into the ice itself.

Inside, Eve was pouring a sample of the toxic lava rock into a vial for some professor while she was on hold with the police.

"What are you doing?"

She turned her back, ignoring me.

Earl showed me his iPad. Have to report the robbery.

"I'm not sticking around here while they send a patrol. We need to be on the road now."

"I can't keep all this a secret," Eve interjected as offensively smooth pop renditions drifted out from her phone. "How would that look?"

"Max still doesn't have a better suspect than you."

"He'll never get a better suspect if we don't report what we've found."

It was useless arguing with her. I skated across the yard, pulled the Evolution as close to the front porch as possible, sanded the shit out of the wheelchair ramp, and got Earl loaded into the back seat. The five-point racing harnesses I had in place of seat belts kept him surprisingly secure. His head still listed a little, but other than that, he sat up taller than most able-bodied adults. Eve showed up with two backpacks as I was getting ready to leave without her.

"What did Max say?"

"I left a message. The operator said unless I was upside down on the side of the road, tomorrow was the soonest I would speak to anyone in the department." She hesitated, one hand on the bag next to Earl. "I packed the gun."

"Good."

As we both buckled in, a push notification popped up. The same tone echoed on Eve's phone and Earl's iPad. The governor of Iowa had declared a statewide emergency. All roads except for I-80 and I-35, the two interstates that carved the state into fourths, were officially closed. The notice advised every Iowan to stay indoors under threat of extremely hazardous and virtually unnavigable conditions.

Eve sucked in a breath.

"Second thoughts?"

"Are you still going?" She arched one perfect eyebrow.

"Yes. I have to."

"Under unnavigable conditions?"

"My car was built for this. I go to the Canadian border every winter and race on frozen lakes."

"You race cars on ice?"

"Yeah."

"For fun?"

"It's more like therapy. But yeah, fun therapy."

She took a deep breath, glanced out the window, and exchanged a look with Earl, who nodded. "Then we shouldn't waste more time."

The car began a gravity-fueled descent down the driveway. I checked the mirrors as we hit the road and spun into a ninety-degree turn. Or it would have been a ninety-degree turn on asphalt. On pure, unsalted ice, the Evolution kept spinning until we'd rotated another 360 degrees, ending in the exact direction I wanted to go, except a few hundred feet farther down the road. We missed hitting a parked Ford by less than a foot.

After the car stopped, there was a moment of silence. Eve had a death grip on the door handle, and the tendons in her neck stood out in stark relief.

"See?" I shot a glance at her profile. "Fun."

A deep and throaty noise came from the back. Earl agreed. "Let's hit it."

The city street lanes were carved into deep ruts. The day's traffic had worn tracks in the slush, which had then frozen into nasty furrows. When I kept the Evolution inside the ruts, we shook like popcorn in our seats. When I tried to avoid them, we slid out of control. Ruts it was.

Eve flipped on the weather station and we listened to repeated warnings to stay off the roads. After a half an hour—for what should have been a five-minute drive—we reached I-80.

The entrance ramp had a semitruck lying on its side and four cars piled in behind it, like some sadistic kid yanked the entire caravan into the ditch by a string. I crawled past the mess, teetering on the knife's edge between sliding back down the ramp or joining the pileup.

We merged into a string of hobbling semis, snowplows, and passenger vehicles going fifteen miles an hour. There were no lanes. There was no visible road. It had sleeted enough to cover the asphalt entirely before everything froze, leaving an unbroken white world where our only option was to follow the car in front of us and hope to god we weren't all doomed.

When the city gave way to open fields, the only markers were the cars crashed every few hundred feet. Semis twisted and jackknifed, overturned with their wheels in the sky. They'd started their hauls on either end of this transcontinental freeway, without enough fear of what the middle could swallow.

This shit show was nothing like ice racing. Lake ice froze to a perfect, smooth crust, a circle of endless possibilities in a ring of pines, the whole world distilled down to me and an engine, sky above and death—quiet and numb—hugging the ice below. Ice racing was speed, adrenaline, and pure joy. This drive was slow-motion terror.

"Oh my god." Eve tensed as a UPS truck with a double trailer, coming the opposite direction, skidded into a truck. They toppled into the white and disappeared. It happened in seconds—a sound-less, colorless end.

My knuckles were white. My eyes bounced in constant rotation between the windshield, rearview, and side mirrors. Eve held on to the door handle like a life preserver while compulsively updating a radar model on her phone. Earl, whatever he was doing in the back, remained silent. The car stunk of fear and adrenaline, and I could barely distinguish whose emotions belonged to whom.

At one point, Eve made a relieved noise and told Earl that their friend Sam had arrived in Davenport. "He wants to know how we're doing."

"Never better," I said as a pickup tried to pass everyone and fishtailed into the median. We inched past the wreck, where steam rose from the idiot's hood.

"I'm just telling him we're hoping for more news soon. I don't want him to worry." She texted back.

"How much farther?"

"Another thirty miles on the interstate, then ten on a county highway and into the back roads."

Those roads probably hadn't been driven on, much less salted. "Forty miles. That's going to take at least two more hours at this pace."

"We'll still have daylight," Eve said. "The worst will be after sundown."

"Yeah, light helps, in theory."

"I mean with the temperature dropping. Ice achieves minimal friction at negative seven degrees Celsius, or nineteen Fahrenheit."

"Can you say that with regular person words?" I didn't risk taking my eyes from the road.

"Friction equals traction. When a surface reaches minimal friction, it becomes the most slippery it can be. Ice, when it reaches nineteen degrees, is at its most hazardous state."

"Oh. Cool."

"We're hovering in the midtwenties right now, but with sundown only four hours away . . ." She didn't finish the thought. She didn't have to.

Each spike of adrenaline from every averted accident drained me a little more, and eventually my arms and shoulders went stiff and started to shake. I wanted my headphones. I needed something to help me relax—or at least pretend to. I didn't realize I'd started muttering until Eve asked who Danica Chase and Angela Garcia were.

"People."

She waited, and when I didn't elaborate, she did it for me. "Danica Chase. She was a runaway in Illinois, right? You helped find her."

Danica, Angela, Kit, George. The found. They were out there somewhere, beyond the ice, alive and home. I had to believe that, had to tell myself it was possible for the dreams to end well. Then Eve said a different name, one I couldn't include on the list.

"Celina."

She was curious. She needed to understand why I was risking my life, or at least my car, in order to look inside a stranger's barn. In the back seat, Earl's attention sharpened.

"What do you want to know?"

"Tell me about her."

I could barely bring my niece's face into focus right now, but maybe that helped. Maybe it was easier that way. I stretched out a cramp in my neck and tried to figure out where to begin.

"I've got a twin, Jason. He and his wife live in New Orleans, and Celina was their oldest child."

"Is he a psychic, too?"

"He's a salesman."

"Oh." She glanced back at Earl. "Fraternal?"

"Identical."

A surge of amusement shot through her and she tried to stifle a smile. I got it. The idea of me, or a copy of me, trying to sell anyone anything was absurd.

"Jason was always the outgoing one. I got the nightmares. He got the people skills."

Clenching the wheel tighter, I stared at the bouncing bumper of the car ahead of us. "I dreamed about Celina before she was born. Not"—I immediately felt Eve's retort—"precognition. It was a formless dream. I don't know anything about souls or spirits, but I sensed whatever she was at that point. Like she was coming to introduce herself: a friendly little zygote." Earl huffed out something that landed near a dry laugh. "When Jason and his wife announced they were having a baby, I told them I'd already met her and she was full of sass.

"Jason's wife always accepted my abilities. She wanted me to be close to Celina and her brother as they grew up, thought it would give them an extra layer of protection. What better way to monitor the health and safety of your children than through your psychic brother-in-law?" My smile turned brittle. "She sent them to summer camps in Iowa, and they stayed with me on the weekends. I'd never been around kids much before that. They don't like me."

"Strange." Eve rooted around in one of the backpacks and pulled out protein bars and water, passing them around.

"Even then Celina was unique. She had this pure joy running through her. I have a hard time in public, but it was easier when I had the kids during those weeks in the summer. I still picked up people's emotions, but they couldn't drown me when Celina was around. The three of us went everywhere together, places I wouldn't dare on my own. We'd start the day at a museum, hit two parks, and end up smuggling a grocery bag full of candy into a movie theater. After she graduated high school, she moved here to study."

"You said she wasn't a student."

"She was studying with me. Celina wanted to be a psychic detective."

They were surprised. They'd thought I was a unicorn in my delusions; they didn't realize there could be more of us, that it might even run in families. I hadn't known at first, either—none of us did—until Celina grew old enough to notice the people around her. *He's all gray and hurty,* she chirped one day when we passed a limping man in a park. *He's making you hurty, too, Uncle Jonah.* I shoved the memory away. I didn't have it in me to resurrect that bouncing, wide-eyed girl right now.

"Celina was . . . like me. Not with the dreams or telepathy, her abilities were more subtle. She could pick up trace emotions, especially when people were in pain. She wanted to develop her focus, to help people, and I agreed to mentor her. She said she was going to be my partner someday.

"The last time I saw her, her mood was bright, almost giddy. She couldn't focus for shit. Said she'd met someone."

Earl piped up from the back, a grunted, "*Who?*"

I shook my head, eyes locked on the road. "I don't know. There was no evidence of anyone else in her apartment when we searched it, no new connections on her social media. When I asked her that day, she grinned and said, 'Someone I can help.'"

I swallowed and finished the story, the reason the three of us were inching across a frozen wasteland.

"The morning Celina disappeared I dreamed about her." The oneiros, according to my mother, except she never imagined I'd dream about her granddaughter. "She called to me from the floor of a barn; she knew I was the only one who could hear. There was blood. Her blood. She was bound and blindfolded, but she still concentrated on every detail she could hear or feel, trying to communicate as much as possible. Her focus"—I backhanded my eyes; I didn't have the luxury of blurred vision right now—"was perfect."

A tissue appeared in front of me. I balled it between my palm and the wheel.

"I haven't seen my niece in four months except when I go to sleep. It's always the same; the terror, the taste of blood in my mouth. I hear a door shutting and footsteps and then I wake up. I know it's not still happening. It's an echo of a scream, an endless replay of that moment when she was trying to reach me."

The tension in my body felt like it could snap me in half. I vibrated with it. The tissue turned to pulp between my fingers. "The nightmares don't matter. I'd take them every night for the rest of my life if I could just find her. If I knew what happened, and why."

"Did the police ever find anything? The person she met?"

I shook my head. "Max tried to help. He wasn't assigned to the case, but he put himself on the line for me anyway. It almost cost him everything."

No one spoke after that. We held on to whatever we could, plowing forward because we had no other choice. At one point,

Earl and Eve passed the iPad back and forth and she reached into her bag for some dried fruit. Earl got sleepy after he ate again, the worry and exhaustion overwhelming him. The haze of sun lowered in the sky until it started to blind me. Finally, after what felt like eight goddamn years on this interstate, a frozen sign with partially obscured letters announced the turnoff to Montezuma.

Eve pointed at the place where an exit ramp might be. "Start turning."

I shifted the wheel out of the tyranny of the ruts, sending the Evolution skidding over an unbroken white plain. I aimed for a cluster of trees in the distance and the gleam of grain bins on the horizon.

"Hold on to something. It's about to get fun again."

Eve

The farm came into view on a long inhale, the breath of an unbroken sight line that brought the curve of the Earth itself into focus. The farmhouse, barn, silo, and outbuildings were all shrouded in a copse of pine, a speck of color that knit the otherwise blank world together, gray above and white below. Rows of colorless apple trees stretched ghostlike over the land behind the buildings. I couldn't see any signs of life—no cars, no lights, no indication that anyone was here. Had the ice prevented Kara from coming? Or had we misinterpreted her journal entry? I'd spent more time googling LRF on the trip here, looking up cities, street names, parks, anything I could think of, until my last bar of cell service had disappeared.

It was an objectively bad idea, driving anywhere in this storm. Earl, who'd lost his wife in a car accident, had to sit and stare at countless wrecks, not knowing how many people had been hurt or even died in them. I saw Helen in every overturned vehicle. Earl watched them, too, with silent tears streaming down his face. I apologized on his iPad for bringing him out in this, but he kept saying it was fine and now I understood why. Even if we found nothing, not a single piece of evidence that Matthew or Kara had ever been at the farm, Earl's face made every danger worthwhile.

He drank in the sight of the house, scanning everything on the property from door latches to outbuilding shingles. We'd visited a few times in the months after Earl was released from the rehab clinic, mostly to pick up items or check on the person who'd leased the land, but the memories had been too painful then, Helen's absence too fresh. Afterward, Earl would retreat to his room for a full day, refusing meals, shunning company. I'd been terrified we were going to lose both of them. But slowly, he got stronger. He participated in his physical therapy, staking small claims against the effects of the stroke. Matthew planted an apple tree mixed with Helen's ashes in the front yard, where Earl could see it from his bedroom window. And we stopped visiting the farm.

Now his entire face lit up, and for a second I saw the Earl Moore I first met, before a car accident and a blood clot had robbed him of almost everything that mattered. Reaching into the back seat, I grabbed his hand. He squeezed my palm, giving me a watery smile.

Kendrick had tears lingering in his gaze, too. Something had shifted on the drive here. It felt like I was beginning to understand this man: his wariness, the way he clocked a room as soon as he entered it, his hunched, defensive posture. It wasn't just delusion or illness. It was trauma.

There were certain things I could never discuss with my colleagues or fit into conversations with my mom or Natalia, experiences my body had that my mind couldn't rationalize. My body had learned, when I was nine years old, that loss had weight. I became heavier after my dad died, as if the tornado had lodged pieces of him inside my bones. I witnessed it with Helen, too, how Earl's body crumpled without her. It wasn't logical. Emotions didn't have mass; they couldn't physically make us more or less, yet somehow they did.

Jonah Kendrick had also lost someone he loved, and he carried the weight of that loss. He surveyed the farm now, bloodshot eyes scanning the barn looming in the center of the pines, and his nightmares echoed inside the car. His niece calling out to him from a barn. Matthew, trapped, with old and new blood. My response to trauma was decidedly different—where Kendrick slipped into delusion and nightmares, I collected data—but somehow both of our reactions had brought us to this exact place and time.

"Turn here." I pointed to the driveway, which dipped into the property. On any other day it would have been a mild decline, but today the road glistened with sheer ice.

Kendrick eased off the accelerator and turned into the driveway. For a moment the car continued to coast, slowly, manageably, but as soon as all four wheels descended onto the hill, we picked up speed. There was no traction, no measurable force working against the gravity. The car slid at an angle, gaining momentum as it sped directly toward the house. A scream built in my throat. Every muscle in my body tensed for impact. Kendrick threw the emergency brake on and turned the wheel, trying to change our course. The car shifted, but it wasn't enough. We careened toward the edge of the foundation, the painted cinder block that would easily stop the car and crush its energy back through the metal frame and the bodies inside. We needed more leftward force.

Unbuckling my seat belt, I tucked my feet up on the seat.

"Let go," I yelled and used my legs like a spring to launch myself across the car. Kendrick's arms shot up. I collided with the driver's side window before hitting his lap.

He grabbed the wheel and turned, digging it across my back and pressing us both hard into the door.

I craned my head up in time to see the house passing inches from the car. Siding, windows, and empty flower boxes floated past before the sky appeared again, a formless expanse of altostratus that meant we hadn't crashed.

The car jerked. We'd reached the fields. My head hit the window and instinctively I curled up. Kendrick spun the car into a tailspin, digging the wheel into my spine again, his arms straining around me as the static force of the bumps and the tires slowed us to a complete stop. When the engine turned off, everything went quiet. I knew I needed to climb off him, but I wasn't sure I could move. My heart raced and I was trembling from head to toe. An answering pound drummed in the chest pressed against mine.

Leaning weakly back, he dropped his head. "Are you all right?"

My shoulder screamed from where it had hit the door and something in my neck felt pinched, but I nodded against his coat. He was so close I could see flecks of amber in his bloodshot eyes, and for a second that's all my brain could process—glowing amber.

"Earl?"

The name snapped me back into reality. Awkwardly, Kendrick helped me up and we both turned to where Earl sat grinning with every facial muscle he could command. A slow, hoarse chuckle began seeping out of his mouth.

"Are you hurt?"

His only answer was a deeper cackle as he let go of the door handle to clap his hands in unsteady applause.

Then Kendrick started laughing, and before I knew it I collapsed against my seat and joined them. We laughed like teenagers who'd gotten away with a reckless stunt, laughed until tears streamed down our faces and my side started to cramp, laughed harder than I remembered laughing in years. After it finally died down, Kendrick stared at me with a strange, fading smile.

"How did you know that would work?"

"I didn't, but the application of a horizontal force to shift the car's center of mass was our only option."

"Yeah, obviously." His mouth twitched. "I hope you've got some studded tires or chains around here, Earl, otherwise we're not going to have any horizontal force for a while."

Our trip had ended in the first row of the orchard beyond the house. The trees surrounding us were encased in ice. Their branches curled and loomed, a forest of twisted icicles, like we'd crossed into some dark fairy tale far from the heart of Iowa.

Apples littered the ground, trapped inside sheets of ice. Some had rotted, while others gleamed bright red inside their icy shells. The vendor we'd leased must not have picked all of them this year, leaving the ground covered with wasted fruit, enough to stop the car from sliding completely through the orchard and down to the creek.

Our final tailspin hid the road from view, but I could make out the kitchen door of the farmhouse thirty yards away. In the distance, the roof of the barn rose above the crest of ice-covered branches. We'd survived the crash, but I had no idea what lay beyond.

Max

I'd never processed so many vehicle accident reports in my life. Traffic incidents didn't fall under the investigations unit, but the captain had mobilized the entire division for the storm. Every able-bodied officer had been on the roads all afternoon. Since I was confined to desk duty with the sling, I'd spent the last six hours logging every incident and the numbers were climbing into triple digits. The mayor had closed all city streets and ordered residents to stay home for anything short of medical emergencies.

"And don't count on help then," Ciseski muttered across the aisle as he logged an ambulance that had skidded into an electrical pole, bringing down the pole and knocking out power for the entire block.

It wasn't Iowa's first ice storm, and it wouldn't be the last. I remembered waiting for these days as a kid, when Clear Lake turned into the world's biggest hockey rink, and school was canceled for days. But I'd never seen a city freeze so fast and hard. Beyond the crashes, parked cars had frozen to the pavement, their doors coated in an impenetrable layer of ice. Tree limbs snapped into streets and onto buildings. The fire department was getting calls from people trapped in their homes.

"That's where they should be."

I had to agree with Ciseski. We'd been head down for most of the shift, regular cases tabled, every new emergency trumping the last. Finally, six o'clock hit and the night patrol came in. We briefed them on the major accidents and the worst roads ("death drives, don't even send a snowplow") as Ciseski grabbed his coat with a limp grunt.

"Careful out there," I called. "I hear it's a little slippery."

"Fuckin' hilarious." He gave me a wave, though—the nicest gesture he'd offered since I'd been back on duty—and lumbered toward the parking garage. I texted Shelley to let her know I was finishing up soon, everything was fine, not to worry, and shut down my computer. I didn't follow Ciseski, though. I walked in the opposite direction, to the corner office, and knocked on the captain's door.

"Come in."

He sounded as exhausted as I felt. I opened the door to a map of Iowa City taped up on the wall behind his desk, marked with red pushpins and slashed with various highlighters.

"What is it?" I heard the unspoken "now" at the end of the sentence and understood. It had been a long day.

"Nothing new. Not yet anyway."

His shoulders relaxed a little, and he gestured for me to sit.

Fifteen years ago, Jon Larsen and I had been sworn in as evening patrol officers together. We'd stood side by side at the ceremony and posed awkwardly for pictures, both of us fresh out of the academy and looking, on the surface, almost like brothers. We were both strapping, corn-fed white kids, tall and bulky under the dark uniforms, a glint of red in his hair, a flame sizzling in mine. Larsen had known the name and rank of everyone in the room. He bantered with the chief and complimented other ranking officers on recent cases they'd closed.

I thought he was a brownnoser at first, but over the years I realized Larsen was simply a cop's cop. He loved the force, almost as much as he loved whiskey and *Mindhunter* and comparing the advantages of strikers to single-action revolvers. He'd been my direct superior for a year now, yet he still treated me like a peer. Like last night, when he offered to have someone else take the Alexis Dwyer case. If I had passed it off, though, I never would have made the connection between the dead woman in the bathtub and a missing chemistry professor with an incinerated car.

"What's going on?"

I briefed him on both cases before circling to the previous allegations against Moore and his potentially inappropriate relationship with Kara Johnson. Then I showed him the bank records from both Matthew Moore and Alexis Dwyer and explained the cryptocurrency connection.

"I haven't gotten into his digital wallet yet, so I can't see if there were any direct transfers between Moore and Dwyer—"

"You think he was keeping her on the side."

"It would track."

"The autopsy points to her being a user. Looks like an accidental overdose. Open-and-shut."

"It could've been self-inflicted, accidentally or intentionally. But the syringe mark on her arm was unusual. No other marks, no scar tissue on her veins. It wasn't her normal method. And where's the syringe?"

"Good question." Larsen leaned back in his chair, rubbing his eyes. "But the ME put her time of death on Tuesday. That's two days before Moore vanished."

"If he had something to do with her death, maybe he needed to disappear. Or maybe his wife found out and made him pay." Eve Roth had gotten angry when I showed her Alexis's picture this morning. It had only been a flash, there and gone, but she was hiding more than she was telling.

"She was in an airplane when his car was torched."

"Great alibi."

Larsen shook his head, more to himself than me. "You'll need more than this to tie the two cases together."

"I know. It's tenuous right now. Could be nothing, but I'll follow it through." I hesitated, fixing every muscle in my face to perfect calm. "I'd also like to look at Celina Kendrick's bank records."

Every trace of camaraderie in the room vanished. Larsen's eyes snapped up, and even bloodshot, they hardened into flinty appraisal.

"Denied."

"But, Captain—"

"I said denied. You have a conflict of interest on that case."

"I want to see if she was receiving cryptocurrency payments, too."

"You might as well ask for anyone's bank records in the city. Why Celina Kendrick? What could she possibly have to do with a dead girl in a bathtub or a torched Tesla?"

The barn.

The image swarmed in my head. Jonah had described it so many times I could've dreamt the thing myself. The idea had chewed at me underneath all the accidents and crashes and emergencies today, a whisper as the entire world devolved into chaos. Jonah was unstable. He'd been losing his sanity by inches since August, but that didn't mean he wasn't right. What if there was a connection between Matthew Moore and his niece? Even Eve Roth seemed to believe it, or she was pretending to. Jonah was chasing a barn that could be anywhere in the Midwest, hundreds of miles in any direction. It was a needle in a haystack. Maybe I had something here that was more solid to go on.

"Celina Kendrick vanished from this city less than four months ago, and we still don't have any leads. This could be a common thread. It doesn't hurt to look."

Larsen stood up, waiting for me to do the same. I didn't.

"You have the gall to come in here today, during this shit storm to end all shit storms, and bring up Celina Kendrick. I thought a six-week vacation would clear your head."

Getting shot in the arm and spending every night cold sweating into the insomniac hours wasn't exactly a vacation, but I didn't argue.

"I'll be honest, Max. When you landed in the hospital and claimed you had a hunting accident, I knew it was bullshit. You don't hunt, not for animals anyway, and no one had to tell me that Jonah Kendrick was with you when it happened."

His anger soured into something between disappointment and pity. I looked away. The story I'd told Larson and everyone else in the department was that I'd sustained a gunshot wound from a hunter in another party. It happened on occasion. Sometimes people drank while hunting; sometimes they didn't stop and check before firing on something in their sights. I said I didn't know who the other hunter was. It was true and not at the same time.

I'd stood face-to-face with the man on a farm south of Des Moines. We had an entire conversation before he shot me, and I still didn't know his real name. Jonah called him Belgrave. But I couldn't talk about Belgrave, or Jonah, or the reason we were out there in the first place. That was a truth that would destroy everything my life was built on.

I stood up, clenching my good hand. "I was off duty. On my own time."

Larsen sighed. "You're a good cop, but you could've been a great one if you hadn't been carting around that freak show. I know he was your friend, you felt sorry for him or whatever, but that's the kind of weakness that landed you exactly where you are. You're not telling me the whole story. And until you do, no one on this force can trust you."

He opened the door. "Dismissed."

Jonah

The farmhouse was cold but not freezing. A gas fireplace took up one whole wall of the living room, the big stone kind that belonged in ski chalets. Floor-to-ceiling shelves lined another wall, crammed with photo albums, novels, framed pictures, old *Farmers' Almanacs*, and a full encyclopedia set with embossed gold lettering on the spines. Fleece blankets were tossed over chairs and couches, and a faded rug softened the dark, hardwood floor. This was a home.

The magnetic pull of it clicked into place when Earl lowered himself into one of two twin recliners. His fingers slid over the microfiber, finding indents in the shape of his arms, as if the chair had been waiting for him all this time. Everything inside the farmhouse shifted an invisible degree, aligning the man into the exact space he fit. It wasn't that he'd been lost in Iowa City—the connections to his family wove around him there—but this was where Earl Moore truly belonged. It was the antidote to my dreams, being in a place where the world didn't crush you but instead held you fast.

"Do you need anything?" Eve asked.

Earl shook his head. His cheeks were wet. I wanted him to soak in that feeling, to wrap it around himself for as long as it lasted.

Most people didn't understand the found moments, how rare they were, how important. Once you've been lost inside the drainpipe, you know what it means to glimpse the sun.

While Earl rested, we searched the house, looking through every closet and shelf. There was no trace of Matthew or anyone else. The air in the rooms smelled like old books and mothballs.

"They met here," Eve said, after checking the last possible crawl space and coming out with cobwebs in her hair. "They arranged it on the burner."

"There's more than one building on this property."

"Wait." She straightened, already knowing where I wanted to go. "I'm coming with you."

The route from the porch to the barn was level, but the trick was staying on it and not sliding sideways down the hill into the orchard. I cracked a path with a tire iron, giving us slightly more traction. Swing, crack, inch. Swing, crack, inch. I could feel Eve's anxiety swelling as we moved toward the shadow of the barn and tried to focus on the exertion, the tendon-jolting vibration of metal hitting ice.

"Did Celina ever mention an older man? Someone like Matthew?" Her question rushed out in an uneasy cloud of breath.

"No." Crack. "But we never located the person she met before she disappeared. The one she wanted to help."

"What have you found? It's been four months. You must have collected some evidence by now, something more reliable than dreams."

I swung the iron harder and a sunburst of shards fissured the ice. "Max and I drove across the entire state. We visited hundreds of farms from Dubuque to Omaha."

"And?"

Every farm we'd gone to, every farmer we interviewed, had turned into another dead end. We canvassed the countryside with blind intent, another barn always looming in our sights, until we went to a place called Belgrave Properties. A lead. And it exploded in our faces.

"We got more information than we could handle."

"There's no such thing as too much data. It's either usable or it isn't."

I straightened up, a vicious ache pinching my shoulder, the tire iron in one hand. "This isn't some lab."

"I know that," she bristled.

"You don't. You have no idea what lives outside your Victorian mansion, your Tesla-and-solar-paneled life. You think Max could *use* PTSD? Does he use his night terrors and the memories of the bodies we've found? You think I can just dismiss my dreams when they're not *useful*, that they don't haunt every fucking moment I'm awake?" Puffs of breath pumped fast and hard from both of us. "You have no idea what you're talking about."

I pivoted and cracked the iron against the ice.

Neither of us spoke the rest of the way to the barn. The rolling doors were coated in thick ice. I got a better grip on the tire iron.

"Stand back."

With a series of deafening whacks that echoed off the silo and across the frozen yard, I beat the doors until they separated. Rolling one back, I took a deep breath and stepped inside.

Stasis. That was the first feeling I got—a lifeless void. But lifeless since when? I couldn't sense anything beyond absence, couldn't smell anything through frozen nostrils. Before my eyes could adjust to the dark, Eve edged behind me and flipped a switch. An overhead floodlight illuminated three tractors parked in a row and tools hung along the length of both walls as precisely as if it were a farming museum. Stairs along the far wall led to an open hayloft in the rafters, and another set led down, into darkness.

"There's a basement?"

"It's a bank barn," she said. "Built into the side of the hill, so both stories are at ground level. The lower door leads out to the orchard."

We circled the perimeter. No one hid between or inside the tractors. The floor was stained with the petrified mud of tire tracks and the loft held nothing but a thick layer of straw covered with feathers and mouse shit.

No Matthew Moore.

The basement had a heavy plastic curtain hanging in front the bottom stairs. Eve flipped another light on, throwing the lower level into sharp fluorescent relief.

"What is this?"

A giant metal funnel dominated the room, surrounded by smaller machines and a conveyer. Pallets of empty glass bottles and plastic bags lined the far wall.

"A cider press. They bottled their own." She walked to the funnel and ran a gloved finger over the metal. "It was a community project, cider-bottling day. Matthew and I always came to help, and Sam and Bella stayed from sunup to sundown. At the end of the day we felt like we'd been rolled in honey. Even the air seemed sticky, and there was always residue on the equipment, bottling day or not." Her glove stopped moving. "It's not sticky anymore."

Back on the main floor, Eve spun in a slow circle. "No one's been here. The house is untouched. Everything is exactly as Earl left it."

I dropped to my hands and knees and lay all the way down on the planks of the floor, closing my eyes.

"What are you doing?"

"Go to the door and close it."

"You want me to lock you in?"

"Just shut the door and don't make any other noise."

She sighed, but after a beat she moved toward the entrance.

"Walk slower."

The walking stopped altogether, then started again at a stiff march. It was louder, if not slower. I squeezed my eyes shut, absorbing the bounce of noise off the walls. When she shut the rolling door, it cracked against the edge of its counterpart with a resounding crash.

"Again," I called. "More deliberate this time."

There was no response, but after a pointed pause the door reopened and shut.

Breathing deep, I invoked the place I usually kept barred shut, the one that led back to the nightmare. I tried to relax, even as my limbs tensed. The sounds came first: the thud of Celina's bound and blindfolded body hitting the floor, the muffled terror rising in her throat, wind moaning over the roof, so high up, and footsteps walking away. The door to the building slid shut, locking her inside. It was the last noise she'd heard for a long time.

I tried to stop it there, to focus on the sound of the door, but the dream kept replaying, forcing itself in. Her thoughts and emotions flooded over me, her fight against the clawing despair. She'd locked on the beat of her own heart, focusing on that one pulsing muscle until she could see my face clearly, and then pushed every sense across that connection. The sounds, the coppery smell of blood smeared in her hair. The bludgeoned spot on her head she was scared to touch, for fear of what her fingers would find. *Hurty, Uncle Jonah.* The little girl, her hand tucked firmly in mine. *All gray and hurty.*

Another set of footsteps superimposed over the girl's voice, pacing around the tractors and stopping near my head. I opened my eyes, water leaking down my temples. Eve's upside-down face hovered directly above me.

"Matthew isn't here."

The door in Celina's barn had creaked; the hinges needed oil. The person who walked away from her had footsteps that echoed through a cavernous, empty space, hollow above and below, not one filled with tractors and sealed off for cider bottling. And the blood. Celina's blood had seeped on to the floor, marking the place I needed to find. The place I still hadn't found.

I swallowed. "Neither is Celina."

We didn't speak on the way back to the house. It was all I could do to creep along the iron-smashed path and not slide down into the orchard, where the curl of ice-covered branches beckoned, promising a slow, numbing end.

Eve was right. Celina had been gone for four months and I was no closer to finding her now than I had been a week ago. All I'd done was open myself to the dream again, and now I was drowning in it. The sound of Celina's hitched breathing filled my ears. Her battered and aching body made my own weak as I staggered across the ice. My skull wasn't broken. I knew that, but my head didn't. I hadn't stopped shaking since I got up.

Inside, Eve searched the house a second time. I didn't have the energy to join her. I dry swallowed a chunk of Xanax and went to the kitchen, leaning against the fridge with my eyes closed, trying to shut out everything I'd felt and heard in the barn. Celina wasn't here. It was an echo, a ghost cry, and I had to force the ghosts back into the growing darkness of the orchard outside the farmhouse windows. Danica Chase. Angela Garcia. I sucked in as much air as I could and let it out on a slow exhale. Kit Freeman. George Marcus Morrow.

I didn't know how much time passed or if I fell asleep like that, staring at the long swallow of twilight, until the energy of the room shifted with a brightness I was starting to know too well.

"Did you find anything?" I couldn't find the will to move, not yet. "No."

"I'm sorry." She didn't reply. "Is Earl all right?"

"Are *you* all right?"

I pushed myself off the appliance and opened the refrigerator door. "He should probably eat something. Food with his medication."

There were a few mason jars filled with brown and red substances—jelly?—and a bag of coffee beans. The freezer had a half-eaten loaf of bread, and I found an unexpired tub of peanut butter and a bottle of pinot noir in the pantry.

Over PB&Js and wine in the living room, we agreed not to drive back to Iowa City tonight. The only local station we could get with the antenna reported hundreds of accidents across the state, with conditions expected to deteriorate. Earl wrote that there were tire chains in one of the sheds behind the garage and, combined with my snow tires and a heavy runway of sand, we could get the Evolution out of the orchard and leave Lovers Ridge tomorrow morning.

This place would be fine for one night, but I wasn't excited about the idea. I lived alone. I had no pets. There was no one to hear or care when I woke up screaming or jumping out of bed.

What would Earl or Eve say if I asked to sleep in the bathtub? If I explained how being that uncomfortable helped me skim the surface of unconsciousness without diving into the nightmares of REM. No, better to shut up and drink more wine. With enough pills and alcohol, I could keep the dreams away.

"We must have misinterpreted something."

Eve had spread our evidence over the coffee table in meticulous order. It was a far cry from the walls I covered in random articles and ripped pieces of notebook paper. She bent over Kara's notebook, as though using an invisible microscope. "Earl, can you pull up the list of LRF acronyms again?"

But Earl wasn't listening. He'd hit Play on an honest-to-god VCR and was engrossed in a home recording of his and his wife's twenty-fifth anniversary party. The man on the screen whirled a blonde around the dance floor of an old town hall, sending her red skirt billowing. Her shoes were kicked off and he had a stain down the front of his shirt. Their foreheads gleamed with sweat as the crowd clapped and whistled.

He was oblivious to Eve and me, to the half of his face that refused to smile, even to his listing slump down the side of the recliner. That whirling skirt lifted everything inside him that could still rise. Eve paused, wiping her eyes and glancing at the empty recliner next to Earl. Red fabric twirled out of the screen and into the living room, dancing across the hearth and reflecting off the pictures framed on the shelves. She was with him, alive in this moment, giving him back pieces of his life. Not everyone gone from this house was lost.

A half an hour later, Earl's snores filled the living room. Eve had asked if he wanted to sleep in the bedroom, but he'd thumped the recliner and pushed a button until he lay almost flat. Using pillows from the master bedroom, we shimmed them between his torso and the armrests, then drew one of the fleece blankets up until he looked like the world's ugliest baby tucked into a bassinet.

We sat on the rug, circling the evidence.

"Alexis Dwyer, your niece, and Kara." Eve drew lines connecting the names and the scant information she'd written about each. "The only common ground they shared was an Iowa City residence and their demographics. Three young, white, cis females."

Turmoil brimmed under the surface, threatening to swamp her, but her voice remained steady. Anyone who wasn't me would have no clue how hard this was for her.

"I thought"—she glanced at Earl, making sure he was asleep— "I thought maybe it had something to do with trafficking, that Matthew was using the farm. You know, bringing girls here."

I picked up the paper with Celina's name etched into it, the letters sinking under the weight of lead. "We don't know what the connection is with Alexis, and I don't see Celina with him at all. This is something else."

"What?"

"I don't know."

"Then we're back to square one."

"No, we're not." I flipped to the last page of Kara's journal. "LRF has to be here. Nowhere else makes any sense. They met here, according to the burner, and Kara was supposed to come again tonight. There's something here."

"Where? We checked the barn and the house. Where would—" Eve sat bolt upright. A spark shot through her body, an electric jolt of nerves connecting. It pinged straight into me.

"I know where to look."

Eve

The first time I visited Lovers Ridge Farm was a postcard-perfect September afternoon, full of blue skies and golden fields. Matthew had proposed the day before in Ryerson's Woods, and the sapphire on my finger transformed the visit into an engagement party.

When we arrived, Helen and Earl were in the orchard with Sam and Bella, the four of them harvesting the apple crop for cider bottling. Helen had pulled a handkerchief off her head, waving it like a beacon from the top of her ladder, and run out of the orchard to meet us. If Matthew planned any speeches, he didn't get a chance to make them. As soon as she spied the ring on my finger, she shoved her basket of Honeycrisps into Matthew's hands and scooped me into a tight hug.

"I finally have my daughter," she whispered. My throat caught, as though I'd floated to the top of a pool and gotten hooked by something eager and light.

The rest of the parents joined us. Bella came over, beaming, her petite frame dwarfed by the apple basket strapped to her front. Earl clapped a hand to Matthew's shoulder, smiling at the ground. Sam congratulated both of us and pulled Matthew into a bear hug.

"Proud of you, kid."

Matthew thumped Sam on the back, tears in his eyes as he pulled away and glanced at his father. Helen took over then, cry-laughing everyone into the house and sending Earl to fetch a bottle of their best champagne.

After the toasts were made and engagement stories told, they gave me a tour of the farm. Helen and Bella sandwiched me between them as the men trailed behind. The wind had picked up while we were inside, carrying a low wall of cumulonimbus clouds on the horizon. I'd already chased hundreds of supercells and studied the physics of storms for years by then. There was no reason to panic, but Matthew and I had spent the entire morning in bed and I hadn't checked the radar or atmospheric models. Normally, it was the first thing I did every day, before breakfast, even before using the bathroom.

I watched the cloud pattern, my eyes tracking the sky even as I nodded and commented on each building and field. It was easier with the women next to me, listening to the bubble of their chatter, but my anxiety grew as we hiked farther and farther from the house.

The orchard ended in a single, sprawling oak sitting at the top of a creek bed. Sam pointed out a clump of buildings on the horizon as his own farm. "Also known as Matthew's other kitchen."

Bella leaned into my arm. "When he was a teenager, he used to have dinner with his own parents and then run right over for a second dinner with us. The boy was bottomless."

"It would've been rude not to clean my plates." Matthew flashed a grin between both mothers as everyone laughed, but all I could see was the sky, which was turning darker by the moment. The champagne began pounding against my temples.

"When the creek freezes in the winter, Earl and Sam plow it off for ice-skating. The five of us have skated here every Christmas morning since Matthew could walk." Helen hugged me to her side. "Now we'll be six."

"We should get inside."

"Oh, it did get a bit cloudy, didn't it?" Helen stepped out from under the heavy oak branches and looked up, finally noticing the menacing swirl. "I've got a few umbrellas in the barn."

The wind gusted. A dark gray cloud dipped lower in the atmosphere. Was there rotation?

The alcohol curdled in my stomach and my breath came shorter and shorter.

"We have to get inside now."

I didn't stop to see if the men followed but grabbed Helen and Bella and half walked, half frog-marched them back through the apple trees, where the leaves whipped in the wind like broken compass needles. I could sense the women's surprise, the bumps of their jostled elbows against my ribs, but whatever they said whistled into white noise in the fury of the wind.

As soon as we reached the house, I turned on the Weather Channel and braced myself against a window frame, staring from sky to barn to silo as the rain began hitting the pane. The glass fogged, and I wiped it away, trying to keep a clear view of the storm. My smartphone, a dinosaur then compared to what I carried now, was useless, far outside the range of any usable signal.

"It's fine," I kept muttering, while Matthew rubbed my back and held off everyone's questions. "An isolated cell. No rotation. Not enough moisture to feed it, anyway."

"It'll be over soon," Matthew tried to reassure me.

"It always is."

No one could comfort me until the cell passed and the sky cleared. At the time, I thought I'd panicked because I was unprepared. I wasn't armed with my usual maps, measurements, and data, but that was only half of it. That storm terrified me because I'd gained a new family and, in gaining them, knew they could be lost in an instant.

"Earl." I nudged Earl until he woke up. His eyes were bleary, unfocused. Kendrick sat on the floor by the coffee table, clearly confused.

"Do you remember the first time I visited the farm?"

He made a few noises I couldn't decipher. I grabbed the iPad and forced his fingers to close over it.

"When Matthew and I left that day, after the storm, you walked us out to the car."

Earl had been quiet during dessert, while I'd explained to everyone about my father and the reason I'd become a physicist uninterested in the big bang or quantum mechanics or any of the more exciting frontiers of my field. Helen asked a dozen questions while holding my hand. Earl listened silently, filling the coffee in everyone's cup. It wasn't until later, when we were getting back into Matthew's car to drive home, that he pulled me aside.

"There's a place here on the farm," Earl said, low and gruff. "A safe room. Built back in the sixties."

"Where?" I scanned the surrounding outbuildings.

"Don't you worry about that." Earl opened my car door for me. "But I want you to know, if a twister ever comes to Lovers Ridge, we'll be fine." He patted the door of the car, two soft thuds of reassurance.

I'd been so embarrassed at the time. I couldn't believe how swift and fierce my reaction had been, how little choice my brain had in the matter. I gave Earl a quick, awkward hug and slid into the car, eager to be home with my models and data. I didn't say anything to Matthew, and in all the years afterward, Earl never mentioned it again. I'd all but forgotten about it, until now.

"You told me about a storm shelter, remember?" A safe room. A secret place. I'd had a few glasses of wine tonight, but I'd never felt more instantly alert. "Where is it?"

Earl still didn't seem fully awake. His good eye rolled groggily, and he typed a few random letters on the iPad.

"The meds," Kendrick said. "They're knocking him out."

I waited until Earl's gaze landed on me and tried to hold his focus. "Did Matthew know about the safe room?"

Earl nodded.

"Where is it?" I propped up the iPad, trying to make it easier for him to write.

te silp

"Slip? Silt?"

"Silo." Kendrick's voice came from over my shoulder, surprising me with how close he'd drawn. "He's thinking about the old silo."

I stiffened, ready to unequivocally dispute the idea that Kendrick heard Earl think anything, but a noise from the chair stopped me. Earl's head fell back against the pillows, and he nodded, breathing the word. *Silo.*

"Is there a key? How do we get in?" But his eyes had already drifted shut, and he almost immediately began snoring again.

* * *

We geared up for another trek outside. I hunted through storage bins full of gloves, ice skates, and coveralls and found two pairs of cleats—rubber straps studded with dozens of metal points. We fastened them over our boots, then layered on coats, hats, scarves, and gloves. Outside, Kendrick lit our way with a floodlight. No other farms were visible on the horizon and only a glimmer of the new moon ghosted the sky.

Bypassing the barn, we inched around three giant grain bins. I'd brought the tire iron, but we didn't need it. The cleats dug tiny holes in the ice with each step, giving us the most traction we'd had since the freeze began.

The old silo loomed above the bins. For as many times as I'd visited the farm, I'd never seen it used. Kendrick shone the flood-light up the dirty cement facade to the top of the cylinder where the dome began, twenty meters above our heads. It was ringed with giant icicles, stalactite-sized formations of ice poised to impale us.

"Jesus." Kendrick exhaled a cloud of breath into the beam of light. "Guess it would be a quick way to go."

"It would be interesting to calculate." He shot me a look. "The parameters of death by icicle. The amount of force needed."

"Yeah, real interesting."

Some of them looked almost a meter long. "I should assign that in my freshman lab next semester."

"Let me know how it turns out."

We inched around the concrete base—poured as a square foundation rather than a circle—to the entrance of the silo. There wasn't a door on the building anymore, making it unlikely to provide much shelter from any storm. The inside smelled dank, even in the dead of winter. Dirt and dead vines covered the walls and a rusting ladder bolted to the concrete led to the top of the dome, where a small square of black opened to the night sky. Some creature had tried to burrow through the petrified silage on one side of the floor, only to be stopped short by stained foundation. Kendrick turned in a slow circle, shining the light over every surface.

"There."

A small patch of cement block near the bottom of the wall was darker than the bricks around it. The rest of the blocks were ringed in frost, all except that one area. A point of warmth. But why?

I crouched down, removing two layers of gloves to touch the block. It wasn't warm, but it wasn't freezing, either.

"What is it?"

"An anomaly." I stood up and lifted the tire iron like a bat. "Stand back."

I hit one of the frozen spots on the concrete block. It made a dull thwack and sent painful vibrations up my arms. Then, repositioning, I used the same force on the warm spot. "Did you hear that?"

"What?"

The pitch was higher. Not by a lot, but the sound waves were definitely shorter. I repeated the experiment, and the second time Kendrick nodded. "So, they're made out of different materials?"

"Or different thicknesses of material. There's something inside this one"—I pointed to the anomaly—"that's making it lighter and warmer."

"What?"

But I was already racing out of the silo and inching my way around the base of the building, until I got to the same place on the outside. Facing away from the farmhouse into the inky-black night was a small vent in the side of the concrete. A ventilation system had been built into the structure of the silo itself—and one that didn't lead inside. The square shape of the foundation suddenly made perfect sense.

"It's underground!" I shouted as Kendrick appeared around the edge of the building. "Air is warmer underground and when it rises through the ventilation system, it heats the surrounding concrete. The safe room is under the silo."

The trapdoor was faintly visible beneath the ice—a thin, shadowy line. We were standing on top of something, and I didn't know how deep it went or what we would find. It felt like Pandora's box, irreversible once opened.

Kendrick went to work on the ice, trying to make a crack deep enough to reach the shadow, but after a hundred blows with the tire iron, his chest heaved and he'd barely made a dent.

"The ice is too thick. The ground is lower here. It probably flooded and froze three times already this winter." His forehead shone with sweat as he leaned against the silo. "Earl doesn't have a blowtorch around here somewhere, does he?"

"I don't—" I inhaled sharply. "The canister."

Kendrick's head snapped up. "The one Earl found in your garage?"

It was right there, the answer to the question I'd been asking since yesterday morning. How does a car burn in the middle of a rainstorm?

"Get a lighter."

Jonah

"Calcium carbide?"

The name was familiar, like a foreign language I'd overheard or a dream fragment that hadn't bubbled to the surface until now.

Eve had gone to the house and brought back the canister from her husband's workbench in Iowa City. The toxic lava rock still looked like toxic lava rock, but Eve crackled with excitement, her entire being lit up with the force of those two words.

"I knew there'd been an accelerant." She tipped the container toward the floodlight, holding it like it was the most precious—or dangerous—thing she'd ever held. "I assumed the substance fought a battle against the rain, that it burned hot enough to defy the cooling effects of the water, but that wasn't it at all."

"What are you talking about?"

"The Tesla. Kara said Matthew started the fire himself. This is what he used."

I tried to work out how black sand could torch a soaked Model S. It was a big conclusion to leap to, especially for Dr. Eve Roth. "What's your evidence?"

Everything in her warmed to the question, and something almost devilish sparked behind her eyes. It caught me square in the chest.

"Get back and stay away from the fumes."

She tipped the canister over the fractured ice. As soon as the tiny rocks hit the ground, smoke billowed from the spot. The ice began to hiss.

"What the hell?" I stumbled backward, keeping the light trained down. Eve poured the rocks along the outline of the door, smoke writhing at her feet. It looked wrong, unnatural.

"Calcium carbide needs water to burn. I should've known. It's one of Matthew's favorite experiments. He performs it every year for his inorganic chemistry seminar."

That's where the name had been familiar. I'd seen it on one of his YouTube videos last night, turning water into fire. Christ.

When the container was empty, she stepped back next to me and crouched down with the lighter. In an instant, the smoking pile of sand burst into flames.

Heat scorched my front, and I threw an arm in front of Eve, pulling her farther away. The fire leapt and spread, crawling wider until it became a giant bonfire licking the side of the silo. The world was suddenly hot and bright. Above, the giant icicles rimming the silo dome grew translucent. Droplets rained down onto the fire, which hissed and drank the water like fuel.

Usually it was my sixth sense turning the world upside down, not the other five. But now I could barely trust what my body screamed was happening—the scorching heat of the flames, the smell of burnt garlic, the creeping menace of the gas as it tried to eat the ice around it. The edges spread farther, chasing us backward, and I had a vision of the entire iced world turning to flame, swallowing us whole. Eve was the one pulling me back now, her glove clamped tightly on my elbow.

After what felt like an hour, the fire died down, leaving a strange bubbled and blackened scar on the earth. The ice covering the door was gone, the world snapped back into place, and the only sound in the night was my own ragged breath.

"Well, that . . . worked." Eve traced the edge of the tire iron along charred ground, trying to find the outline of the door again.

"So, we know the who and the how of Ryerson's Woods. Your husband torched his own car with freaky chemical rocks." I looked at Eve's profile. "Why?"

She shook her head, eyes on the trapdoor, and inched toward it.

"Be careful."

"The reaction is done. It can't reignite without more gas."

She started hitting the edge of the tire iron against the cement, vibrating the exposed foundation with each blow. A creaking noise came from overhead, followed by a snap.

I tackled Eve. We hit the still-warm ground seconds before one of the giant icicles crashed on top of the safe room door, shattering into a thousand pieces.

"Oh my god." She crawled away on elbows and heels, slipping and skidding. Daggers hovered above us, the remaining icicles poised and ready to fall.

"Death by icicle?"

"It was supposed to be a thought experiment."

"Don't think of any more experiments tonight, okay?"

We waited until the scorch mark had cooled and the icicles stopped glistening before creeping back to the door. With my heart in my throat and the hair on the back of my neck standing on end, I carefully chiseled out the outline of the door, revealing the entrance to the safe room inch by inch. When the handle was exposed, we each gripped one side and pulled.

The door opened on a gust of scorched chemicals and frozen dirt. Narrow wooden steps disappeared into darkness between slabs of solid concrete. There was no hint of what lay beyond, no trace emotion or energy. Every time I'd stepped into a barn in the last four months, I knew what I was looking for, my head tensed into a crash position for the worst-case scenario. But this, this was a dead zone, a gaping blank. I had no idea what scenario waited in front of us. Eve's energy stretched tight over a war of adrenaline, exhaustion, and nerves, but her face was intent, her gaze laser focused. She was braced to crash.

Silently, we descended the staircase. I went first, wielding the tire iron, opening myself up to sense any danger ahead. Eve followed with the floodlight, shining it over my shoulder and casting more shadows than light.

At the bottom, we pivoted, back-to-back, in a slow circle. The room was an eight-by-eight-foot concrete cube with an air filtration system, an old bomb shelter probably built during the nuclear panic of the sixties. Wall-to-wall shelves lined the space from floor to ceiling, but instead of rations and emergency supplies, they held clear tubs filled with stacks of identical plastic bags.

"What is this?" Eve moved to the closest shelf and reached for one of the tubs. I grabbed her wrist.

"Don't touch anything." I'd worked with Max long enough to know not to contaminate a scene.

"But—"

"No."

"Fine." She pulled her hand free and shined the light into the tub. Every plastic bag was full of round, white, unmarked pills, at least five hundred in the top bag alone.

"Jesus Christ."

"Are these drugs?" Her energy reeled, recoiling.

I was doing too much math to answer, adding up the number of bags in each tub, the number of tubs in the room. A few hundred thousand pills—and that was on the low end. Depending on what they were—and I'd bet hard on opioids—we could be surrounded by a fortune.

Eve's breath hitched. Her emotions spiked, bleeding into the claustrophobic room. "Why are they here?"

"Storage." I started pacing, picking up her churn of frantic analysis and riding the crest of it, letting her mind carry me forward. Cryptocurrency, untraceable payments. That giant house, full of smart, rich-people toys. Alexis Dwyer, killed by an overdose. Of fucking course.

"No, not here. Not on Earl and Helen's farm." Her voice broke.

"It's perfect," I muttered. Here in the middle of the country, surrounded by nothing but fields and sky. No one to see. No one to hear.

But something must have gone wrong. The car fire, the ransacked office.

Matthew Moore was a trafficker but not of girls. And he'd made someone very, very mad.

Max

I punched out of my shift and left the station with Larsen's words still clouding my head. *No one had to tell me Jonah Kendrick was with you when it happened.* Did he think Jonah was the one who shot me? That I was covering for him? It hadn't occurred to me before now, but it tracked. It would explain why Jonah had been banned from working with ICPD, why they'd all treated him like garbage on Thursday morning. The whole department must've believed it, with their sidelong glances, their clipped greetings and awkward pauses. Ciseski, leaning on the vending machine: *Did'ja hear about the cop who got shot by his best friend?*

I never meant for my omissions to throw Jonah under the bus, but the truth was if they thought that, they wouldn't suspect what really happened. Though I'd only seen the man who shot me for a few minutes, his face was imprinted in my brain. I looked through endless mug shots, social media feeds, local newspaper stories, and precinct blotters across Iowa. I didn't have the resources at home that I would've if I was on duty, but I searched anyway. He could turn up anywhere. He could pass me on the street someday or be pulled over for a traffic violation five counties away. I hadn't found him yet, but I had an endless supply of sleepless nights ahead of me, and it didn't matter what Larsen or anyone else in the department thought.

I headed south instead of driving home, sliding through the dark and frozen wasteland that covered my city. Street markings, curbs, and sidewalks had disappeared. Wrecked cars littered the streets. The tow trucks had given up, three hundred bucks a car not worth it under these conditions. Only snowplows and emergency vehicles hacked their way through the city now. I careened sideways into a parking lot just as the snowplow I'd been following threw a chunk of asphalt the size of my head off its bucket, narrowly missing my car.

The lot was full of vehicles frozen to the ground. I tried double-parking in front of them, but the cruiser slid an extra ten feet before bouncing off a chain-link fence, sending ice chips pinging across my hood and windshield.

I killed the engine and checked my phone.

Where are you? Are you stranded? Can you get home?

Shelley. She'd been worried about me starting work again before my arm was fully healed, and she'd suggested a therapist more than once. Not the rehab kind—or at least not rehab for my arm. Now the storm was sending her anxiety into overdrive. I typed a quick reply, telling her I was fine, not to worry. I'd be home as soon as I could. One of those things, at least, was probably true.

Alexis Dwyer's landlady stood under the eaves of her apartment building, her posture hunched and indignant at the same time.

When I skated close enough, she gestured at the fence I'd slid into with my cruiser. "Who's going to pay for that dent?"

"Bill the city. Put my name on it."

She huffed and made a few more noises before leading me in to a pitch-black entryway.

"Power out?"

"Five hours now. You want to see Alexis's place again?"

I did, but not yet. I pulled out my phone and showed her the university staff photo for Matthew Moore. "Is this the man who visited Alexis? The one she had the fight with on Tuesday?"

"No." The landlady turned and went into her apartment. I stayed by the door as the beam of her flashlight disappeared down a short hallway.

"You sure?" I called into the belly of the black apartment. "You want to look at it one more time?"

Rummaging noises came from the other room. She didn't have any candles lit in the main living area. All I could see was a shaft of dull moonlight filtering through her front window. I imagined waiting out this storm in a dark building where a neighbor had been lying dead for days and was glad to be going home after this, to a warm house with my wife and son.

"Here." The bobbing flashlight beam reappeared, moving to a spot near the window. A beat later a laptop screen flashed to life. "Come look at this. I was going to call you before the storm hit."

I moved closer as she sifted through computer files, clicking on each one and muttering to herself.

"I checked Alexis's bank records."

The landlady went quiet.

"You said she didn't pay rent this month. Looked to me like her check cleared on December first."

Her hands stilled on the keyboard. "I was worried. Alexis was so sad and alone. Then I didn't see her for days. But I couldn't enter the apartment without cause. And worry isn't a cause."

No, it wasn't. You couldn't put that on a form and not get sued. But I understood. I knew the things worry could make you do.

"I won't say anything. Next time, though, call in a welfare check."

She nodded, one sharp bob of agreement, and resumed her search. "I won't bill the city for the fence. It was already dented."

Eventually, she found the file she wanted. "Here." She pulled up a video and hit Play. The image was grainy security footage, a fishbowl shot of the apartment building's parking lot from a camera mounted right above the entrance. I checked the date. Tuesday, at 1:00 p.m.

"There they come."

A pickup truck pulled into the lot. It was black, a late-model Silverado from the shape of the taillights. The license plate was too blurry to make out. I squinted as Alexis and the blond man walked across the lot, coming closer and closer to the camera. They were turned toward each other, arguing already. Alexis stopped in the middle of the lot, throwing her arms wide. The man grabbed her and kept moving, forcing her shoulder into a locked position. He was blond and skinny, dressed in jeans, boots, and a long, dark jacket. The face looked too lean, the frame too gaunt to be Matthew Moore. Then they came closer, and I stopped breathing.

"Pause it."

She froze the video right before the couple went inside. I leaned in. The shot was still pixelated and washed out, but everything in me had gone as cold as the world outside.

The landlady was right. The man walking Alexis Dwyer to her death wasn't Matthew Moore. It was Belgrave.

Saturday

*Science is the acceptance of what works and the rejection of what does not.
That needs more courage than we might think.*

—Jacob Bronowski

Eve

A high-pitched, buzzing whine woke me up. I sat up, disoriented, and reached for the coffee table.

"Kendrick?"

The room was completely black. Earl still snored in his chair, but the other noise grew louder and louder, eclipsing his nasal breathing. It sounded like a chainsaw, coming from outside.

I moved to the front windows, feeling my way around furniture, and pulled the curtain open.

Lights crested the hill along the road and zoomed toward the farm. Snowmobiles. I relaxed a little, watching their progress, until they slowed down in front of the driveway.

The one in the lead swerved off the road and the others followed, disappearing behind the grain bins. The buzzing became metallic, echoing off the metal, and their headlights flashed around the outer edge of the buildings. When they reached the old silo, the buzzing idled and the lights stopped moving.

"Kara."

I jumped. Kendrick had snuck up behind me. I could barely make out his face in the darkness. Earl woke up with a snort and a jerk.

"You think she's . . ."

"Coming to LRF tonight? Yeah. And she's finding out she wasn't the first one here."

The calcium carbide. We'd left a gaping scorch mark on the ground. I whipped back to the window in time to see two headlights swerve around the grain bins and head straight for the house. One of them turned too sharply and went spiraling across the road, catching us in its beam for fractions of a second on each revolution. Frozen, breath held, we waited. The other snowmobile idled, aiming their light at the one who'd flown out of control.

"We have to hide. Now."

I ran to the front door and locked it while Kendrick whispered explanations to Earl as he hauled him to his feet.

"He can't go up or down stairs."

"Pantry. It's the closest option."

Together, we muscled Earl through the living room and into the kitchen, pulling him into the darkest corner of the pantry. It was big enough for all of Helen's canning and baking supplies, and the three of us could fit inside easily, but we knocked into a shelf as we moved through the dark. A thud shook my arm and Earl's weight dropped, falling to the floor.

He grunted, slumping sideways.

"Earl." I traced the shape of his shoulders and back, trying to feel where he'd been hurt. "Are you okay?"

The buzz of snowmobile motors roared up to the house. Kendrick's car was out of sight in the apple orchard. If they didn't go into the trees or shine a headlight directly at it, it might stay hidden. Earl's chest heaved in and out, and I could tell he was trying to muzzle his pain. His good hand moved to mine, I assumed to pull himself upright, but his fingers pressed against mine. They formed the shape of a gun.

"The gun's in the backpack on the porch," I whispered—then gasped—remembering the other thing we'd taken from Kara: the notebook. It was sitting next to Matthew's formulas and all my notes and data, spread over the coffee table for anyone to find.

"Eve—" Kendrick started, but I'd already bolted up. I slipped out of the pantry as the front door shook in its frame. Someone was trying to get in.

A flashlight shone through the front porch. I dropped to the floor and crawled back to the living room beneath the thin beam of light, grabbing everything off the coffee table and shoving it under the couch. A loud bang made me jump. Two more followed. It sounded like they were kicking in the door.

I crawled to Earl's recliner, where a mountain of pillows and blankets still sat, and stuffed as many as I could behind the chairs. When the sound of shattering glass echoed through the house, I dove behind the recliner and tried to make myself as small as possible.

"Shoot the fucking lock."

More breaking glass. Someone was making the hole wider, clearing the edges. "And have it ricochet into your dumb head? That's not a bad idea."

I sucked in a breath. The second voice was monotone, female, and familiar—Kara Johnson. God, we'd been right. The journal, the barn swallow. The ice storm hadn't stopped her from coming; it had only delayed her.

The door creaked open and boots thudded into the house. Two sets. Kara and someone else, someone with significantly more mass. I squeezed myself as small as possible, trying not to disturb the curtains or rock the chair. The lights in the kitchen turned on and my breath caught in my throat. We'd cleaned up after dinner, but what if they saw the wine bottle in the recycling bin or the plates stacked in the drying rack? Earl was only a meter away, one turn of the pantry door handle. He was completely defenseless.

A voice shouted outside over the buzz of the engines. It echoed off the grain bins with other, harder to distinguish noises. Thumps, slaps, a dull hum of activity. For a strangled moment I thought they might follow Kara into the house, until I realized what was happening: they were emptying the safe room, and we couldn't do a thing to stop them.

I'd almost collapsed inside that room earlier. The number of tubs filled with white tablets was staggering. I couldn't process it, couldn't connect what I was seeing to any rational explanation. My whole body had gone numb.

"Fucking Walter White," Kendrick said, as he'd counted the boxes.

"Who?"

"Are you kidding me?" He pointed the floodlight in my direction, blinding me. *"Breaking Bad?"*

I had no idea what he was talking about. It was like I'd stepped into a parallel universe. He explained the show—some TV drug drama—concluding, "Kara must be his partner. He's cooking and she's selling out of that store. That's why they logged so many sales for used jeans. Right in the middle of downtown. Christ, it's brilliant."

I felt like I was choking. The man who'd proposed to me in a sun-dappled forest, who'd built me a weather station and cared for his disabled father was a drug lord? I stuttered over everything it would mean. Our life, over. Our marriage, our home, our family, gone. My heart tried to turn away, to reject it out of hand, but my brain—my incessant, insisting, cataloging mind—kept combing through the data, weighing the evidence until more things clicked into place.

Matthew had never wanted to talk about money. When I asked about the renovations to the house, the trips to Paris, the Tesla in the driveway, he always had a ready answer. A Bitcoin sale. A great deal with a contractor. A refinance. And I accepted it every time. I was too preoccupied with my classes and research to question anything. Maybe that's why he married me. He'd put a widow's walk on the roof and a skylight over our bed to keep my gaze lifted, to shift all my attention to the sky.

Kendrick and I left the silo untouched. We'd planned to call the police in the morning as soon as we could get a cell signal on our way home. But now they were emptying the safe room. And we might not be leaving Lovers Ridge at all.

Footfalls moved into the hallway. One set of boots. The door to the cellar opened. A light switched on and the stairs creaked as someone went downstairs. The other person moved quietly through the first floor, so softly I couldn't be sure exactly where they were.

My heart pounded so hard in my ears it drowned the activity outside, insisting I do something—anything—to insure its continued beat. I had nothing. No weapons, no plan. If they found us, we would die.

They continued searching the house and eventually met in the living room. On the other side of the chair, I could see a sliver of a silhouette. Hooded, petite. Kara.

"No one upstairs. Place is empty." The voice was male and deep.

"There's a giant slice of scorched earth out there that says different," Kara replied.

A third snowmobile roared up to the house, sliding into the foundation with a string of shouted curses. Then more footsteps, the door opening.

"We're loaded," a new voice called, this one with a hint of an accent.

"Anything seem off?" Kara asked. "Were the bags opened or moved?"

The guy grunted a negative. "Can we get the fuck out of here already?"

"If Matthew talked to someone . . ."

"He can't talk to anyone anymore."

The sound came before I could control it. A small, strangled bubble in the back of my throat, followed by an immediate jolt of panic.

Kara started to say something else, but she cut off midsentence and I knew: she'd heard me. My entire body tensed, bracing itself as I traced the sliver of boot, up the leg, torso, and shoulder of the person on the other side of the chair. She moved a fraction to the side and her eyes locked on mine. I was a deer in headlights, trapped, frozen.

"What should we do? Leave the stuff? Torch it?" the accented voice asked. "Boss isn't gonna be happy about that."

"No." Kara's gaze shifted smoothly away from my hiding spot behind the chair. "We're taking it."

"What if it's fucking tampered? What if there's tracking—"

"Don't worry your pretty head." Kara moved out of sight as they all went to the front door.

"But the boss—"

"Leave Belgrave to me."

Jonah

The door flew open, hitting the wall with a bang.

I jerked, reaching for Earl—or was it Celina?—reaching for the person I was trying to protect and finding nothing but porcelain.

Someone walked across the room and crouched in front of me. I scrambled up, hitting my head and slipping on the smooth surface. I was damp, dizzy, frantically trying to figure out which world I'd been tossed into.

"Kendrick."

The voice came like an anchor. Firm. Rational. Not a threat. I moved toward it without thinking, and my hand hit the lip of the clawfoot tub. Eve's cap of reddish hair shone in the moonlight filtering in from the bathroom window. We were at Lovers Ridge. The snowmobiles had left hours ago. We were safe.

"What is it?"

"You were screaming. You said, 'Save her. I can save her.'"

I'd been in the barn with Celina, feeling the graze of tears down her temples, her unbearable, quiet acceptance of whatever rolled open those creaking doors to come for her, but I didn't remember saying that. I didn't know any part of me was still capable of that much hope.

Save her? Sometimes when I dreamt about her now, the barn itself cracked open, swallowing her in its dark, gaping mouth, sucking her down with all the others I'd lost. Four months was a lifetime in missing person cases. I'd never found anyone who'd been gone this long. When I called my brother, we sat on the phone, all the things we dreaded seeping into the silence. After four months, hope had congealed into desperation. We would take any answer, the worst possible answer.

"Sorry." I doubled over, putting my head between my knees, and waited for the rest of the room to orient around Eve's voice, for my mind to retract into the cage of the tub and strangle the insanity of subconscious fantasies. "That's why I live alone."

Gradually, the dream faded and the events of the night came back into focus. Kara and the muscle she'd brought with her; he'd reeked of dumb brutality even through the pantry door. The two of them had searched the house quickly and left abruptly, and I didn't know why. Eve hadn't wanted to talk about it, but something had happened. Her energy was stunted, cut off at the knees.

"Is Earl okay?" I rubbed cold sweat from my forehead and gave sitting up another shot. The dizziness slowed into the dull rotation of a tilted carousel ride, and the contents of my stomach seemed like they were going to stay put.

"You didn't wake him up. I think the medicine . . . We didn't give him too much, did we?"

There it was again. The usual humming drive of Eve's mind had a hitch in it, tiny spasms of emotion trying to hijack her. She'd been fighting them off since the snowmobiles left and we moved Earl back to his recliner. He'd fallen hard in the pantry, hitting a shelf on his bad side. He couldn't put any weight on that leg. It didn't feel broken, but it didn't feel exactly whole either.

Eve had pulled out a giant plastic bag of prescription bottles and sorted through them with shaking fingers.

"What were they?"

I didn't have to ask what she meant.

"The pill market is still mostly opioids. Fentanyl. Oxy." I hunted through the labels until I found the right one and picked up the bottle, rattling it. "Oxycodone hydrochloride. Ten milligrams orally every twelve hours as needed."

"So, Matthew was making pain pills? Illegal pain pills?"

I shook out two of the tablets. They weren't the same as what had been in the bunker. Tiny writing marked them as property of the legal drug traffickers, the ones who'd pushed opioids until they trended hard into morgues across the country. I'd worked more than one drug-related case in my career. Sometimes it was the first way someone became lost—in the slippery fog of chemicals—before they disappeared completely. And the drug companies didn't give a single shit about any of them. I couldn't hate them completely, though. Those same companies made Xanax, and I'd probably have been agoraphobic by now without it—or locked up in an institution somewhere.

We debated giving Earl one pill or two. Eve pushed for none until she registered her father-in-law's face, clenched and blotchy, trying to swallow the pain. We gave him one, and she sat by him until he finally fell asleep. At some point after that, I'd gone to the bathroom and climbed into the clawfoot tub.

"Is he breathing steadily?" I asked now.

Eve sat on the tile on the other side of the tub, her face sliced in half by moonlight. She nodded.

"Then he's fine. Stable. He's probably been taking those for a while."

She nodded again, not speaking or making any move to leave. We sat in the dark, facing each other on either side of the tub, listening to the unsteadiness of our own breath and marking where on the stability scale we might land in this moment. Whether it was better or worse than the moment before.

Eve broke the silence with the last thing I expected.

"My father died in a tornado when I was nine years old."

She swallowed and rested her temple on the lip of the tub, staring at something beyond me. "Search crews went out in the days and weeks afterward, combing the nearby land and streams, the gullies and thatches of woods between fields. They didn't find anything. The tornado never gave him back. For the rest of my childhood, it felt like he was caught somewhere between the land and sky. We never knew."

She trailed off and her eyes filled, brimming with dark, unshed tears.

"Most people dream about tornadoes coming to get them, ones they can't outrun. After my father disappeared, I dreamt about tornadoes I couldn't see. It was all around me, the wind whipping everything into a blur, the noise like a scream in my ears but invisible. I couldn't find the tornado until it was gone, until it had taken him again.

"I would race after it, desperate to chase it down. I ran through fields of debris shouting my dad's name, but I could never reach it.

I had that dream hundreds of times. Sometimes I still do, thirty years later, and it's always the same. I still think I can catch the funnel cloud and that if I can reach it, I can make it give back everything it took."

Her pain was old and new, a scabbed wound rubbed raw and shimmering with nerves. "Enhypnion."

"What?" Her head still rested on the tub but she shifted, meeting my eyes.

"The ancient Greeks believed in Oneiroi. They were winged, bat-like creatures who were the embodiment of dreams. Every night the Oneiroi flew out from their cave through one of two gates, one made of ivory and the other horn, and the gate they took determined what kind of dream they would become—enhypnion or oneiros. The tornado and your father, it's an enhypnion dream, a dream of things past. You can't change it or act on it. That's why you never catch the tornado."

"And you think your dreams are the other? Oneiros?"

I shrugged. My mom had believed it, had wanted so desperately for my dreams to be important, not insane. She'd never admitted they could be both. "The Greeks thought oneiros were divine, messages from the gods. I don't know what kinds of gods would send the things I see."

We fell quiet, Earl's steady snores from the living room the only sound in the house. I leaned against my side of the tub, pressing cold porcelain to my temple. Eve's energy had calmed slightly, but her emotions were still there, quaking beneath the surface. I pictured a nine-year-old girl with long, reddish brown hair, staring at the sky, waiting for answers that would never come.

"Are you familiar with quantum entanglement?" she asked after a while.

"No."

"Einstein didn't believe in it at first. He called it spooky action. Entanglement happens when two particles interact and then separate, but the connection between them remains. They can be great distances apart from each other and when one particle spins, the other will spin in the same direction. They become tied to each other, regardless of space and time, for as long as the entanglement lasts."

Nerves pricked up and down my arms and legs, like particles in me were spinning, too.

"I don't know much about ancient Greek philosophy, and I've never accepted the idea of psychics—"

"They're mostly garbage people running easy cons."

"—but maybe the connection between you and Celina has something to do with entanglement. She was your niece, your protégé. You loved her very much."

I couldn't answer and she didn't need me to. It wasn't a question. She understood loving someone that society didn't require you to protect. A niece. A father-in-law. Family didn't always grow in direct lines. My connection to the world wasn't as simple as she wanted it to be—or as rational—but she was willing to offer that compromise, to adjust her paradigm to include me, and for a moment I couldn't speak. I never expected generosity and didn't know what to do with Eve's. Before I could recover, a strangled sound came from the other side of the porcelain. Her fingers appeared next to her hair, holding the tub as if for balance.

"When they were searching the house, they said . . . they said Matthew couldn't talk to anyone anymore." Another gasp, cut off before it could build. "I don't understand what he was, or why he lied about so many things. I want to scream at him, to make him explain, to pin him in one place until I get the answers I need, but he's gone. It's the tornado all over again and he's gone."

The words poured out of her. She was grieving without knowing what she'd lost. I hesitated before reaching up and covering the hand that gripped the edge of the tub, absorbing the heat and rush of emotion, taking what I could bear.

Her fingers clenched and bit into mine, holding fast.

Eve

Saturday dawned cloudless and cold, the clear troposphere calling me outside before either Kendrick or Earl woke up.

I didn't have my instruments or models or even a cell signal to pull local readings. I couldn't see what was coming over the horizon, but maybe it didn't matter anymore. Maybe the worst had already come.

Using the cleats, I went to the old silo, where pieces of icicles still clung to the dome and dozens of tracks crisscrossed each other on the ice below. In the daylight, it looked like the safe room had exploded. Scorch marks climbed the cement block of the silo and rimmed the edges of the door with chemical char. Inside, the shelves were empty, the tubs of plastic bags gone. We had no evidence, no samples or pictures, nothing to prove what had been here yesterday.

I climbed back outside and sat on the ice, letting the cold freeze through layers of clothing into my skin, and did the only thing I knew how to do; I looked up. It was like being in a planetarium here, the unbroken bowl of blue. I could almost see the gases that hugged the planet, incubating the life inside. Our atmosphere was so thin compared to the circumference of the Earth and virtually nothing next to the vast and empty space beyond it, yet we lived our whole lives here—in the razor's edge between rock and darkness. I wished I could be up in the atmosphere now, flying at the edge of the sky, where every complication receded into insignificance. I always felt closer to my father when I was flying. Would it be the same with Matthew someday?

My eyelids, already swollen and red rimmed from last night, stung with a cold slap of wind. I blinked the water away, refusing to cry anymore, not when I didn't know who I was crying for.

Two days ago, my life made sense. I had a home and a family. We weren't perfect, but I knew we loved each other and were trying our best. It was the foundation the rest of my life was built on, as solid as the laws of motion or gravity. Today, nothing made sense. My husband was missing and probably dead. Millions of dollars' worth of drugs had been hidden on my father-in-law's farm. And I had no evidence to prove any of it, to help me understand how the foundations of my life had been ripped away.

The only person who knew for sure could have killed me last night. She could've and she didn't. I should have felt nothing but grateful, but something rankled beneath the relief. Kara had stared right through me. I was nothing to her, not even worth exposing as I cowered behind the chair. Two days ago, I'd looked at Jonah Kendrick the same way, yet he was the one who'd held my hand last night as my world fell apart.

I needed new laws, the kind that made fire from ice, that explained the kindness of haunted psychics, laws that could pull tornadoes from the sky.

I stood up. The wind blew me forward a step, onto the tracks that sliced through the ice from the safe room, across the fields, and disappeared in the horizon. And just like that, I knew what I had to do.

"You're what?"

Kendrick and Earl were at the kitchen table when I got back, hunched over the exploded birds in Kara's notebook.

"I'm going after them." The tracks in the ice were pristine, untouched. Maybe we'd left them glaring evidence that we'd discovered their cache, but they'd also left us a perfect trail.

"Across country?" Kendrick glanced out the window, toward the orchard. "The Evolution isn't built for off-roading."

"I'm not driving."

"Do you have a snowmobile?" Kendrick asked Earl, who shook his head.

"Too loud. I don't want them to know I'm coming." I went to the closet and pulled out one of the tote bins of outerwear and equipment.

"Then how—" Kendrick cut off as I appeared with a set of ice skates and cross-country poles.

"I know the fields are completely iced over," Kendrick said, "but they're still bumpy as fuck. You can't ice skate over jagged tracks of farmland."

"I'm not going to." I dropped to my knees next to Earl's wheelchair. "How's your hip?"

He waved off the question, dismissing my concern. His eyes focused better this morning, the medication no longer fogging his gaze. I wondered how long he'd been taking the pills we'd given him last night, how much his body depended on them. If he was in pain, I would give him more without any hesitation. I didn't know what that made me, and I didn't have time to find out now.

"The landline is still dead." The power companies wouldn't be able to repair downed lines for days, maybe weeks, and there had never been cell service on the farm. "I can't call anyone, and Sam's not home next door." He'd stayed over in Davenport last night. He was stuck there because of us, because I'd asked him to stay with Earl and delay his trip. Now I was leaving a second father stranded.

Earl picked up his tablet and jabbed a message. Go.

"Are you sure?"

I'm home.

"Kendrick, will you—" Earl cut me off with an emphatic grunt and elbowed Kendrick in the arm, pointing him toward me. I argued for a minute, unwilling to leave Earl completely alone, but there was no changing his mind. Kendrick hesitated, and the two of them seemed to have an unspoken conversation. Finally he nodded and stood up.

"Let's go."

We inched through the orchard on cleats until we came to the giant oak tree above the bank of the creek, the perfectly smooth ice where we skated every Christmas morning. The meandering waterline paralleled the path of the snowmobiles.

"We don't know when the tracks will leave the creek bed." Kendrick pointed out as we laced up the skates and packed our cleats into backpacks stuffed with supplies. I'd debated leaving the gun with Earl for protection, but he insisted we take it with us, that we would need it more. I hoped he wasn't right.

"They didn't want to be spotted by any bordering farms. That's why they stayed at a lower elevation. Simple geometry. I'm guessing they followed the creek as long as they could."

"Is that a hypothesis?" Kendrick asked.

"Only one way to test it."

I pushed off with a pole and started skating. It was heady, almost like flying, moving with an ease and speed we hadn't enjoyed since the state froze. The wind bit at my face and eyes, stinging them clean and new. I didn't know exactly what I was chasing, but I had mass and force and energy singing through my veins, and right now that was enough.

I glanced back to check on Kendrick. He skated easily behind me, leaning into long strides that matched his frame, poles tucked under his arms. His cheeks were red, and when we got to a wide enough place in the creek, he put on enough speed to pass me, eyes flashing like the starting gleam of a dare. I bent forward and pushed harder, heart pumping fast and light.

We skated for at least an hour, following the thin skidding lines left by the snowmobiles. Occasionally a set of tracks veered above the creek bank and we stopped, changed into cleats, and used the poles to climb up the bank and see where they'd gone, but the marks simply skimmed along the top of the embankment and then dipped back down again. A lookout, checking their position.

A few farms dotted the horizon and at one point I was able to get two bars of cell coverage. My phone beeped with multiple incoming messages from Natalia.

Sitting down with the group now. Told them this is an extra credit assignment.

Matthew's notes. I'd almost forgotten I'd sent a picture of them to Natalia. Her next text was time-stamped a half hour later.

One of the formulas is an opioid, semisynthetic. It doesn't match anything we can find in databases. The rest of the notes are simple, mostly organic compounds. Looks like a messy grocery list. But for what store? Putting our heads together over Gallo pinto and gallons of coffee.

And after another twenty minutes:

We identified five different plants and a few chemicals. One of my students did a study on Roundup last semester, and she ID'd that on the list— second from the end. Besides the opioid formula, the notes appear to be a trace chemicals or heavy metals analysis, the kind of results you'd expect from mass spectrometry. Did you find out anything else?

Too much had happened since I'd last talked to Natalia, more than I could ever convey via text, and I didn't have the energy to spare. I sent her a thank you with heart emojis and told her I'd call soon.

There was also a voice mail from Investigator Summerlin. I played it on speaker.

"Hi, Dr. Roth. This is Max Summerlin with the Iowa City PD returning your call. I'm sorry I missed you earlier, but we've had our hands full with the storm, as I'm sure you can understand. I wish I could share more with you about your husband's case. We don't have any concrete indication of his whereabouts yet, but it's an active investigation and we're pursuing all possible leads." His voice sounded clipped and tired, like he'd been giving variations of this boilerplate message for a while. He paused for a moment before continuing. "I'd like to speak with you, as soon as possible. You were in the company of Jonah Kendrick earlier." He cleared his throat. "There are things about Jonah you don't know. Please call as soon as you can."

Kendrick listened to the entire recording with an implacable expression. The first time I'd seen both of them in the police station, Summerlin had reached into Kendrick's pocket to put headphones on him. It was something Natalia would do for me, those small moments of guardianship between friends. But he'd also kicked Kendrick out of the station and warned him to leave town. And I couldn't ignore the fact that he was right; there was so much I didn't know about the man standing in front of me.

"What's he going to tell me?"

Kendrick shrugged. "The truth. That you shouldn't trust me. That I'll probably get you hurt. Or killed."

"Why would he think that?"

Kendrick's gaze didn't falter. His expression was resigned, accepting.

"Because that's what I did to him."

Jonah

There'd been a moment this morning. Sitting around Earl's kitchen table, connected by coffee steam, sleep-deprivation, and the spidery grain of polished oak between our elbows, something pulled at me, sly and insidious, an addiction burned into my organs no matter how long I'd gone since a hit.

It felt like I belonged. Like I was part of something. And that was the most dangerous part of this entire trip.

People didn't last long in my life. They shouldn't. Look at my brother. Look at Celina. My head lived in rotting drainpipes, in the decay of every good intention. When Eve told me about her father last night, I could feel the tornado ripping through her chest. I sensed her grief, her every tremor, whether she wanted me to or not, and the creepiness of that alone was more than anyone should fucking tolerate.

But she'd chosen to tell me. She'd shown me what shaped her, the empty place no data could fill. I had to do the same.

We skated through a white and silent world, side by side and slower now, not the leapfrogging, adrenaline-fueled pace from earlier. There were no planes, no cars revving in the distance, no roads, fences, or any signs of life rimming the creek bank beyond us. We could've been the only two people in Iowa.

"When Celina went missing, my brother and his family came immediately. They combed through her apartment and interrogated everyone on her block. Jason badgered the police, demanding updates and resources. He begged local TV stations to keep airing Celina's picture. After weeks of nothing, no leads, no suspects, no explanations for how she could vanish, they had to go back to New Orleans. My nephew's still in high school, and Jason and his wife have jobs they can't afford to lose."

"But you stayed," Eve said.

"I stayed."

A warmth grew in her as she skated next to me, a welling of respect I didn't deserve. I couldn't have gone back to work even if I wanted to. Celina's absence shook every waking hour of my life; her fear consumed the rest.

Every morning, I analyzed the dream. I relived each moment a thousand times, searching for something new and not knowing if my brain was fabricating the evidence I desperately wanted to find. I charted every county in the upper Midwest and compiled addresses for farms a hundred miles in every direction.

"I leaned on Max hard." The investigator in charge assumed Celina had run off, *like a lot of kids do*, and he wasn't lifting a goddamn finger. If she'd been a blond hometown quarterback, they wouldn't have left a rock unturned, but Celina worked the graveyard shift at a diner. She was from out of state. They weren't even losing tuition on her. Her life couldn't have mattered less to them, and Max knew it.

"You wanted him to take over the case?" Eve asked.

"It was my case. But I needed Max."

My relationship with ICPD had always been tenuous. Whenever I helped them, it went through the filter of Max, and afterward they called it an anonymous tip. Max always walked that line for me, one foot in both worlds, but he wasn't supposed to be working Celina's case. He'd been told it was a conflict of interest. I knew that, and I didn't care.

He and Shelley got used to me showing up at their house on Saturday mornings with a bag of donuts and a thermos of coffee. "I'll bring him right back," I always lied, while his kid played video games and Shelley simmered with resentment over whatever weekend plans I'd hijacked. I could feel Max's loyalties tear— between his family, his badge, and me—and I took advantage every time.

We scoured the countryside, flashing Celina's photo in front of countless farmhouses and stockyards full of grunting hogs. We went to the Amana Colonies, the massive corporate farms, even an animal sanctuary with a menagerie of whiskered pigs and three-legged cows. Every place we went people frowned at the picture, shook their heads, and wished us luck. She'd been gone a month, and not one person knew a thing.

When no one answered the door at a place outside Decorah, I went to their barn. It was a tall A-frame, with the kinds of rafters that could produce the same whistling wind I'd heard in the dream. Max chased after me and pointed out the NO TRESPASSING sign. I ignored him, trying doors and circling the building until I found a window to look inside. As September wore on, I cared less and less about laws or the ethics of investigation. I checked garbage cans. I looked at people's mail. At another empty property with a barn that gave me a bad feeling, I picked the lock, ignoring Max's yelling until he stormed back to his car and drove away. He picked me up a half hour later walking down the road. Neither of us spoke the whole way back to Iowa City.

Belgrave Properties was one of the addresses on my list of South Central Iowa farms, a region we hit in mid-October as combines churned the fields into dust and mulch. Most of the places around here were family farms and corporate names I was getting familiar with, but I hadn't seen this one before.

"You heard of these guys?"

Max shrugged. "An investment company, maybe." Then, after a pause, "You know I can't keep doing this."

He wasn't freaked out that I was inside his head, only asking me to acknowledge what we both knew.

"A couple more weeks and we can finish the list. Someone's seen her."

"Jonah—"

"No one in your bullshit department is even looking. We're the only people she's got left." It was a cheap move, appealing to Max's hero complex, and I didn't think twice about it.

"If my department finds out I'm investigating against orders—"

"They won't."

"—with someone who's trespassing, breaking and entering—"

"I'll stop. I promise."

He gave me a hard look.

"You have to keep it together and follow my lead. If I tell you to get in the car, you get in the car."

"Done."

"I'm putting my job on the line."

"Christ, I get it."

We drove in silence for a while, heading past a suburban development south of Des Moines and into the countryside that rolled toward Kansas City. Maybe it was the hills. Maybe it was Max's anger. But somewhere along the way my stomach started rolling, too. Every rise and fall in the road created a bigger pitch and fall in my gut. The coffee tasted foul. Sweat broke out on my forehead and back.

"What?" Max turned as I palmed my face.

"Nothing." I breathed through my mouth. I wasn't giving him any reasons to turn around. "Belgrave Properties is the next one. Up here on the right."

We turned onto a long driveway that snaked past a creek and over a pine-shrouded hill. A combine harvested rows of corn along the horizon, but there were no barns or outbuildings on the property. Three RV campers lined up next to a decaying farmhouse with paint flecking from faded and splintering boards. My skin started crawling. Nothing about this place looked like an investment company would acquire it.

Four men stood in front of the campers smoking, three Latinos and a white guy. They watched us pull in as a mangy-looking dog on a chain leapt up and began barking like its life depended on it. The air smelled foul, burning chemicals and something else, something I couldn't place and didn't want to. My stomach threatened to heave.

"Max."

He glanced at me, and I could feel his resignation. He wanted to get this over with. Before I could warn him, he climbed out of the car.

Max left the door cracked and walked toward the group. The white guy moved forward, meeting him halfway to the car. Their conversation filtered over the barking, even as I slid down in the seat and fought to wrestle my body back from whatever forces were clawing their way into me.

"Howdy." Max flashed his badge.

"You a cop? You ain't dressed like a cop."

"I'm an investigator with the Iowa City police. Have you seen this girl?" Max held up the photo of Celina.

Tobacco juice ejected from his mouth, splatting on the ground. "Nope."

"She was last seen in August, so several weeks back now."

"What makes you think I seen her? This ain't even your jurisdiction."

The man was all sharp angles and sunken eyes, a skeleton who'd scraped together a bit of gristle and flesh. His buzzed hair barely shaded the bleached-bone sheen of his scalp. The others arranged themselves behind him.

"I know it's a long shot, but we're working on a tip that she may have been seen at a farm around here."

"Said no already. You can leave now."

"Are you Mr. Belgrave?"

No answer.

"Is Mr. Belgrave available?"

"Nope." Another squirt of tobacco juice hit the ground. I staggered out of the car; the smell was worse out here.

"He's lying."

Max turned to me and pieces of him strained against each other. I could feel my best friend from college rearing up, the one who craved adventure and justice and needed to solve the mystery above all other things, but that Max was diluted by Investigator

Summerlin, a man sanded down by years of protocol and following rank.

"What'd you say?" The skeletal man turned, spoiling for a fight. He was on edge. The picture of Celina had made him nervous.

"I said you're lying."

Max stepped in front of me, the officer in him winning out. "Come on. Let's go."

"And I said get the hell off my property," the man said, and the other three closed ranks behind him. The dog whined, running the circumference of its chain. Bare patches were scratched red and raw in its coat.

"We don't want any trouble." Max put his diffusing voice on, every word calm and measured despite the adrenaline spiking in his chest, and I hated him in that minute. I hated the caution, the rule following. He was going to let this goddamn skeleton lie to us and get away with it.

"He knows Celina. I can feel it. He knows what happened to her."

"Get in the car." Max tried pushing me, but I wasn't going anywhere. Not when I could smell the reek of lies, the fear pulsing like a living thing in front of me.

I shoved Max off and lunged toward the closest camper. Trash bags covered its windows, hiding whatever—or whomever—lay inside.

Everything happened quickly then.

The Latinos moved to block me, and the skeleton pulled a gun. Max was armed, too, but he was focused on chasing me down and didn't see the revolver in the skeleton's hand in time. I shouted or maybe someone else did. The sound rose up in my head and I lunged for Max.

The first shot went wide, the second knocked us to the ground. I didn't know which of us was hit at first. Pain and confusion mixed together as Max fell on top of me, then a boot caught me in the ribs. Someone else kicked Max in the head. I grabbed for the foot and missed. Hands came from above, pulling Max off me. As he fought them, something dark glinted at his hip. I reached for his holster and drew the gun.

A Glock. No safety. I fired, and the explosion scattered the men on top of us. The skeleton had gone to unleash the dog, who was howling and gnashing at his chain, panting to be in this fight. He turned, but I shot first. I hit the camper and the ground, forcing him to take cover behind the vehicle.

Max intercepted a guy with a knife, fighting him off before he could stab me. I pulled Max to the car, firing behind us, not knowing how many rounds we had, how many more feet we would get before the skeleton took us out. Somehow, we made it to the car and I hit the gas, gunning the cruiser backward through the trees as Max grabbed his rifle and sent warning shots through the window. His sleeve was dark with blood, dripping down his hand. He had a gash on his head. It hurt to breathe, maybe for me, maybe for both of us.

Spinning around at the end of the driveway, I threw the car into gear and buried the needle, heading for Des Moines and the closest hospital.

"We need reinforcements. We need a goddamn SWAT team, now."

"No. Don't tell anyone about this," he said, clutching the rifle with bloody fingers. "I can't . . ."

"He knows Celina. That guy is the key to everything."

Max's energy was uneven, there and gone, like shadows skittering on a wall. His head lolled against the seat. "Say it was a hunting accident."

"Are you fucking kidding me?"

But he didn't answer. He'd passed out.

The emergency room doctors wouldn't tell me how bad off Max was. They taped my ribs and let me call Shelley, then put me in a room with a rookie officer who didn't buy the bullshit hunting accident story until Max woke up and confirmed it.

I tried to get him to change his mind, but Shelley had arrived by then. She stood between me and Max's bed and told me to go. When I kept arguing, she pointed to the exit and screamed, her voice breaking in a thousand quivering places.

I went. I left and didn't come back.

"Did you go back to Belgrave Properties?" Eve asked. Her breath puffed out in wisps of cloud behind us, a disappearing trail as we skated through the frozen world.

"They were gone. The RVs, the men, even the dog. The farmhouse was abandoned. No one had been inside for years. The land had been leased to a neighboring farmer who didn't know anything."

Belgrave Properties hadn't led anywhere, either. It turned out to be a shell company, the real owner buried under impenetrable layers of legal firms and LLCs. I couldn't trace it back to a name. The skeleton, Belgrave or whoever he was, had vanished.

Eve was silent for a while. I could feel her mind humming, sorting information into patterns and anomalies, examining the pieces she couldn't reconcile. She pulled her phone out again.

"Why wouldn't Summerlin tell the truth?"

"He wasn't supposed to be working Celina's case. He was out of his jurisdiction, abusing his badge and rank."

"But he was shot."

"And beaten and stabbed." Regret clotted my throat, the same useless emotion that carved hollows out of my chest night after night, as Celina's whisper drifted from a barn to an RV to the mouth of a black drainpipe, inviting me inside.

"My best friend almost died because of me."

Max

The day was too bright. Sunlight bounced off the ice-covered back-yard and glared inside the patio doors. I sat at the kitchen table, squinting and guzzling coffee while Shelley read the newspaper coverage of the storm, stopping every once in a while to ask, "Did you handle this one?"

Most I hadn't, or maybe I didn't remember. The image of Belgrave, forcing a soon-to-be-dead Alexis Dwyer into her apartment building had consumed me. I sat up half the night, grateful for my insomnia as I pored through Alexis's contacts and connections, looking through every social media comment, tracing every phone number she'd called or texted. A list of a half dozen possible matches was shoved into my sling, crinkling with each gulp of coffee. I needed to get to the station.

"I wish you didn't have to work on Saturday." Shelley had been ecstatic when I was promoted to Investigations and started a nine-to-five schedule. She liked having me home on weekends and curling next to me at night, even if she was the only one sleeping.

"The whole division was called in." I tried not to sound too eager to get to my desk and the databases I could access between storm triage duties. Crossing each name off the list until I found the one I could finally circle. "It's a state of emergency."

"Be careful." Her brow furrowed. We'd been married as long as I'd been on the force, and she always knew when something was off—with a case or with my head. She could sense something this morning, but it was better if she didn't know what. Telling Shelley I'd found the man who shot me wouldn't comfort her and it sure as hell wouldn't excite her the way the knowledge hummed through me.

When she first met Jonah, she'd treated him with respect and wariness, like he was some kind of exotic pet. But after we got married and Garrett was born, their relationship went south. Every investigation I helped Jonah with meant time away from my family. Shelley became worried the friendship would jeopardize my career. When it ended up jeopardizing my life, she lost it. She'd tossed him out of my hospital room and asked me never to work with Jonah again. She didn't say it was him or her, not in so many words, but that's what it boiled down to: choosing between my best friend and my wife.

She touched my good hand across the table now, an invitation, but I shook my head. "It'll be fine. Another long day."

She went to check on Garrett, who'd been playing some shooter game on his Xbox since dawn. I cleared the cereal bowls from the table and was strapping on my holster when the call came in.

I stopped, glanced at the living room, and slipped out to the garage. "Dr. Roth?"

"Yes." Her voice sounded cautious and strangely out of breath. A whistling sound cut through her end of the line. Wind, maybe. She was outside. I waited for her to ask for an update on the investigation and prepared to give her the standard answer. *We're following all possible leads*, etc. But she didn't ask.

"Investigator, a lot has happened since we last spoke."

The hair on the back of my neck went up and my gut tensed, waiting.

"I'm all ears." I set the phone on my shop bench, turned it on speaker, and started recording a voice memo.

"Have you heard of calcium carbide?" I jotted notes, trying to figure out where this was going as she listed chemical properties and how apparently the stuff could easily incinerate a Tesla in a pouring rain. She claimed she'd found a container of it in their garage. I glanced around my own, where the most hazardous thing was paint thinner and maybe some rusty nails.

"Are you accusing Matthew of setting his own car on fire?"

"No, I'm telling you this was probably the accelerant. Have your lab test the residue. It should be a fairly simple analysis."

"I'll mention it." I paused, checking to make sure the garage door was closed. "Are you with Jonah?"

She took a while to answer. "Why?"

Because I wanted to talk to him. Because I was dying to share this lead, that I'd found the first solid path to Belgrave and he was connected to an investigation I had every right to pursue. I wanted Jonah to know I hadn't given up, on him or on Celina. And I couldn't say any of that, not while I wore an ICPD badge and recorded this conversation. Not with Shelley a room away.

I chose my words carefully. "It might not have been clear yesterday, but Jonah's been instructed not to interfere with this investigation or any other investigation conducted by the Iowa City police. He's got some history you might not be aware of. I don't know what he's told you."

"He's told me he's a psychic detective. That he dreams about a barn stained with blood. He said he can help me find Matthew." She paused. "And I believe him."

Then she gave me an address.

"Are you there now?" I wrote it down, trying to figure out where the hell in the state that was.

"No, but Earl is, and he has some data for you." Then she told me about a bunker full of drugs at a farm, white pills there and gone, and how she believed Matthew was involved in making them. The story spiraled beyond credibility, beyond anything I'd uncovered on this case so far. I wanted to dismiss it out of hand, to chalk it up to a suspect casting blame anywhere but on herself, but other facts bubbled up, making me pause. The large cryptocurrency transfers. Alexis Dwyer's probable overdose. Even the fertilizer truck we'd bagged last summer, millions of dollars of pills couched between layers of nitrogen, hiding in plain sight.

There were two truths in every story, and the truth beneath the missing professor and his scorched car was coming closer into focus. Pieces of it were still missing, giant gaps just out of my reach. I couldn't fully trust Dr. Eve Roth, or Jonah, or even myself right now, not with the grainy image of Belgrave consuming the edges of my thoughts. I watched the voice memo sound bars expand, recording everything as another whistle of wind came through the line.

"Can you please pick Earl up?" Her voice wavered a little. "I wouldn't ask, but his neighbor is out of town, and you need to collect the evidence as soon as possible." The evidence, from what I could determine so far, was an empty canister, an empty bunker, and a piece of paper scrawled with formulas. Not exactly a smoking gun.

"I'm on duty today. I can't leave the city."

"Please. His life could still be in danger and he shouldn't be on his own."

"Why is he on his own? Where are you and Jonah?" She didn't answer. "Eve." I switched to her first name and enunciated every word as carefully as if I were reading her rights. "I need to know exactly what's happening."

"So do I."

The line went dead.

Jonah

She believed me.

I skated into the wind, half-frozen, my fingers and toes long past numb. If I lost all of them to frostbite it didn't matter. I'd gotten so used to being a freak, being at the fringe, categorized and marginalized by anyone who knew what I was, that I'd forgotten what it felt like to be included, to be trusted. Dr. Eve Roth—a physicist who had the respect of her field, of professionals, academics, students, and the world at large—believed in me.

We skated on, through stretches of trees where the weight of ice bent branches so low we had to duck under them, and then back to open land, baring us to the wind and sky. When the sun had risen to a forty-five-degree angle and my shins ached, we reached a sharp left bend in the creek where the snowmobile tracks veered right. Not one rogue set of tracks checking their position. All of them left the creek. At the top of the bank, dividing the path of the water from the tracks, stood a small grove of trees.

We stopped, both of us breathing hard. In the distance came the whine of a high-pitched engine. It didn't change pitch or volume and I felt the thought in Eve's head at the same time as mine—an idling snowmobile. Changing wordlessly into cleats again, we climbed up the side of the bank and into the cover of trees.

The tracks made a straight path toward a group of buildings. Two of them were low, prefab boxes made of corrugated sheet metal and white roofs, like thousands of others scattered across Iowa, but the third building stood out. It loomed over the other two, a giant silver half cylinder stretching as long as a football field.

There was no movement outside the buildings and the sun reflected off the windows, making it impossible to see anything happening inside, but I could feel a hum riding beneath the engine noise, the energy of people working.

"What is this place?"

Eve pulled out an old road map. Tracing a finger along the winding creek, she arrived at a gray tract of land bordering a county road.

"Lars Field."

An airport? It looked more like an off-brand storage facility. "There's no tower, no lights. I can't even see a runway."

She shook her head, eyes scanning the perimeter. "It's not municipal. It must be a private field for crop dusters in the spring and summer."

"And drug traffickers in the winter?"

Carefully, we slid back down the hill and out of sight.

"It's plausible." Eve paced, staring at the map. "The airfield gives access to Lovers Ridge, which feeds almost directly onto the interstate, and from there you can be in Des Moines in an hour or Chicago in five."

"It's less than that to Minneapolis."

"Kansas City and St. Louis are both easy drives south." She kept pacing, her voice low.

"The entire Midwest is within reach."

"This isn't just one farm. Not with the quantity of drugs we uncovered. It's bigger than that. Belgrave Properties isn't that far south of Des Moines, maybe fifty miles from here. And Celina's barn might be nearby, too. This airfield could be a hub for an entire network of locations."

"You're speculating. We need data," Eve said, folding up the map. "We have to find out who, or what, is up there."

A scarf covered most of her face, but I could feel the determination rising from her, the same resolve that coated my gut every single morning. She needed the truth. She needed answers no matter how much they cost or what horrors they would bring. And she believed in me.

"Let's go."

There was zero cover between the grove and the airfield. The buildings were at least a hundred yards past the trees, but the ground was flat, not the tilled-up, bumpy landscape of farm fields. We could cross it on skates.

The engine noise, whatever it was, provided sound cover. "Our only real obstacle," Eve whispered, "is sight."

There were two windows, one in each of the smaller buildings and both reflected the sun. It was impossible to see past the glare, at least until Eve turned on her phone and took pictures of the buildings, switched the filter to an X-ray setting, and examined the results. As far as we could tell, the edges of the windows outside of the solar halo were dark, the rooms unoccupied.

"But this filter is inadequate. And we don't have enough information about the purpose of each building, or the number—"

I watched the airfield, looking for any signs of life beside the vague rumble of energy coming from the hangar. Either we went now or we waited for sunset, which might be too late. We might already be too late.

I cut her off midanalysis. "Save it for your students."

Grabbing her arm, I tugged us both out of the trees and we skated like hell. Heart pounding, breath pumping, it felt like days. When we reached the halfway mark, the space between one of the smaller buildings and the hangar opened up, revealing a parking lot of snowmobiles. They were all turned off, no exhaust rising from any of them. One had a cargo sled attached to the back, but the sled was empty.

Beyond the snowmobiles, someone appeared on a strip of the airfield. He faced away, walking toward a large machine halfway down the runway, but I didn't stop to watch. I poured everything I had into crossing the remaining yards and skidded to a halt inches shy of slamming into the back of the hangar. Eve staggered on her stop, and I grabbed her before she could crash into the metal siding. We stood stock-still, our exertion mixing into a cloud of breath that rose into the blue overhead. Before we could recover, someone shouted from inside the building.

Eve stiffened. Her camera had been right about the windows on the other buildings: they both had shades drawn. No one could have seen us crossing the field. More voices chimed in—a half dozen?—in a buzz of activity, but individual words were impossible to make out over the engine.

Eve turned to the far side of the hangar, away from the other two buildings, and I followed.

We half skated, half walked to the edge of the wall. Across a thin line of trees, the county highway ran parallel to the hangar. There were no cars in either direction, and the shimmer of sheer, unrutted ice meant the roads were still closed.

We couldn't see the runway from here. Eve motioned ahead with one gloved finger. We moved along the side, braced against the building and using blades, toe picks, and ski poles to negotiate the uneven ground. If they caught us out here, there would be no escape.

At the front of the hangar, we pressed ourselves flat against the side and Eve peeked around the corner. One second. Two. My heart slammed in my throat, growing louder the longer she looked.

Finally, she pulled back with an expression I was starting to know too well—lips parted, eyes downcast and sweeping the perimeter of things beyond what could be seen—her information-processing face. She motioned for us to change places.

Two pickup trucks were parked inside the open garage door of one of the smaller buildings, with no one inside. The other building had only a regular door and a window, like an office, with the lights on. I couldn't see inside the hangar from this angle, but the entire runway was in view. The guy was still out there, dragging a machine that looked like someone had stuffed a fan and a helium tank inside a metal cage.

Beyond him, at the far end of the runway, a small airplane lay tilted on its side, the skyward propeller smashed and one wing crushed against the ground. Debris was scattered around it. They must've tried to fly the drugs out already and failed.

The guy pulling the machine slipped and fell, landing in a puddle of water. Christ, were they trying to *thaw* the entire runway? From inside the building, someone laughed. "Watch your step!"

The guy flipped around, cursing, and I drew back before he could see me. "None of you are getting off your fucking asses."

"You first, sweet cheeks." A female voice. Kara.

Eve tugged on my sleeve and handed me a compact mirror and a roll of electrical tape. Securing the mirror to the end of one of the ski poles, I slid it past the edge of the building.

The mirror reflected metal siding, then a space of black, followed by a slash of silver and white: the wing of another plane inside the hangar. I angled the pole, tracing the wing down to the body of the plane. An open door revealed layers of sacks inside. They were bigger than the bags we'd found at Lovers Ridge, but it was clearly cargo.

Two people walked between the mirror and the plane and I retracted the ski pole as slowly as I could force myself to move. The footsteps came closer. Eve's hand tightened on my coat and I turned my head so the frozen clouds of breath wouldn't give us away. If we ran, they would hear us. We locked eyes and waited.

The footsteps stopped a few feet from the end of the building and the smell of cigarette smoke drifted around the corner.

"You want to tell me what really happened on the farm?" The man's words instantly made the hair on the back of my neck stand up.

"Nothing. We collected the goods like we were supposed to." Kara. Inches away, Eve's eyes widened. She was tense and focused, memorizing every word.

There was a grunt and a pause around the corner. A swelling of contempt. "Trick said the space had been opened already. Someone else had already been there."

I knew that voice. The connection hovered, waiting for my head to catch up with my ears.

"It was nothing. You don't need to worry."

"Oh, I'm not worried. If I was worried, you'd know it."

"You think you can hurt me?" Kara's voice went deadly flat. The amount of hatred seething around the corner, from both of them, was palpable. "I don't do hurt. You think you can scare me? You have nothing left to scare me with."

Silence stretched out, long and dark. I started shaking. Sweat popped out on my forehead. I didn't know how much longer I could balance on two blades of metal. If I fell, they would be on us in an instant. Eve grabbed my elbow, steadying me.

A shout from the runway drew their attention. A cigarette butt flew past the corner and landed on the ice, smoldering for a second before it went out. The sound of footsteps trudged away from the building.

Kara didn't say anything, didn't make any noise. Alone, her energy became clearer. She was quaking, enraged and unsettled by the confrontation. She wanted to do something. She felt trapped. I gripped the corrugated metal of the building, desperate to hold on, to stay upright even as it felt like I was free-falling into darkness. I knew the man who'd threatened her. It was the same person who'd almost killed me and Max.

Belgrave.

After an eternity, a second, quieter set of footsteps moved away from the corner, heading back inside the hangar, and I lost my grip on the building.

Eve caught me, tugging me back, tracing the same slow and agonizing path along the hangar until we reached the back side of the building again.

"Are you okay?" she asked as soon as it was safe to speak.

I couldn't answer. I dug my hands into the sides of my head, trying to wrench it back from Belgrave and the dripping water, the stagnant pool of decay and darkness. I wasn't in the drainpipe. I just had to make myself believe it.

"Danica Chase. Angela Garcia." The talismans filtered in like beams of light and it took a minute before I realized it wasn't me speaking them. Eve crouched in front of me, murmuring, giving me the names of the found.

"Kit Freeman," I said.

She nodded. "George Marcus Morrow."

The nausea faded. It hadn't been a full-blown attack, but I knew what triggered it. Eve pulled out her phone and powered it up.

"Eve—"

"Hang on."

She texted Earl. Kendrick and I found something at Lars Field. We're bringing it to Iowa City.

"What?" I had trouble keeping my voice to a whisper. Even with the sudden intent ringing in her mind, it was impossible to believe what she was thinking.

She looked up at me, her eyes bright and fierce. "We're taking the plane."

Eve

"Steal the plane?"

Even if I wasn't perfectly serious, it would have been worth saying just for the expression on Kendrick's face. He'd seemed like he was having a panic attack on the side of the hangar, but now he looked like I'd physically slapped him.

"It's an airplane." He emphasized "air"—as though I might have confused it with some other kind—and wiped a sheen of cold sweat from his forehead. "We can't drive it away."

"No, we'll fly it."

"How?"

"I have a pilot's license." Compared to Joan, my sleek, sophisticated air lab, the crop duster in the hangar would be like riding a tricycle.

"You want to hijack a plane?" We barely spoke above whispers, but the disbelief in his voice was plain. He lowered himself to the ground and put his head on his knees. I wondered if he was going to have trouble breathing again, if I should keep reciting the names of the people he'd been chanting in the car.

"We need the evidence inside the plane." I pointed through the wall of the hangar, where voices rumbled unintelligibly. "How else do you propose we get it?"

"We'll grab one of the sacks. We can create a diversion, sneak inside the hangar."

"A diversion, good idea." We'd have to get them all out of the building, preferably after they'd warmed up the plane, because that would be our most vulnerable point. Between starting the engine and throttling down the runway, we'd be sitting ducks.

"God, I know how Max feels now." He closed his eyes and pressed the heels of his hands to his forehead. "Eve"—his breath was evening out—"the runway is practically solid ice. We'd crash like they did the first time they tried to fly out of here."

I squatted next to him, balancing on the skates. "There's an ice runway in New Hampshire that operates every winter on the bay of a frozen lake. It's a question of forces—thrust, drag, lift, and weight." He didn't respond, so I pulled his hands away from his face. "When you go ice racing, is it more dangerous to be the first or the last car to run the track?"

A spark of understanding flared in his eyes. "The first."

"Correct, because the more tires that have scarred the surface, the more friction you have. Did you see that runway? There were tracks everywhere. When they unloaded the crashed plane, they must have used snowmobiles to haul the cargo back to the second plane. They don't know it, but that's all the traction the second plane's going to need."

"There's something else." He opened his mouth and then closed it, looking down at my hand still resting on his arm. He looked sick, more than I'd ever seen him outside of that first encounter in the police station. Did he not trust me? Did he think I was going to get us both killed? I wanted to reassure him, but he might not be wrong.

"The guy—" He stopped and sucked in an unsteady breath, then tried again. "The one talking to Kara."

"Belgrave, right? The man who shot Summerlin."

Kendrick's head snapped up. "How did you know?"

It was the only logical conclusion. The man's voice alone had sent Kendrick into a panic attack. I shrugged. "Observation and analysis."

"I've been looking for him since that day. He knows what happened to Celina."

"And likely Matthew, too. But we don't have any chance of kidnapping him, so we'll have to settle for the plane." I dropped my hand, giving him the space he needed. "Are you coming with me?"

A smile crept over his face and his breath puffed out in a ghost of a laugh. "Here's to a fiery death."

We got to work. I inventoried the contents of my backpack looking for something we could use to create a distraction, and ordered Kendrick to do the same. Beside the gun, there wasn't much to work with. I'd brought granola bars and water, extra clothing, a map, a campfire lighter, a tire iron, and a multipurpose tool bearing a prominent corkscrew, in case we had to fight off any bottles of wine. I sighed and kept digging. There had to be something here. We needed Kara, Belgrave, and the rest of them not only out of the hangar but also far enough away so we could get the plane moving before they figured out what was happening. Or at least before they stopped us.

Kendrick crept to the corner of the hangar, peering around the side to where the snowmobiles were parked. When he came back from his reconnaissance, he picked up the gun. "Did you see the heater they're using on the runway? It's a propane tank."

I nodded. It clearly wasn't designed to defrost an entire runway, which was lucky for us. If they'd had a salt or sand truck, they would've flown the second plane out of here before we ever caught up with them.

"*Jaws*," Kendrick said.

"What?" I frowned at his chin.

"The end of *Jaws*." He lifted the gun, shaking it, as if that explained something. "The last scene."

He was talking about a shark movie? "I never saw it."

Kendrick made a deeply disgusted noise, then explained how we could shoot the propane tank and make it explode, creating the "perfect" diversion.

"With that?" I shook my head long before he finished. "It's highly unlikely a bullet would meet the temperature requirements to ignite propane."

"In English."

"*Jaws* is bullshit."

"Do you have a better idea?"

I skated to the same corner and peeked around the edge. The snowmobiles were parked in a row between the buildings. Halfway down the runway, two guys moved the heater again. The propane tank was big, but if they'd been running it all morning, it would be close to empty, meaning even less fuel for Kendrick's imaginary explosion, which wouldn't work in any case. They'd take cover, protect their inventory. We needed something that did the opposite, a way to draw them out.

When both figures on the runway faced away, I skated quickly across the open space. Sounds came from inside the first of the smaller buildings. I couldn't tell how many people were inside. The voices were low, indistinct. As silently as I could, I moved to the next building—the garage—where all was quiet. I tried the windows. The first one was sealed tight, but the second opened. Carefully I pushed up the pane and lifted the blinds. Tools and canisters littered the workbenches lining the back of the garage, along with old rags and an assortment of random papers. An idea formed.

I returned to Kendrick, who was crouched behind the hangar with one hand braced on the side and his eyes closed. When I told him my plan, he listened without interrupting, nodded at various points, and—to his credit—didn't once break in with another "shoot the propane tank" idea.

"Well?" I asked after I finished and he still hadn't said anything.

He stared at the hangar wall like he could see through it. "The guys moving the heater around are pure muscle. They do what they're told. There might be three or four of them. Someone, I think it's Belgrave, is angry. He's hurt, too, maybe from when they crashed the first plane. That means he's not moving fast. He'll be the last to leave."

"And Kara?" I asked.

"I don't know. I get the feeling everyone else is giving her a wide berth. They could be cutting her out, or just scared."

Judging from the guy at the thrift store ducking out the minute she ordered him to leave or the man searching the farmhouse with her last night, I guessed fear. Belgrave was the only person who'd tried to challenge her, and she'd practically dared him to take his best shot.

A loud, scuffing noise came from inside the hangar, like something being dragged across the floor, and we both fell silent. After a few seconds it stopped. I scanned the edges of the building.

"There's at least two more people in the office."

"So, seven or more in total." He lifted the gun. "If there's any problems, I might have to use this."

"Do you know how?"

"Yes."

I hesitated, hearing Summerlin's voice again, telling me there was a lot I didn't know about Jonah Kendrick. "Have you ever killed anyone?"

He didn't answer.

"Kendrick"—I leaned in—"I'm done with liars. I can handle whatever you are, as long as you're honest about it."

He mirrored me, probing my gaze as we crouched on the ice. "You want honesty?"

I nodded.

"*Breaking Bad* is one thing, but *Jaws*? Come on. If we don't die in the next few minutes, you and Earl and I are going to watch that movie and I don't want to hear shit about how it defies the laws of physics. It's the best film ever made."

"I'm serious," I said, even as a smile threatened to derail my serious expression.

"So am I."

He shifted, leaning against the side of the hangar. He seemed to be searching for words, and it took a full minute before he spoke again.

"It feels like I've killed every person I didn't find in time." His gaze dropped to the ice. "Bodies decomposing in fields and drain-pipes, the ripping grief of the families when they find out; it all feels like my fault, and it doesn't matter what my head says or how many people I do find alive. The ones I fail . . . they're always here."

He pulled the hammer back on the gun, looking inside the chamber. "But I haven't shot anyone. I tried, at Belgrave Proper-ties. I would've shot any one of them and never gave it a second thought. People like that? They're why I have nightmares. They're the reason Celina's gone."

His voice was gritty with sincerity, and I believed he would shoot anyone inside the hangar without hesitation. It was exactly what I needed to hear.

I held out a hand and we pulled each other to standing. It was time.

Jonah

I followed Eve behind the buildings, both of us moving as quickly and quietly as we could. We changed back into cleats, then climbed through the open window into the garage. Two Silverados were parked inside, one brand-new and the other a workhorse that smelled like manure even in the dead of December. Beyond the trucks, the garage door was open, giving us our first clear view across the field to the front of the hangar. Someone moved in the cockpit of the plane, which looked tiny, like a model of a real airplane. If the Silverados had wings and propellers, they would dwarf the thing Eve wanted to fly out of here.

I knew shit about airplanes beyond the standard safety lectures given by bored flight attendants, and I avoided flying whenever possible. I wasn't scared of the mechanics or the idea of soaring thirty thousand feet over the Earth; the problem was being trapped with that many people. I'd rather sail a dinghy by myself across the ocean than board a commercial jet full of heightened anxieties and frustrations bottled up like rotten champagne.

This would be different, though. This was Eve. She'd clung to my hand on the tub last night as she mourned the lives that had been ripped away from her. She was in my head now, telling me what we were attempting was possible, even reasonable. It was a particular insanity I'd sensed in other people. Faith, they called it. Or the brand of crazy that made you think you could steal a plane.

We could hear but not see two guys struggling with the generator. The engine noise gave us plenty of sound cover. Kara climbed out of the cockpit and pulled out her phone, ignoring the curses from the runway. Belgrave and the rest were out of sight. Keeping to the shadows and not making any sudden movements, we laid a trail from the back of the garage by the windows through the space between the two pickups: papers, rags, empty oil cans, and plastic containers. Our goal wasn't a bonfire, Eve said, but a smoke signal.

I was stuffing a filthy rag into the newer Silverado's wheel rim when Eve sucked in a breath. A man walked out of the hangar. Belgrave. He was still bone thin, his face hollowed out, eye sockets swallowed in shadow. His head was tilted down, watching his step on the ice, but he was headed straight for us.

We had nowhere to go. Eve shifted back, crouching next to one of the workbenches. I ducked behind the wheel well. He might not see us immediately, but as soon as he stepped out of the sun and into the interior of the garage, the path of junk we'd planted across the floor would give us away.

The sound of his footsteps became clearer over the generator noise. I dropped to my stomach on the oil- and dirt-stained concrete and watched the progress of his boots. He walked toward us until he hit the shadow line, then disappeared to one side of the garage door.

A door opened and slammed shut. He'd gone into the office next door. I sat up and caught Eve's eye, trying to communicate some sense of reassurance. She nodded, reassuring me.

We finished setting up the decoy. Eve climbed out the garage window while I watched the field from the edge of the doorway. The two guys handling the generator slid back to the hangar for a smoke break with three others. One of them wore his jacket open and I could see a holster at his waist. I assumed the others were armed and Kara, too. That made at least six guns in the hangar alone.

After they finished smoking, two different guys inched back down the runway and the others disappeared into the hangar. Swapping shifts. Belgrave hadn't come out of the office. Unless a SWAT team showed up, this was as good a situation as we were going to get.

I lit an invoice underneath a pile of rags and climbed out the window, which was harder than it looked when you had a gun in your pocket, fire at your back, and couldn't risk making a sound. As soon as I cleared the frame, Eve closed the window and we moved behind the office. On the other side of the wall, Belgrave's sharp tenor cut over other voices. I couldn't tell how many.

Dropping to our hands and knees, we crawled along the back of the office until we reached the snowmobiles and crouched behind them. I squeezed my eyes shut, concentrating on Kara's energy inside the hangar, the one I might be able to pick out from the rest. I couldn't sense anything until a shout went up from the heater.

"Fire!"

A curse and the pound of running feet on the other side of the wall. Kara swung around the corner and past the snowmobiles, followed by the others. The two on the runway abandoned the heater and slid toward the garage, too. They'd spot us if they turned, but they were facing the smoke. We wouldn't get a better chance.

"Come on."

Keeping low, we crawled around the snowmobiles and into the hangar. As soon as we cleared the threshold, we sprinted for the airplane, cleats pinging against the cement floor. Three other planes—small, one-seat crop dusters—lined the back of the building and a single fluorescent light illuminated a worktable in the corner. A game of cards had been abandoned next to an assortment of Glocks.

"Got the keys!" Eve shouted from inside the cockpit. I pulled blocks away from the wheels, scraping them across the cement.

At the garage, black smoke seeped out of the building and into the sky, obscuring the people rushing inside and crowding around it. The door to the office opened and Belgrave and two others barreled into the fray.

Behind me, the propeller caught and began rotating. Belgrave jerked at the noise. For a second, we both froze, staring at each other. He may not have recognized me, but this was the man who shot Max. He knew what happened to Celina, to Matthew Moore, and probably dozens of others. Reaching for his waistband, he lunged toward us but didn't get two steps before falling flat on the ice.

Eve banged on the windshield, springing me into action. I spun around and climbed inside. A shout came from the garage, a mixture of fury, surprise, and pain. The back seat of the plane was crammed with heavy, oversized sacks. I squeezed into the front next to Eve and slammed the door.

"What were you waiting for?" she yelled over the engine.

I pulled the gun out of my pocket, hands shaking, and cracked open the window vent. Belgrave rolled up to his knees and pulled a striker out of his waistband. Three more guys ran across the ice. One fell and I shot toward the other two. One guy hit the ground hard. The other ducked behind the snowmobiles. Belgrave dove into the cover of the smoke and disappeared in the garage.

"Let's go!"

But we didn't. Eve shook her head, adjusting switches and pulling on a set of headphones. The propeller sped up, whirring faster and louder against the spray of bullets I sent toward the garage, trying to keep the area clear.

"We have to go now!"

Eve pulled a black lever and with a jerk the plane lurched forward out of the hangar. We rolled onto the runway, but it wasn't fast enough. Pickup taillights appeared out of the smoke billowing from the garage, tires skidding and slipping as the truck gunned straight for us.

"Faster!"

I grabbed her hand and pulled the throttle back harder. The plane sped up, swerving dangerously. We cleared the pickup as it shot across the runway, nearly hitting the tail fin. The truck swung around, trying to back into a turn and shift into drive, but it lost control and kept spinning, spraying water as it skidded through heater-made puddles. I slammed the window shut and pressed my face against it, trying to see around the cargo. Eve yelled something I couldn't hear over the roar of the engine or the gunshots still ringing in my ears. The plane sped up.

The propane heater flashed past and I yanked the seat belt on, trying not to bump into the controls. The crashed plane at the end of the runway was getting closer. It didn't look like we could clear it. We were going at least 55 mph, maybe 60. The obstacle grew larger and more real by the second—the broken wing, the pieces of smashed metal scattered across the runway—when suddenly its rear windshield shattered. I spun around to see Kara silhouetted in the hangar door, legs braced wide and arms outstretched, aiming.

Eve pulled the wheel back just in time to soar above the debris. The hangar receded, getting smaller and smaller, an insignificant speck in a white, frozen world. Someone shouted. It might have been me.

We were flying.

Max

"Let's go over this again. You found the drugs where?"

The guy sitting across from me had been out of prison for all of two months. Twenty-four years old with a spray of acne covering barely there stubble, he looked like he wanted nothing more than to bolt out of the interview room.

"On the street. Someone must've tossed them."

A baggie of capsules filled with white powder sat on the table between us, confiscated when an officer pulled up behind his car stuck in a ditch off Highway 6. The guy ran, and on any other day he might've gotten farther than ten feet without slipping on the ice and cracking his skull. Beside the baggie, he had two cell phones, a half-smoked joint, and a knife on him at the time of arrest. His parole officer was going to be thrilled.

This storm was racking up casualties like a gleeful pinball score. The worst so far was an SUV that skidded out of control into a couple crossing the road to get groceries. The man was killed on impact, and the woman lost consciousness and died before the ambulance arrived. That incident went to Ciseski, but domestics were starting to come in, too, people stuck inside together who shouldn't be together, and since patrol was still on traffic triage, most of the remaining investigators had been sent to deal with the logical results of stress and isolation.

Normally, I wouldn't have bothered interviewing this guy and especially not during a storm like this. Let him sit in a cell pissing himself until the courts opened on Monday. But I'd spent every spare minute today hunting for clues that could connect the missing and the dead. More and more names swirled around me, the net growing wider, the scope of what I was dealing with expanding almost faster than I could keep up. Between calls, I worked on the time line, laying the pieces out one by one.

August 19: Celina Kendrick punched out of her overnight shift to go home. Her car was found parked in her building's lot and there was no evidence of forced entry in the apartment. She was never seen again.

October 12: Jonah and I visited Belgrave Properties, an untraceable shell company, while searching for Celina. We met four unidentified men who claimed they hadn't seen her. They assaulted us when Jonah accused them of lying, and the leader, "Belgrave," shot me in the arm. Afterward, the property was abandoned.

December 10: Belgrave, who maintained a relationship with Alexis Dwyer, was caught on tape forcing her into her apartment building. The landlady overheard an argument and witnessed Belgrave leaving the building. Two days later, Alexis was found dead in her bathtub of an apparent overdose. I was still waiting on the toxicology report from the ME. The lab, like everything else in the state, had been shut down ahead of the freeze.

December 12: Matthew Moore lied to his father and wife and drove to Ryerson's Woods Park, where his car was incinerated with a specialized chemical. He hadn't been seen since.

I added the last date to the time line after listening twice more to the recording of Eve Roth's phone call this morning:

December 13: Eve Roth and Jonah Kendrick allegedly discovered a cache of drugs on the Moore family farm—before it was taken in the middle of the night.

It wasn't verified, and it wouldn't be until law enforcement actually went to the farm, but I added it anyway, because drugs started to make more and more sense. The thing that might connect everything. Celina worked a graveyard shift. She could've easily witnessed something she shouldn't have—a deal, a transfer of product. Before she disappeared, she told Jonah that she'd met someone she wanted to help. Maybe she'd confronted someone, tried to intervene, and they'd retaliated. And why else would Belgrave have shot a cop in broad daylight, if not to protect an illegal operation we'd stumbled on in our search for Celina?

The RVs parked on the property had disappeared with the men. Dirt coated their undercarriages, but each of them had sported almost brand-new tires. They'd traveled a lot of dirt roads, the least patrolled routes, and were equipped to leave at a moment's notice. If what Eve Roth said proved true, they'd used ideal storage locations, too, remote farms where scatterings of residents minded their own land and interests. You didn't have to hide if there was no one to see.

When the dealer was brought into booking, I'd been reviewing last summer's fertilizer truck bust again. The driver claimed he had no clue he'd been muling millions of dollars' worth of drugs. He'd been a longtime employee of the company with no priors or any association with known cartels out of Mexico or Chicago. The DEA organized a task force for the bust and took over the case immediately afterward, which was where our files ended. All I could see in NCIC was that the driver got five years, and the drugs were listed as a derivative of oxycodone hydrochloride.

The baggie on the interview table in front of me was nothing in comparison. Thirty capsules—barely possession with intent to distribute—but I was stuck in this station with no end of the day in sight. The guy hunched in his chair, holding an ice pack to his head.

"What is it? Fentanyl?"

He shrugged and mumbled something indecipherable.

"You know we're testing it anyway. Save us some time and help yourself out by cooperating."

He mumbled something.

"Speak up."

"Molly, okay? For some finals parties this weekend."

"Are you kidding me? Two years ago, you were busted with enough oxy to sedate an elephant. Now you're throwing dorm raves?"

He clutched the ice pack and nodded.

"Why the change in business model? You want customers who depend on your product, not broke freshmen who'll give out your number to anyone who asks. Jesus, don't they teach you kids anything in school?"

I leaned on him some more, told him how much this arrest would add to his sentence. Eventually he asked if he could cut a deal.

"I don't want the name of your molly dealer."

"Then what?"

"The oxy, when you got busted the first time."

"That's over, man. That whole supply dried up."

"How? Who was your supplier?"

"Lex." He shrugged. "I didn't know her real name."

"Her?"

"She just held the stuff, divvied it up for pickups." He gave me an address on the south side, one I already knew. My gut tightened. When I asked him to describe the woman, he said he had a picture. I got one of his cell phones and let him pull it up. It was older, a shot from a club the guy didn't look old enough to get into. The girl he leaned into for the selfie was the same one I'd seen two days ago, dead in a bathtub.

Alexis Dwyer.

My pulse hummed as pieces of the investigation clicked into place. The landlady said she'd seen men going in and out at all hours. The space in her closet, empty and vacuumed clean. The regular Binance deposits every month.

"When you say the supply vanished . . ."

"I went to see Lex after I got out, but she told me the whole thing was done, over. It sounded like something went down higher up the chain. She was really weird about it."

"Weird how?"

"Like sick, maybe? She was wearing sweats and looked like shit. She didn't even want to let me into the apartment. I thought someone was in there with her, but she said she was alone, that she couldn't trust anyone."

"Why not?"

"I don't know, man. She acted like someone had died, or they were about to. That's all I know."

I was hauling him back to booking when my phone buzzed. The number was Eve Roth's but the message was from Jonah.

Found their cache.
And Belgrave.

I stopped in front of the booking desk. The dealer shifted a glance at me, but I barely registered him. If Jonah had actually located Belgrave, I could bring in reinforcements. He was a person of interest in Alexis Dwyer's death, and I had a witness who could put him in the middle of a drug trafficking ring. I had every reason to pursue this lead.

Where are you?
In the wind. We're bringing it to you.

I tried calling, but the call disconnected and another text immediately popped up.

Can't talk. Too loud up here.
Send the cavalry to Iowa City airport. We're coming in.

Shoving the dealer at the booking sergeant, I sprinted for the captain's office.

Eve

From three thousand feet up, Iowa became a canvas of whites. The skies were clear and open. A few commercial jets soared above us in the thirty- to forty-thousand-foot stratus—coast people flying over the vast and seemingly empty middle—but no other personal or hobby fliers had been cleared for takeoff today. We were alone in our airspace, without a cloud or weather system in sight, and for the first time since Thursday morning, I breathed easy. I wasn't the same person I'd been in my air lab. I might never be her again but looking down at the world beneath us brought echoes of that woman back.

Kendrick put on the other headset, and the electronic sound of his voice cut through the engine's overpowering buzz. "Max wants to know our position."

I gave it and, after he'd texted our coordinates, told him to turn the phone off.

"Why?"

"It's interfering with the radio." I needed every instrument this plane had. It was holding together so far, despite being shot at, but a single-engine crop duster was a great-grandmother compared to Joan, my mobile lab. And on top of that, a great-grandmother I barely knew. I'd never in my life piloted a plane without reading the manual first, testing every control and gauge, and doing a thorough preflight safety check of the entire craft. The fuel line read a quarter of a tank. Either the drug traffickers hadn't planned to fly far, or they hadn't fueled up the plane before we stole it.

Kendrick turned his attention to the sacks piled behind our seats. He pulled one of them onto his lap and shifted it label-side up. "Seed corn. Fifty pounds."

Grabbing a utility knife from one of the cupholders, he stabbed the sack, cutting a line through the middle of the logo. Corn kernels spilled everywhere. Reaching in, Kendrick pulled out ten plastic bags filled with pills, the same drugs—as far as I could tell—as we'd found in the safe room. They'd hidden their inventory inside the most innocuous currency in Iowa.

"Is that everything?"

"From Lovers Ridge? Probably." Kendrick counted the sacks, multiplying. "But this is only one cache. There's more out there."

"You can't know that."

"They shot a cop in broad daylight. They've murdered two people and probably more."

Something seized in my chest, a sharp, unexpected pain. Matthew had been murdered. We could be flying over his body right now: his too-big ears, the toes curling slightly out, the perfectly round black moles just below his shoulder blades that looked like peppercorns had been scattered on his back. All the landmarks I'd mapped on my husband's body were gone, decaying back into the earth. Would I ever get to know where or why?

It had taken me decades to make peace with my father's death, and I couldn't imagine even coming to terms with Matthew's, not when I understood so little about it. It wasn't just his body that had been ripped away but also everything I'd known about him. Ten years of memories, our shared dreams and ambitions, the jokes meant only for each other. How could I process any of that now? How could I remember what I might never have known?

"Hey—" Kendrick's voice sounded distant in the headphones, but the hand that reached out to squeeze mine was warm and strong. "You did this. You found the connection. Matthew to Kara. Kara to Belgrave. And now we've got a fortune of drugs tying them all together. We've got them." He paused and corrected. "You got them."

I forced a smile. "I'll share credit on the byline."

Kendrick picked up the phone again, waving off my objection. "It's in airplane mode, relax." He took pictures of everything: the plastic bags, the ripped-open sack, and the identical ones stacked floor to ceiling behind us. While Kendrick counted pills, I counted pounds, calculating the weight of the cargo and how much extra fuel each seed bag was burning. The needle had dipped below a quarter tank now.

As we crossed an empty highway, a scratchy, tar-coated voice hailed us on the radio.

"Gail?" I couldn't believe my ears.

"Living the dream, Dr. Roth. Living the Disney *Frozen* dream." The Iowa City air traffic controller confirmed my position and told me we were thirty miles out. We could make it that far. I was almost positive.

Then Gail informed us we had to reroute.

"They were trying to deice the runway for you and crashed two plows right in the middle of the strip. On a normal day, you could get around it, but today . . ."

Kendrick fell still, listening to the conversation through his headset. I took the coordinates of the new strip, south of Iowa City, where the authorities were already en route.

"How much farther is it?"

"If you turn south now, an extra twelve miles."

Forty-two miles. I glanced at the fuel gauge, swallowing.

Gail confirmed the airport's arrival area was as clear as it would get. "It's a shorter strip, though." Her voice broke, chopped up by the electronic static, not her usual coffee- and cigarette-fueled calm. "Line it up and go around if you need to. Wind's five knots due west. Take her down as slow and easy as you can."

We wouldn't be circling to scout the runway or carefully planning the least hazardous descent. We'd be lucky to get there at all. I thanked her, signed off, and turned south.

Kendrick slumped in his seat, corn seed shifting and spilling around him. "I didn't even think about how we were going to land this thing."

"Newton's third law of motion states that every action has an equal and opposite reaction."

"Meaning?"

The fuel gauge hovered above the E, a hair's breadth of space before it dropped into the red. "Gravity takes care of everything eventually."

Jonah

"Have you ever landed on sheer ice before?"

Eve didn't answer. She didn't have to. The adrenaline flooding her system told me exactly what I didn't want to hear.

Biting down on the "oh, fucks" that wanted to pour out my mouth, I tried to hold it together. It would be like ice racing, with a few extra thousand feet of elevation tossed in. No problem. I sucked in air and braced myself against the window, a heartbeat ahead of a panic attack, until Eve added, "And we're running out of fuel."

I snapped around, hunting for the gauge in the maze of instruments. It wasn't that I didn't believe her, but I couldn't fucking believe her until I saw it for myself, right there, the needle sitting on empty. The buzz of the engine created a blanket of white noise around us. My lungs stopped working. Everything slowed down, suspended like a freeze-frame in a movie, the bomb before the explosion, close-up, ticking down.

"Are we going to make it to the airport?"

"If we can get close enough, we might be able to glide the rest of the way in."

So, no. I locked eyes with Eve. "We're going to glide . . . onto the glacier."

"Yeah." She nodded, but the motion dissolved into a tight shaking of her head. "Everything's fine."

Something bubbled in the air between us. A tendon jumped in Eve's throat, her mouth twitched, and without warning we both burst out laughing. It was uncontrollable, insane, cannibalizing every other emotion until there was nothing else left. I slid down the seat, corn seed digging into my legs and feet, which made me laugh harder. Eve laughed until tears poured down her cheeks and she swiped at her eyes, arms shaking as she tried to keep the plane steady.

We could make it. Thousands of feet in the air with a plane full of stolen drugs, out of fuel, and no airport in sight. Fuck it, why not? Eve's energy soared, full of possibility and determination. I'd spent months tortured, cold sweating in bathtubs and getting nowhere in my search for Celina, and after two days with Eve Roth we had more evidence than even the Iowa City PD could ignore.

"Let's do this."

The land spread blank and bright beneath us. We scanned the horizon and counted miles, pointing out silos and grain elevators, a snaking river that broke the symmetry of frozen fields. Each marker we passed got us closer. The fuel needle cut through the E, dipping into the bottom of the red zone. Neither of us said anything about it.

Somewhere down there, Max was driving to the airport, preparing the runway, carving another space in the world for me. At least I was bringing him something in return this time. Information on Belgrave and enough pills to launch a full-blown multiagency investigation. It wasn't anywhere close to what I owed him, but it was a start.

Twenty minutes later, the airport hailed us. They'd salted the runway and marked it with flares two miles ahead. The navigation system pinged soon after, telling us we were approaching our coordinates.

"It should be—" Eve cut off as the engine sputtered. We glanced at each other.

"There!" Cresting into view was a low, brown building with a radio tower and vehicles clustered around it. We'd descended enough to see our own shadow flying over the ice.

People moved like ants in front of the building. As two sparks flared to life, illuminating the beginning of the runway, the plane's engine coughed and died.

In the sudden quiet, Eve's energy spiked. She gripped the controls with white, bloodless fingers. The wind whistled around the cab and wings as I yanked both of our seat belts tighter. "You can do this. We're nearly there."

She muttered something about altitude, lift over drag, as her eyes played a tennis match with the instrument panel and the landing strip. The plane dipped lower, slowing down. Ahead, the runway shone like an icicle in the sun, blinding and dangerous.

Details appeared beneath us: ditches, fences, individual branches on trees. The ground rose up faster than it should. The two flares burned, hailing us from at least a quarter mile away. My heart thudded inside the headphones, drowning out anything Eve said. Nothing mattered except distance and angles, our lives reduced to geometry. And the geometry told me we weren't going to reach the runway.

In the last seconds before we hit the ground, I looked for Max, trying to find his cruiser among the parked trucks or his uniform among the scattering of people on the ice, but they were too far away. I couldn't make out any of them before we collided with the field in front of the runway.

The plane shook on impact. Our bodies bounced, jerking in our seats. The cab shuddered like the whole thing was about to implode. Eve pulled on the wheel, trying to keep us upright, but the field was tilled up under the ice. We hit a giant rut, which threw us to the right. Eve corrected, but we were going too fast. The world tilted, the wing hit the ground with an earsplitting crunch, and corn seed sacks slammed over the seats into our heads. Eve's body jolted forward as pain exploded in my skull. G-forces threw us in every direction.

The plane stopped and there was a moment of terrifying silence.

"Eve!" I sensed her before I could see her, a stutter of shock and disorientation but alive. Achingly alive. A dozen sacks of corn seed had crashed over the back seat between us. Corn kernels and pill-stuffed plastic bags were everywhere, filling the cabin. I couldn't see around them.

I unbuckled my seat belt and fell forward. We'd crashed into a snowbank, nose down, the windshield blanketed in a press of dark white. Light filtered through from somewhere on Eve's side of the plane. Her shock was fading, but I couldn't tell if it was because she was losing consciousness.

"Can you hear me?" I tore at the sacks. Corn seed poured out of them, threatening to bury me.

"I'm here," came a muffled reply.

A hand protruded between two bags and I grabbed it, squeezing her bones together. She squeezed back.

The sound of the plane door opening on Eve's side stopped me cold.

"Get out."

It wasn't Max's voice. The tone didn't sound like law enforcement or first responders and nothing I felt on the other side of the sacks gave me any reassurance. My skin started to crawl.

"Where's Investigator Summerlin?"

No one answered. Eve's hand stiffened in mine and before I could process what was happening, her fingers were yanked away. She made a noise, a muffled gasp of surprise and fear.

No. This wasn't right. I shoved a hand in my pocket, looking for Kara's gun, but it wasn't there. It must have fallen out during the crash.

The voice instructed Eve to move slowly. Then a dull thud sounded from somewhere outside the plane, followed by a cry.

I twisted in my seat, searching for the gun, the utility knife, a phone, anything. The sacks shifted like quicksand as two hands reached through the debris. I burrowed farther down, feeling along the seat and what I could reach of the floor. Seeds. Seeds and pills and nothing else. I shoved a handful down my sock as the hands dragged me through the sacks and out of the plane.

Eve lay on the ground, her forehead smeared with blood. A guy in a camo hoodie drove a knee into her chest as he bound her wrists with duct tape. Another one stood over her with a gun.

"The police are on their way." She choked the words out. "They'll be here any minute."

The one with the gun laughed, a dumb bark of glee. "That right?"

The flares sputtered less than a stone's throw away, dying on the ice. Beyond them, the airport building was dark. The trucks that had been parked there ringed the crash site now, with tricked-out suspensions and oversized, studded tires. Half a dozen men circled us.

Had the air traffic controller set us up? She was the one who said there were crashed plows in Iowa City. She'd diverted us to a remote, rural airfield, and I never thought to confirm it with Max. Christ, she probably worked for Belgrave. We flew exactly where they wanted us to go.

Eve kept talking, but the intent reeking from the gun-wielding man's head was a wall. There was no getting out of this. After they bound her hands, feet, and mouth, they did the same to me. They emptied our pockets, including my notebook and prescription bottle, and tossed everything into the plane. Then they hauled us to the back of a covered pickup.

"Why can't we fuckin' torch them with the plane?" the one dragging Eve complained to the one dragging me.

My guy didn't answer.

They left us on the ground as they unlocked the tailgate. The rest unloaded the plane, hauling sacks to another truck outfitted with chained tires and a snowplow.

Eve's eyes were wide and her hair was matted with blood. She wasn't panicking, not yet. She probably still thought we could get out of this, that someone would come before it was too late.

The two guys tugged at something inside the pickup. They didn't like this part. I could feel them getting uncomfortable, nauseous even. A sled fell to the ground between us, carrying what looked like mannequins. No energy or emotion came from the limp pile of torsos and limbs. Then it hit me.

One guy dragged the sled toward the plane while the other yanked at Eve. "Stand up, honey, or it's going to hurt a lot more."

She complied, still staring at the bodies. Both had black hair, one short and the other trailing behind on the ice.

The guy put me in the back of the truck after Eve. Across the field, two guys hoisted the first body into the plane as another one doused the cab with fuel. It was Matthew Moore's car all over again, except this time they were planting corpses at the scene.

The tailgate slammed shut, locking us inside. I rolled to my back and bumped into Eve. The bed of the pickup was completely sealed. Except for a few pinpricks of light at the edges of the gate, we were in total darkness. I couldn't see her, but I could feel the question reflected in her. Or maybe it had been her question all along, mirrored in me.

Why hadn't they left us in the plane? Why keep us alive when they could dispose of us here and now? A bang on the topper made us both jump. "Y'all stay quiet back there. Don't go trying to get loose unless you want to end up on a sled of your own."

The front doors of the pickup opened and slammed shut. Two people started talking as the truck reversed in a sharp, fast arc, sending us crashing into the back side of the cab.

Someone in front laughed.

A series of cracks and hisses sounded outside the truck and one of the guys in the cab hollered in appreciation. The blunt hollows of their skulls lit with a flare of red and orange. Cavemen, gaping at a blaze. They'd set the plane on fire.

The truck gunned into drive, heading for somewhere that—no matter what else it was—would be our final destination. I knew that much. If I'd been alone in the back of this truck, on my way to the end of everything, no more nightmares or panic attacks or the torture of being in this world without any ability to actually live in it, I could have accepted this for what it was. I could have let go.

But Eve. Her heart thrummed next to me. Her body twitched, aching with every bump and slide. Adrenaline and confusion battled inside her. She wanted to live. She had theories to form and storms to conquer. It made me want to die twice, first for me and again for her. But there wasn't any saving Eve. I couldn't save anyone, and that might be the only answer death gave me.

Sunday

Nothing in life is to be feared. It is only to be understood.
Now is the time to understand more, so that we may fear less.
—Marie Curie

Max

There are two truths in every story. In the first version, I got a text from my best friend, telling me he'd hijacked a plane full of illegal drugs in the middle of an ice storm. I went to Larsen, got authorization to pull people from their emergency duties, and brought two patrol officers and a forensics team to the Iowa City Municipal Airport. I drove to an equipment operator's home and physically brought him to the airport to deice the runway. And we waited, minutes ticking by, watching the sky as no plane appeared. The team got restless, muttering to each other and wandering off. I went to the air traffic controller at one point, a spindly, leather-skinned woman with a permanent hunch in her back, and demanded to see the radar again.

"Nothing yet." She pointed to a screen that might as well have been in braille for all I could read of it.

"What's that?" I tracked a dot moving through a corner of the screen.

"Delta 1372, on its way to Atlanta." She pulled a Marlboro out of a pack and tapped it on the table. "You sure they're coming in?"

I was less sure every minute.

"Can't you track 'em somehow?"

"Can't you?" I fired back.

The woman shrugged and slipped her phone into a purse that had a gold chain and two interlocking C's on its front. It looked like the kind Eve Roth would carry around. When she saw me looking at it, she stuffed it into a drawer. I sighed and turned to the cleared and empty runway.

"Don't you have a way of hailing them?"

"No one out there to contact, far as I can see."

Two hours. I waited two hours at the airport for Jonah, texting and calling both his and Eve Roth's phones. Both went immediately to voice mail. The GPS coordinates Jonah had given me put them due west of us, just south of the freeway. They should've landed twenty minutes after we'd arrived.

At 6:30, Larsen pulled everyone from the airport. He was livid, to put it mildly, and he sent me home, stripped of all my cases. Without a plane full of drugs arriving like a Hail Mary at the end of the fourth quarter, I had no evidence to back up my emergency request. I'd wasted critical department resources three days after being declared fit for duty and was headed for disciplinary action.

That was the first truth, the one that would fit easily in the notes of my personnel record. A shitty cop making a shitty call.

The other truth was more complicated because I didn't go home on Saturday night. I didn't follow the orders I'd been given because deep in my bones I knew something was wrong.

Something had happened to Jonah.

I texted Shelley that I wasn't coming home. I told her everything was fine, not to worry, and turned off my phone before she could reply. Then I drove west.

I went to the only place I knew to look, the last place I could trace them—Lovers Ridge Farm. I'd called in a welfare check earlier that day, but the local sheriff's office said they were so backed up he couldn't promise a man out there until Sunday at the earliest.

It took me half the evening to get to the address. I parked on the road, not trusting the sheer ice coating the yard. At the front door, Earl Moore met me with a kitchen knife clutched against his walker.

I raised my good hand and eased a step back. "I'm Investigator Summerlin, from Iowa City. Do you remember me?"

He did, thank god, and dropped the knife with relief and exhaustion. He didn't look good. Cold sweat stuck what was left of his hair to his head, and a fetid sense of fear hung over the house. It looked like he'd tried making a sandwich at one point, spilled an entire Ziploc bag of pill bottles over the kitchen floor, and had pulled all the curtains down in the living room.

He didn't know anything about an airplane. The last contact he'd had with Eve or Jonah was Saturday morning, when they headed out on ice skates to chase after drug traffickers. Jesus Christ.

They took a gun.

I handed the iPad back to him and pointed at my arm. "I had one, too, when this happened."

They wouldn't have gotten far on skates, a ten-mile radius tops, which practically eliminated finding any kind of high tech or commercial jet. This was crop duster and hobby flier country.

The sky was clear and dripping with stars when I went out to the bunker. Scorch marks and snowmobile tracks ringed the base of the old silo like a macabre circus had come and gone, leaving nothing useful behind. Jonah's car was empty, too.

The old man slept fitfully for the rest of the night, waking in jerks and starts, while I put chains on Jonah's tires. The Evolution could navigate ice infinitely better than my city-issue sedan, and Jonah owed me at least that much. Then I sanded a runway up the driveway, took a gray nap, and tried pointlessly to get a cell signal.

At dawn, I loaded Earl Moore into the front seat of Jonah's car and we headed back to Iowa City. I wasn't sure what to do with him when we got there, but I couldn't leave him on that farm by himself. It should have been an hour-long drive, but it had taken me five last night, and I expected at least that on the way back. No one in Iowa was going anywhere fast this weekend.

As soon as we got to the freeway, Earl's iPad pinged with an incoming message. It was from Eve, dated yesterday, telling him they were taking something from Lars Field. There were no messages after that.

"No point going there now. They were airborne last I talked to them."

He nodded tightly and turned to the window.

We listened to traffic reports and the news for a while, but the sheer number of crashes and incidents made it impossible to know if any of them related to Jonah or Eve Roth. I turned on a country station, and we listened to Cash and Willie in silence. The old man watched the sky, like some hint of his daughter-in-law might appear in the dawning blue above.

A pickup with a covered bed passed on my left, the driver's profile framed for an instant before it pulled ahead of us. Something tugged at me, a nagging feeling I couldn't place until the truck was a car length ahead and I registered the tailgate. It was a black Silverado, same as the one on the security footage at Alexis Dwyer's apartment.

Belgrave.

I reached for the radio automatically, ready to call in backup before remembering this was Jonah's car, and Larsen had relieved me of duty last night. I wasn't in my jurisdiction and didn't have a case to investigate even if I was.

Cursing, I gripped the wheel with both hands, ignoring the twinge of pain in the left, and cut across jagged furrows of ice into the lane behind the Silverado. The semi behind us honked and slammed on the brakes, fishtailing into two lanes. Earl's body thudded against the door.

"Hang on. The guy ahead of us is the one Jonah and Eve found with the drugs from your property." I hesitated, then added, "He's also the reason I'm wearing this sling."

Earl pulled himself as upright as he could, which wasn't much, and rearranged the iPad that had fallen off his lap. I waited for his objection or for him to tell me to keep driving to Iowa City. Instead, with shaking fingers, he began recording the Silverado's license plate.

I couldn't see much from behind, only the general outline of the driver. No one rode in the passenger seat. The bed of the pickup was completely covered with a snapped-on tarp, and every so often the tarp rippled and bulged, as if the load inside had shifted. The ice trenches on the road bucked and broke in unexpected places, sending the Silverado skidding dangerously in front of us. I followed, closer than I should, willing it to crash right here in the middle of this hobbled freeway.

But it didn't. The pickup powered on, and I followed, without knowing where or how this would end.

Eve

We rode for hours. Every rut threw us into the air. Every flat surface sent the truck fishtailing and tossed us against the wheel wells. At some point I managed to turn, bracing my feet against the side and my back against Kendrick, and we held there, waiting for whatever came next.

I couldn't remember the exact sequence of events after the plane landed. The wheels touched down, the plane shook, and the next thing I knew Kendrick was shouting my name. He'd sounded underwater, or maybe I was underwater, but I hung on to the sound waves, weak as they were, following them back into the wrecked, grounded plane. There was a jumble of hands, voices, and bright, sharp stabs of pain. And now we lay in the back of a covered pickup, a space the size of a double casket, where two bodies had lain before us. A puddle of something stuck to my coat, and a faint, putrid scent clung to the air. I willed myself not to collect the data, to resist analyzing any of these inputs.

Why had Gail sent us to the other airport? Had she known what was waiting for us there? The back of my head throbbed; something must have struck me when we landed. I tried to recall exactly what the air traffic controller said, to remember the coordinates of where we'd landed, but every piece of information disintegrated the moment I stopped focusing on it, as though layers of cirrus, altostratus, and cumulus clouds kept drifting into my brain and obscuring any sense of the sun. It could've been twelve or thirty turns later when the truck stopped and we heard the people in the cab get out.

A bang on the side bed. A dull thwack. I jumped.

"Y'all hang tight now. If I hear so much as a peep . . ."

Someone walked away. Kendrick turned his head, listening. There were more engines, and a background noise that sounded vaguely animal. A distant rumbling of snorts, squeals, and metal on metal, punctured by an intermittent ringing. I didn't know which noises were real and which ones lived only in my head.

I moved as much as I dared, trying to find the edges of the binding. There was no air between my wrists or ankles, and they'd wrapped each at least ten layers thick. Beyond the stickiness of the pickup bed, there didn't seem to be anything in the back of the truck with us, nothing we could use to free ourselves. Kendrick moved, stretching and flexing. He was trying to break the tape.

Were they out there somewhere, digging our graves? I'd flown over this land so many times. Shades of green in the summer, golden in the fall, a patchwork of whites in the winter and all of it laid open to the sky. The sky gave, and the sky took, and Iowa became whatever the sky made of it, ready to soak in anything that blew over the horizon. This land had swallowed my dad, and now it was going to swallow me.

Minutes dragged out, turning into an hour, maybe more. The metal bed of the truck stole heat from our bodies and we shivered uncontrollably, trying to stay warm. I wished we could talk but at the same time I didn't know what to say beyond, *I'm sorry. I was wrong. I should never have tried to steal the plane, and now because of me, we're going to die.*

Eventually Kendrick gave up trying to break the tape. He pressed his shoulder gently against my forehead, as if he could feel the vicious pounding inside my skull. I let myself rest against him, absorbing his body heat, his comfort, and waited.

A truck door slammed, jolting me awake. The truck started moving again, and for another freezing jumble of time, we braced ourselves against each other and the sides of the truck.

By the time we stopped a second time, I couldn't feel my hands or feet and I couldn't say with any certainty whether the numbness came from the plane crash, the car ride, or the duct tape binding my ankles and wrists. The vehicle doors opened and shut, and heavy footsteps thudded around to the back. Kendrick nudged me with an elbow, a warm touch I took for a welfare check. I made a noise that came out sounding smaller and more frightened than I'd intended. His elbow pressed firmly against me and I took a deep breath. Whatever came next, I hoped they would let us face it together.

Someone opened the gate of the pickup and rolled the cover back. It was barely lighter outside than it had been in the sealed bed. The stars winked and blurred, and I squinted at an upside-down Orion, the hunter upended. Someone hacked at my feet until the tape broke and pulled me out of the truck. Shadowed buildings surrounded us, the outlines of machines, snowmobiles, and beyond that, the horizon hinting at dawn. We'd been in the truck all night.

A push from behind. "Walk."

I did, stumbling on limbs that couldn't feel themselves. The ground was still crusted with ice, but it crunched; someone had laid a path of sand leading to the tallest shadow. I made the mistake of looking up and hit the ground almost before I felt the vertigo tilting my sense of gravity. A hand hauled me back up and pushed me forward again.

"Why did you have to steal the goddamn plane? Why couldn't you just go to the cops?"

It was the question drumming in my head, but it wasn't my voice. It came from outside me, a whisper in the cold. Before I could place it, someone pulled open a creaking, rusting door. A barn door. The hinges squealed like an echo of pigs in the night, revealing a sliver of light and then a larger and larger rectangle. The person holding my wrists steered me inside the barn.

The walls were made of thin planks rattling in the wind. High, bare beams crossed the ceiling, strewn with the remnants of nests long abandoned. The space was empty except for a single fluorescent light and a man lying in the center of the broken floor. His hands and feet were tied together, mouth covered, skin bloodless and white, but his eyes were open and gazing right at me.

Matthew.

Jonah

The barn. Celina's barn.

Light bloomed on a black canvas, the doorway between consciousness and unconsciousness revealing itself, like it had been in front of me the whole time, waiting for me to open the right set of eyes.

Someone pushed Eve through the doorway and I followed, stepping out of the Iowa landscape, off the map, and into the depths of my nightmare. The man lying on the floor wasn't any man on any floor. It was Matthew Moore, bleeding like Celina had lain bleeding. When the wind whistled through the cracks in the building, it played a song I'd memorized every night. The same one-word dirge: *Look, look.*

Eve dropped next to her husband, putting up no fight against Kara, who'd brought her inside. I barely registered the guy pushing me or the gun he pointed. Everything receded behind the knowledge that somehow, despite every wrong step and failure, I was here.

I traced a path along the creaking, uneven floor toward Eve. This was where the nightmare footsteps had walked, making their way to Celina. I knelt in the spot where the boards wavered, where the sound of the wind whipping the slats of the building hit the exact pitch I'd heard night after night. The oneiros had led me exactly here, hurtling through the horned gate into the place where reality superimposed itself over the dream.

This was where Celina lay.

Doubling over, I bent my head to the floor and breathed a final hello in the place she'd said goodbye.

"The fuck is this?" said the guy. "Take the tape off their mouths."

He yanked me up, making the floorboards shake beneath us, and ripped off the duct tape. Kara did the same to Eve. A trickle of blood appeared next to Eve's mouth. Her gaze trailed unsteadily from her husband to the spot I crouched over, as if she could see the imprint of a body, too.

"Celina?"

Kara whipped toward Eve, her mind stuttering with shock. It was strong enough to break through everything else: the barn, the man lying half-dead between us, even the wind that flapped like bat wings, Oneroi at the gate.

"How do you know Celina?"

The guy turned. "Who?"

Kara ignored him. "How do you know her?"

"I'm her uncle."

"The psychic?"

My shock mirrored hers. I stared at Kara, covered in tattoos and piercings, her strength like a wall holding her apart from everyone around her. She'd spared our lives at Lovers Ridge and when she shot at us at Lars Field, she'd hit the crashed plane instead.

The windshield exploded again in my mind, slow motion, like the birds in her notebook, with their wings and feet and eyes splayed and frozen forever in time. Then the pieces fused back together, creating an entirely new whole.

"You're the one Celina met. The one she was so excited about."

Kara's jaw tightened as a chasm of pain cracked open inside her. She struggled to look impassive. She wasn't going to say anything in front of the guy, but connections began firing anyway, fueled by everything that had happened in the last few days.

When I collided into Kara at the thrift shop, I'd thought of Celina. I'd sensed my niece in the air and dismissed it. I hadn't trusted my own instincts. Maybe, though, Celina had been whispering to me from that first moment, pointing to Kara, showing me the key to understanding everything.

"Tell me." I fought to sit up straighter, to hear every thought and emotion swarming through the barn. "You're getting rid of us anyway." I glanced at the guy who was trying to keep up with the conversation. "Please, I need to know."

"Is this about your little girlfriend?" the guy asked. He started to laugh.

"Fuck you." Kara turned on him, but he was already primed. The gossip in him couldn't wait to dish.

"That little bitch cozied up to Kara and right off started getting information from her."

"Shut it, Trick."

"Names, dates, drop-offs, and she was feeding it all to the fucking DEA."

"I said shut it."

"Boss plugged the leak before she did too much damage. Only reason you're still around." He waved the gun in Kara's direction, still grinning until she jabbed him in the face. He stumbled back and swore, wobbling as the floor bent and creaked.

"You need your mouth stapled shut."

"What does it fucking matter?"

"That's what we're gonna find out." Kara took the gun from him. "Tie their feet."

He did, grumbling as he duct-taped our ankles again. I barely noticed. They took Celina because she was working with the DEA? She said she wanted to be a detective, that she wanted to help people, but she never told me she'd been involved in anything like this.

Christ, how did a nineteen-year-old girl expect to take down a drug trafficking ring?

Trick wound the tape tighter and tighter.

"Did you kill her?"

Trick snorted as he ripped the end of the tape off and gave my legs a shove, making the floorboards groan. "She didn't have a clue. Didn't even know it went down until afterward."

When Kara rounded on him this time, he knew enough to shut up, sputtering excuses and wiping blood from his nose. She waited until his back hit the door of the barn before turning around, looking from Matthew to Eve to me. Leaning down to grip my shoulder, she spoke in a voice only I could hear.

"I did kill her." Kara's eyes swam with tears and the pain inside her seized. She could barely contain it. "I killed her the first time I met her."

Her fingers dug into me, creating a lightning rod of connection. I shut out the confused terror rising from Eve, the stink of death on Matthew, the wind and the cold, everything, and focused on the hand bruising my shoulder, the information Kara's wrenching gaze told me to take.

I felt love first, the kind of love that happened in spite of everything. Kara wasn't supposed to love Celina—it wasn't in the plan—but she had anyway. Blisteringly. Openly. She'd confessed everything to her. In the space between sheets and shadows, between graveyard shifts and sleepless sunrises, it had all poured out. The memories came, ballooning in my head: Kara nuzzling Celina's hair, the two of them racing along the Riverwalk together, dinners at dawn in a cramped kitchen. She lingered on each moment, making me see, knowing I could. And then, as suddenly as it swelled, the balloon of memories popped, and her energy exploded into guilt and darkness. Kara hadn't known Celina was gone until she went to her apartment and found Belgrave instead, his skull-like face twisted in grim threat.

I remembered the conversation we'd overheard at the hangar. *You think you can scare me? You have nothing left to scare me with.*

The growing sound of an engine cut through my focus and Kara blinked as she registered it, too. She released my shoulder, which felt branded now, a permanent scar of memory. The engine grew louder, eclipsing the murmur of voices and moving bodies outside the barn. A truck was coming.

"He's here," Kara told Trick, straightening up. "Let's go check in."

Trick grinned. "Y'all have fun catching up now."

A security camera was mounted above the door, its red eye trained on us as Kara and Trick left. They slammed the rolling door shut, shaking the beams of the barn, and a chain rattled against the outside of the door, followed by a heavy click. They'd locked us inside.

Max

We inched along the endless horizon, following the Silverado in an otherwise unbroken line of semis chancing their way through the icy wasteland. Neither of us spoke. Earl clutched the strap of his seat belt with his good hand, and I gripped the steering wheel with mine.

For an hour we followed the truck, switching lanes whenever he did. I didn't care if Belgrave figured out he was being tailed. He couldn't go anywhere. He had nowhere to disappear this time and with every excruciating mile, I became more convinced that this was it. I had my badge, handcuffs, and gun, and I was prepared to use all three to get the answers I needed.

Forty miles outside of Iowa City, the game changed. The semi in front of the Silverado swerved onto an exit ramp for a closed weigh station and Belgrave followed.

"What the hell?"

Heart pounding, I cranked the wheel over the jagged ruts at the edge of the lane and skidded after them. No plows had come through the weigh station yet, and the ramp was covered in an unbroken sheet of ice.

The semi's brake lights lit up well before the station building, but the truck kept moving, sliding like a toy past the signs and into the scale lane, before finally bouncing off the curbs enough to stop at an angle on top of the scale. The Silverado took the bypass lane, coasting next to the semi and fishtailing to a stop.

They were working together. And they had blocked us in.

I pulled the emergency brake well before the scale, skidding to a halt fifty yards behind them. The weigh station building windows were dark and empty. A row of pine trees hid the freeway and its caravan of suicide drivers from view.

"Great."

Earl made a noise that sounded like a question.

"Don't worry." I reached for my phone and nodded toward the dark building. "There's cameras everywhere here. This is all being recorded. I'm going to—"

The windshield exploded.

I hit the floor, reaching across the console for Earl and shoving him down. I couldn't tell if he'd been hit or not. Putting the car in reverse, I slammed the gas pedal down and tried to steer. Two more shots hit us, but they pinged off metal instead of glass. The car fishtailed and spun, revolving a full 360 before crashing into something behind us. Throwing open the driver's door, I waited for more shots. None came.

I pulled my Glock and checked the chamber, making sure I had a round ready. Earl's head lolled, but his eyes followed the gun.

"Stay down."

Using the door as a shield, I checked our position. We'd skidded into an outbuilding farther away from the semi and Silverado.

I fired three shots toward the cars and waited for any return fire. None came. Smoke hissed out of the Evolution's hood.

Ducking around the back of the outbuilding, I moved into the pine trees for cover. The ice was patchier here, and I stumbled from branch to branch, trying to get close enough for a decent shot. It felt like I'd been sucked back in time. I was at Belgrave Properties all over again, surrounded by gunfire, submerged in sudden violence. I braced myself against a thick trunk and took aim through the bottom branches. My bad arm shook as waves of pain sent tremors from wrist to shoulder. I focused on the shaking sight, looking for a target.

Movement near the semi drew my eye. Belgrave climbed into the passenger side of the cab. My gun shook. I was too far away for a clean shot and would only give away my position. I ran instead. Skating out into the open, I crossed the ice and barreled into the Silverado, crouching behind the front wheel well.

The semi's engine ground into gear, vibrating through the pickup. They were leaving.

I took position, steadying the gun on the hood of the pickup and fired into the cab. A volley of shots came back, ricocheting off the Silverado. Heat sliced through my shoulder, but I kept firing, chasing the truck as it pulled away.

For a moment, an agonizing moment that caught me by the throat, I thought I would lose him again. That Belgrave would get back on the road and disappear in the endless chain of semis. But the cab slid. Its wheels turned too sharp and the whole thing jack-knifed before crashing onto its side halfway down the exit ramp.

I ran, fell on the ice, got up, and ran again. Adrenaline flooded my chest, a surge of pure fuel. When I reached the cab, the driver's side door kicked open into the sky and Belgrave dragged himself out. I took a wide stance and fired. The bullet slammed him back and he disappeared into the belly of the cab.

I waited, aiming at empty sky for what felt like an eternity, my whole life distilled into a clenched breath and a finger poised on a trigger. My arm cramped and locked. A dark patch of blood soaked the shoulder of my coat.

Holding the gun in my bad hand, I scaled the steaming cab as quietly as I could, biting back the burn of pain. I'd lived with pain for months. Pain was nothing. I needed answers.

On top of the truck, I paused, staring at the open door, listening to the dark silence inside. My heart threatened to pound out of my chest. Finally, I leaned in.

Belgrave lay on top of the body of another man, facing the sky. Blood streamed down one of his arms, and in the other hand he held a gun.

When he saw me, he pulled the trigger.

Eve

I was here and yet I wasn't. My head pounded and spun, and everything I concentrated on made the throbbing worse. I'd shattered, and I had no idea how any of the shards fit together again. Two words pulsed against the edges, breaking and reforming with every breath. Matthew. Alive.

My husband was alive.

We were in a barn stained with blood. With Matthew. Somehow he was exactly where Kendrick said he would be. I didn't understand how or why we were here and I didn't care. The minutes of my life were ticking down, slipping away. I could only hold the most important things now.

After they left and locked us inside, I half knelt, half lay next to him, struggling to keep myself upright on bound, bloodless hands. Parts of Matthew wavered in and out of focus. His too-large ears that always stuck out more than he wanted. The slope of his neck, dotted with tiny moles. The place where his side met his hip, the smooth skin beneath his ribs where I curled my hand as we slept. He'd shattered, too, flashes from another life, and each one cut into my heart.

"They said you were dead." Tears blurred my vision.

He made a noise and a matted clump of hair fell into his face. I brushed it back with numb hands, shaking with the effort.

His sunken eyes swam with tears. For a moment he crystallized into the man I'd married, the one who'd held out a sapphire ring in the woods, who'd offered me his family and stood with me on the top of a roof, circling us to see the entire wide, unbroken sky. I thought I'd lost him or that somehow the man I'd known and loved for ten years of my life may never have existed. But here he was, breathing in jerks and starts, looking back at me with the same disbelief.

Outside, a truck engine turned off and everything shifted again. Matthew's face distorted into gray skin and bloodshot eyes. He became someone else, blurring into the men's voices rumbling back and forth outside. A door slammed in the distance. How much distance? Formulas disintegrated in my head. They had no order, no form. I couldn't find their edges or shape and began to panic. How could I function if I couldn't think? Was I even me? The single fluorescent light hanging from the ceiling glared like the sun, and the world felt like it had tilted beneath me. I'd never had a concussion before. This is what it would sound like if brains could scream.

With clumsy fingers, I ripped the tape off Matthew's mouth. He didn't flinch. His skin was cold and unyielding. How long had he been lying on these wet planks? Maybe hours, or days.

"Eve," he breathed. The sound of his voice pricked fresh tears into my eyes. "Why?"

His question was barely more than a whisper. I didn't know what he was asking. Why was I here? Why had I loved him? Why did I come all this way so we could both die? I said the only thing I could think of.

"The tornado." The words felt strange in my mouth, a foreign message from a foreign woman. I couldn't bring her into focus—or the thing she needed so badly to chase down. I shook my head, trying to clear the fog for even a second. There were questions I needed to ask, but I'd misplaced them all in some dark, slippery room in my mind.

Somehow Kendrick knew. He inched over and grabbed Matthew's wrist. "How long have you been working with Belgrave?"

Matthew looked confused.

"Your boss, the drug lord." Kendrick leaned in, making the duct tape on his own wrists squeak. "Were you just storing the pills or did you cook them, too?"

Matthew made a noise that didn't sound like anything, but Kendrick nodded. "Yeah, we found your stockpile."

He shuddered, and his throat whistled with the effort. "I designed and tested the formulas."

Before I even knew what I was doing, I shoved my duct-taped hands like a battering ram into his chest. Kendrick flinched. Matthew cried out as his body slid across the floor. The wood was warped, rotting and falling apart. There were splintered places where some of the boards had already given way. I wanted to push him through one.

He'd lied to me. He'd lied about everything. Fury flooded my veins as I stared at the beaten, half-frozen man I'd married. I loved him, and I despised what he'd done with that love, how he'd betrayed every single person in his life. What would Earl say? How would Sam react, knowing what their son had chosen to become?

"How, Matthew? How could you do it?"

Apologies choked out of his mouth. Tears welled and spilled down his temples. "I thought . . . I tried . . . wanted to do the right thing."

"You thought dealing narcotics was the right thing?" I shoved him again, and his body felt like a dead thing, cold and stiff. The boards beneath us wobbled.

Kendrick, still holding Matthew by the arm, shook his head. "He's thinking about Kara now."

"Did he sleep with her?"

"No." Matthew answered for himself, his words barely more than breath and pain. "That night, with the pictures, she told me what happened to her girlfriend. She was devastated. I couldn't believe he would do that, that he could kill an innocent girl. I had to stop him, to end it." Matthew's voice broke.

Kendrick turned away, as if he couldn't face the emotion head-on. "He's telling the truth."

"Then why are you here? What happened on Thursday? Why did you set the Tesla on fire?" The questions emerged from the fog in my head, tumbling out almost faster than I could speak.

"I wanted to trap him into admitting what he'd done. Arranged to meet him at Ryerson's. I was recording him. Knew it was a risk. He'd gotten so paranoid. Knew if he caught on, I'd have to get out fast." Each sentence ended in a choked exhale, but he kept whispering, desperate to tell the story, as if it might be his last chance. "I had the diversion ready. Fire and rain. Time to get into the woods. To the airport, and you."

"You were trying to find me?"

"Supposed to be just him and me, but he had more. Surrounded me. Fire . . . didn't work."

Matthew's whispers became less and less intelligible. He started rambling about tracing particles. Then something about a fight, cutting off—he cut something off or something had been cut off from him? The words made less and less sense: a cop, a mass spectrometer, suppliers. His breath rattled in and out. His eyes went glassy.

"Wanted . . . the whole sky." He trailed off as tears streaked down his face. It was what he'd told me after the house renovation, when he'd taken me up to the widow's walk outfitted with weather station instruments and a 360-degree view. *It's yours, Eve, the whole sky.*

I'd never thought about Matthew's sky, how his view could look completely different from mine. I'd seen one sky my entire life. But there were billions, one for every person looking up. Mine brought tornadoes and storms, the monsters I'd learned to dissect. Matthew had courted the monsters in his sky, beckoning them until they'd swallowed him whole.

I curled up as another wave of pain crested. It was too much. I couldn't hold all these skies in my head. Everything went black and sharp. All I wanted was to make it stop, to make everything stop—my brain, these people, Matthew. I couldn't do this.

Then I heard it: a deep inhale and long, scratchy exhale. Kendrick was breathing for me, showing me how. The sound was an anchor, the first thing I trusted since we'd walked into the barn. I closed my eyes and let the bite of cold oxygen purge the noise in my head.

The floorboards groaned as he moved closer. "Stop it."

"I'm not doing anything." I could hardly move.

"You're thinking too loud. It's giving me a headache."

He pressed his forehead against mine and the comfort of that simple connection worked its way behind my eyes, calming the ache of my traumatized brain. With every breath we took together, the throbbing dulled and the dizziness faded. The walls stopped moving around us.

Before I wanted him to, Kendrick lifted his head. "Better. Now, we need to—"

But whatever we needed to do was lost as Kendrick turned to Matthew.

His shudders had stopped. There was no rasp of weak breath moving in or out of his mouth, and his eyes, tinged the white-blue of pure ice, had closed.

Jonah

"Matthew!"

Eve checked his breath while I felt for a pulse. It was there but weak and so slow it could fade to nothing at any minute, like his heart was freezing solid. His thoughts had slipped from chemicals and machines to Kara and regret, before blurring into a dreamlike state where sapphires bloomed between the rotting floorboards of the barn. His brain had disconnected itself, floating away from his solidifying body.

"Should we cover him? Try to warm him up?" Eve bent over her husband, her concern knotted up inside the anger that had shoved him across the creaking floor.

"He's too far gone. If we move him or apply too much heat, he could go into cardiac arrest."

We didn't have many options for any kind of warmth. The single fluorescent light hanging from a rafter gave off no heat. The hay loft had partially collapsed in one corner, covering the floor with a second skin of moldy wood and nails but no hay. A single, sickly bale of straw next to the door was the only possible blanket. Eve crawled toward it, but before she'd gone two feet one of the floorboards cracked and gave way. She screamed, her arms disappearing to the shoulder as the board crashed and echoed below. Her head cracked against the floor, and another board, bowing dangerously low, started to splinter.

I grabbed her feet. The space below us was black and smelled like foul water and meat. It felt like the drainpipe, a gaping mouth beneath us. I'd dreamed this. I'd seen the barn crack open and swallow Celina whole. I'd thought it was only a nightmare, my own dread seeping into the oneiros, but this was real: Eve's scream, her body struggling to pull itself up, to not slide into the oblivion.

Together, we inched back over boards that bent and quivered. We got to a higher spot near Matthew's feet, the crest of a wooden wave, but Eve shook her head and pointed to the tremors of the nails holding the slats together, so we inched to another crest, a more stable one in the middle of the barn, where the supporting beam beneath us felt intact. Eve pushed herself up next to me. Her entire body shook. She ran her hands over the floor surrounding us, warped and waving, the ice frozen in the eyes and ridges, trying to calculate which one would give way next.

"Are you okay?" Her wrists over the duct tape were as red and raw as her eyes and a new cut sliced across her cheekbone.

She stared at her husband, who was lying a few feet from the floorboards that had broken, in a trough with clearly no supporting beam underneath him. He was between us and the door now, exactly as I'd first seen him in the dream.

"What difference does it make now?"

I felt the pounding in her temple, the sinking weight of her battered body. Her headache had become my headache and her gash, blooming with fresh blood, burned on my own cheek. What had she called it? Entanglement. When one particle spun, the other did, too, regardless of space or time. Somehow we were entangled now. Our lives, as different as any two could be, had collided in the same unlikely place. I listened to her thoughts for a moment. I was past caring about how creepy and unnatural it was. She was scared, reliving memories of being trapped on a farm by forces larger than she was. Resigning herself to meeting her end the same way.

"I'm sorry."

I felt her words as much as I heard them. "Stop."

"I should never have left Earl alone. I don't know why I thought I could chase them down. I don't even know who I was doing it for." Eve drew her knees up and pushed her forehead into them, drawing herself into a ball. "Matthew. My father. It doesn't matter. My families disappear and die."

It wasn't a scientist sitting next to me anymore, the one who'd questioned, pushed, and calculated her way to uncovering an illicit drug operation in less than three days. She rocked in despair, and I couldn't stand it. It was one thing for me to know I'd failed, to be sitting on the mouth of a monster and waiting for it to unhinge its jaws, but I couldn't take Eve's defeat, not when she was so goddamn wrong about the whole thing.

"Oh, screw that."

I waited until she looked up.

"You wanted the truth? This guy." I shot a glance at Matthew Moore's lifeless form. "He's an asshole. A drug-making, sneaking, lying asshole. I get how Max figured you murdered him, because honestly? You should have. He never deserved you and you still came to save him."

She shook her head, the denial poised and ready, but it was my turn to talk.

"Your father. I don't know who you think you are, but you can't stop a tornado. Not when you're nine and not when you're a badass airplane-hijacking scientist. I'm no doctor of physics, but I've got a solid handle on the betting odds of humans versus cyclones."

Her mouth opened and nothing came out. I slid one of her gloves between mine and pressed our numb hands together. I knew shit about the universe or why anything happened. The principles and theories working in Eve's mind were completely beyond me. Family, though, I understood, and how the people we loved bound us more than any duct tape ever could.

"Celina was the only person in the world like me, but better. She was so much better, in every way. I existed, but she lived. I wish you could've met her." I choked on the thought, knowing it would never happen, that Celina was gone and what was left of her body was probably lying beneath us right now. Part of me had always known, had given up hope weeks ago, but it was one thing to brace yourself in a crash position without knowing which direction the truth was going to slam into you and another to feel the punch of it ripping into your bones. And still, I was grateful. To be here. To have found any part of her. The worst possible answer was better than no answer.

I tried to explain that to Eve, to put into words what it meant to have this terrible, shredding truth inside me. To be kneeling on Celina's deathbed, inside the place that had swallowed her, and to know her nightmare was over. I never would've had that without Eve. "You should've seen yourself, lighting ice on fire, skating across the frozen state, chasing down drug traffickers and murderers like some comic book hero."

"Or an insane person," she said, her head still resting on her knees. "The two are very close."

Her eyes were bright with tears, her nose and cheeks glowing red with cold, the gash on her face darkening with unshed blood.

I squeezed her hand so hard the duct tape squeaked. "Can we get out of here already?"

Something small and good happened, a warmth that had no right to live in a frozen, bloodstained barn, that couldn't be explained by anything outside or around us. Entanglement. Molecules moving in sync. I spun, and she moved, too.

A trace of a smile ghosted her face. "I've been thinking."

"Of course you have."

"This has to be a bank barn." It took a second before I remembered Earl's barn on Lovers Ridge, built into the side of the hill so it had two ground floors. She scanned the sagging floor and the darkness beneath us. "We must be on the top floor, and if there's another floor underneath . . ."

"There's another way out."

Not a mouth but an escape, if we could survive it. I'd spent most of my adult life resisting the drainpipe, trying to keep the nightmares at bay. Now Eve was telling me to let go, to let the drainpipe swallow us and follow Celina through the darkness.

"How do we get down?"

The place where the stairs were in Earl's barn was a gaping hole in this one, past the straw bale on the side of the door. If we could find a safe path across the floor, there might be a way to climb down. The security camera pointed at the middle of the barn, where

Matthew lay. It might not record us that close to the wall. I got to my knees, trying to see into the hole, and the shape of it suddenly became clear.

He can't move, but he sees a stone. The ring he gave her in the woods, a blue stone to match her eyes. The shape of Eve's ring was outlined in the floor.

"Did they take your wedding ring?"

"No." She pulled her glove free of the duct tape and tilted her hand. The sapphire was rectangular, with long, precise edges.

"Is that thing sharp enough to cut duct tape?"

Her eyes lit up. "It could be."

We worked slowly, hearts racing faster than any movement we dared to make. Facing away from the security camera, Eve sliced the ring against the tape on my hands, back and forth until the layers began to split. As I yanked my wrists free, a door slammed outside. Voices came from somewhere on the property. They were moving, but I couldn't tell if they were getting closer or farther away. I slid the ring off Eve's finger and attacked the tape on her wrists.

An engine fired up as I cut through the last layer.

"Hurry." The voices were getting louder now, definitely closing in. I caught snatches of words, guttural instructions. Footsteps crunched over sand. I moved to our ankles, cutting frantically, kicking numb feet outward as hard as I could until the tape gave way. We scrambled on hands and knees along the supporting beam toward the remains of the stairway. The floorboards creaked but held. We were halfway across the barn when Eve stopped short.

"Look." The camera above the door had gone dark, its red eye dead. The chain on the barn door rattled and the deadbolt slid open. There was no time to hide, no time to be swallowed. I slipped the ring into my pocket and put myself between Eve and whatever was coming.

The door rolled open, screaming in protest, and Kara walked in, followed by Trick and another guy I didn't recognize. Kara had a shotgun. The other two carried Glocks. In the distance at least four others stood around an idling box truck, the exhaust belching up into a clear, morning sky. The side of the truck advertised a fertilizer company.

Another man appeared, blocking the view of the truck as he stepped into the barn behind Kara. He was different from the others, unarmed, a giant, grizzled old man wearing coveralls and muddy work boots. He carried a battered metal thermos in one hand. Eve shot to her feet and gasped but not out of surprise or fear. It was a noise of pure and utter relief.

"Sam!"

Eve

Sam Olson, Earl's best friend, Matthew's second father, who'd delayed his trip to Davenport for us on Friday morning, stood in the doorway to the barn. Water filled my eyes at the sight of his familiar, hulking form. He braced knuckles on hips, his expression unreadable as he took in everything from Matthew unconscious on the floor to the piles of duct tape Kendrick and I had hacked through with my wedding ring.

"Sam." I took a step toward him, ready to throw myself into one of his bear hugs and cry with relief, but the second I moved, two strange things happened. One of the men stepped in front of Sam, and Kendrick's arm shot out, preventing me from getting any closer to either of them. I stared at everyone in the room, trying to make my aching brain understand as the floor dipped underneath my foot. Kara pulled the barn door shut with a high-pitched squeal and crash that made the entire wall shudder.

"Grab him," Sam said.

Kendrick's arm tightened against me, but Kara and the guy who'd hauled us into the barn earlier moved toward Matthew. They stepped uneasily over the creaking floor.

"Whole fucking thing's going to cave in," Kara muttered.

I swallowed. "Sam, what is this?"

Sam rubbed his jaw, finally looking at me. He had the expression of a man resigned. A man in charge. It was impossible, but the evidence was right in front of me. The others were taking orders from him, protecting him. Sam Olson, a drug lord? Everything in me reeled as the world tilted completely upside down, no longer obeying any laws I recognized or understood.

He heaved out a sigh and sat on the bale of straw. His bodyguard stood next to him, bracing himself against the wall. "I didn't want to have to do this."

Kara and her partner dragged Matthew by his ankles across the groaning floor, picking their way carefully to avoid the holes. His head bumped and jostled, but his eyes remained closed and his skin was even grayer than before.

"Matthew is dying. Is he here because of you? Did you do this to him?"

Sam leaned forward, elbows to knees, looking for all the world like a weathered grandfather about to tell the kids a story.

"No man who's worked the land takes life lightly. He knows what goes into making it, every day from sunup to sundown, gambling on the weather, the market, breaking his back turning seed into crop, and praying it'll be enough to last his family the winter."

Kara and her partner dropped Matthew's ankles in front of Sam and stepped aside. One of the floorboards cracked and Kara skipped away from it, springing back to the door. Outside, the truck doors slammed and the engine shifted into gear, driving away, leaving nothing but the sound of the wind against the slats and the seven of us here alone. Sam steepled his fingers, contemplating Matthew's limp form.

"You can't save every life on a farm. You've got to hunt the pests and cull the weak from the herd. Sometimes life doesn't have a chance. We had a Labrador once that got run over by a car right after she had a litter of puppies. Tiny, whimpering things. Wouldn't take a bottle. Bella was beside herself." He shook his head, his features pulled tight with memory and regret. "You do what you have to do."

Kendrick's arm, still stretched in front of me, began to shake, and a muscle in his jaw twitched. "You're Belgrave. Not the guy who shot Max. It's you."

"No." I turned toward Kendrick and the room kept spinning. I needed it to stop. I needed everything to stop right now, but Sam—or something that looked exactly like him—kept talking.

"Guess I got a bit carried away with the name, but I was heartsick. She died right before we started buying property. She was the inspiration for everything." He paused and his eyes unfocused. "My Bella had stomach cancer."

I remembered. She'd come to our wedding but stayed only for the ceremony—so small and frail by then. She'd petted the lace on my dress with quiet affection before Sam took her home. That was the Sam I knew—the caring husband, the neighbor who picked apples and bottled cider, the man who lived alone and watched too much TV. I had no idea who the man in front of me was.

"The doctors, they were getting up in arms about the opioid epidemic, wouldn't prescribe anything that could even touch her pain, said she might get addicted. Like that mattered. She couldn't eat, couldn't rest, couldn't hardly take a breath without suffering for it. She tried to hide the worst from me, but there were nights she couldn't contain it. The pain was eating her and taking its goddamn time with every bite.

"Matthew visited one day, and I showed him Bella's poppies in the garden. I'd been watching them for days, waving their orange faces at the sun. He hesitated about that first batch, until he saw how bad she'd gotten. Boy understood what family meant and what we have to do to take care of them." He nudged Matthew's leg with his boot. Matthew didn't stir.

"You made opium together," Kendrick said.

"Morphine, opium's main alkaloid." Sam huffed out a laugh. "Matthew wasn't the only one who knew some chemistry."

Kara shifted her weight against the door, making the boards creak. The man next to her, Trick, with one eye swelling red from where she punched him, lit a cigarette.

"After Bella died, we knew we had a crop the market needed. Morphine was too expensive on a mass scale. Too risky, too. Matthew designed a formula for a new product and I created the infrastructure, all right here. Made in the USA."

Matthew said he inherited investments from Bella. It was right there. He'd told me exactly where the money came from, and I had no idea.

I remembered the snowblower Sam was hauling to Davenport the other day. If the corn seed sacks were filled with pills, what had been inside that machine? What lived beneath the facade of his farm? It was a simple, perfect plan, playing into every bias. Someone like Kendrick, who made wild claims and had panic attacks and was out of place in every room he walked into, was

thrown out of the police station and barred from the entire city
for trying to find his niece, while Sam, who looked and talked
and thought like one of them, transported millions of dollars of
narcotics through the state unnoticed. Who would suspect him?
He was an aging white farmer, as ubiquitous to Iowa as a field
of corn. If his truck had broken down in the storm, he would've
gotten a police escort.

"Why are we here?"

"Took the words right out of my mouth." Sam stood up, and
his knees popped. "I visited you and Earl on Friday and neither
one of you knew a thing. I made sure you were both out of harm's
way. Then, the next goddamn day, you steal an entire planeload of
inventory." The floor groaned under the clump of heavy work boots,
boards vibrating with every step he took. He leaned over Matthew,
and the hand he put up to his nose, checking for breathing, was
huge and gnarled. It could crush Matthew's entire head.

"I combed through the house. Kara and the boys took care of
the office. There shouldn't have been any trail for you to follow, yet
here you are. Either you talked to someone or you found something."
Sam straightened. "Which is it?"

"I . . ." The faces in the room blurred out of focus, and my head
throbbed. If I told Sam about Matthew's formulas, I'd endanger
Natalia. If I told him about the notebook with the bird drawings
leading us to Lovers Ridge, I'd expose Kara. I shouldn't've cared
about protecting her, not while she stood guard at the door, doing
nothing to help us, but she'd saved us the other night at the farm.
She'd seen me and hadn't said anything. And Earl—my heart stuttered over my father-in-law. He'd been with us every step of the

way; he knew almost everything that had happened. What would they do to Earl?

Kendrick's face was the only thing I could see clearly, his bloodshot, steady eyes locked on mine. He nodded, and I understood.

"Him." I swallowed, pointing at Jonah. "This man showed up at my door. He told me Matthew was trafficking drugs."

"And you are?"

"Jonah Kendrick. I'm a private investigator."

"Kendrick." Sam tried to place the name.

Kara spoke up. "He's Celina Kendrick's uncle."

"I brought the cop to Belgrave Properties. The one your people shot."

The connection flared in Sam's eyes. "You almost stumbled right into Matthew's kitchens."

Kendrick said three RVs were parked on the property when he and Max arrived, and when he came back after the hospital, they were gone.

"That was the day I knew it was time to retire. There's never just one rootworm in a cornfield. If you see one, there's a thousand more in the soil." Sam picked up the thermos sitting on the straw bale. "How'd you find the property?"

"Jonah's a psychic."

"Come again?"

"A psychic," I repeated. "He dreamed about Celina and Matthew, both of them trapped in this barn."

Sam let out a chestful of air like a steam engine after a hard day's work and surveyed the faces of the people in the room like he was waiting for the punch line. The bodyguard shook his head. Trick laughed. Kara looked away.

"That's rich. You expect me to believe that you, Dr. Eve Roth, put your faith into a psychic? That you followed him across the country and hijacked my business on account of some dream?" He barked a sharp laugh, and the sound seized my throat. "You're going to have to do a little better than that."

"I'm serious."

"So am I." Sam unscrewed the lid of the thermos. Steam billowed out of it, obscuring his face. He braced one boot on Matthew's chest, and—before I could process what he planned to do—poured a stream of scalding water directly onto Matthew.

Screams ripped through the barn. Matthew's eyes popped open, frantic and rolling in their sockets. He thrashed underneath Sam's boot, and the floorboards bounced and cracked. I lunged toward Sam, not caring if the whole barn buckled underneath us, but before I'd gotten a step someone pushed me to the floor. Kara and the guy with the black eye had moved behind us, holding Kendrick and me immobile.

"Information, Doc. I need the truth from you now." Sam recapped the thermos, grinding his boot down harder.

Matthew panted and tried to claw the water away from his face and chest. He sounded more animal than human. His skin had turned purple where the water had splashed it. I fought against Kara's hold and begged her, begged Sam, begged anyone who would listen to stop this before Matthew went into cardiac arrest.

"Matthew won't tell me shit about the evidence he claims he's got against me. Thought the boy was going to be a lost cause." Sam leaned into his boot, compressing Matthew's chest. "Then you show up out of the blue. Like an answering angel, wings and all."

Matthew's head lolled toward me and he made a sound between a hiccup and a sob. "You can make this stop, Doc. Tell me what you know and who else knows it."

Natalia. Kara. Max. Earl. Another inhuman sound. I didn't know if it came from Matthew or me. Sickness welled in my throat and the room quaked.

Sam unscrewed the thermos again.

Max

Belgrave pulled the trigger before I could react.

Nothing happened.

My heart thudded. One staggering beat that could have been my last. The end, and I hadn't even flashed to Shelley or Garrett, the faces I loved and would have died for without question. The only thing I'd felt as I stared into the barrel of that revolver was a throat-clutching rage that the ghost I'd been chasing had beat me after all.

But he didn't. He was out of ammunition.

I dropped into the sideways semi cab feetfirst, landing on his chest and knocking the air out of him. He fought, but I had fifty pounds, gravity, and a hell of a grudge on my side, and within thirty seconds I had his good arm handcuffed to the passenger door and the rest of him pressed facedown to the unmoving, blood-splattered body beneath him.

"Howdy. You remember me?"

He didn't answer. I checked for a pulse on the other guy, the driver, but couldn't find one. The window underneath his head had shattered into a thousand-point snowflake, and his neck twisted at an impossible angle.

"I'm Investigator Maxwell Summerlin. The cop you shot on Belgrave Properties." I flashed a badge at his back. His blond hair was shaved so close to his head I could see skin and moles and veins snaking underneath. "And your name is?"

Still nothing. Blood seeped out of his injured arm at a steady trickle. I stepped on it.

He grunted and thrashed, tossing me against the seats, but I pressed my boot down until he told me.

"Ash. Russell Ash."

Russell. It was so normal, a nothing name, the kind you immediately forgot after the guy introduced himself at a party. I glanced out the windshield, where a thin line of semis forged a path down the freeway. They'd seen a hundred wrecks this weekend, most worse than this. None of them were going to pull into a closed weigh station to check on a single jackknifed truck, not when their own rigs still balanced on the knife edge of disaster.

I took the empty gun and checked the cab for other weapons, patting down the dead man and the living one, making sure Russell Ash remained unarmed. Then I left him to his makeshift cell and went to see what the semi was hauling.

When the cargo door opened, hitting the ice, a dozen boxes tumbled out of the back. Most were wrapped tight in plastic, but a few burst open. The writing on the side said CAUTION: DE-ICING AGENT, and I recognized the bags of white pellets that coated sidewalks and driveways everywhere this time of year, little balls of salt and chemicals that ate the ice and left a nasty white film coating the cement. I ripped open one of the bags, spilling pellets everywhere. Nothing. A sinking feeling swarmed my gut as I ripped open another, then another. On the fourth box, I found it. Hidden among the pellets were three plastic bladders the size of hot water bottles, stuffed with pills.

There were hundreds of identical boxes inside the truck. It was packed from floor to ceiling, and if even a tenth of them had pills it would be a staggering fortune, enough drugs to end a thousand lives and ruin tens of thousands more.

Grabbing one of the bladders, I skidded back to the Evolution.

Earl was miraculously uninjured—sitting as straight as he could with a lapful of broken glass while making a text-to-voice call to 911. He had a few cuts on his arms and face. Nothing serious.

I brushed the glass away and tried making him more comfortable as he pointed to the blood on my arm.

"Just a scratch."

Earl told the operator about the drugs while I inspected the weigh station, now a crime scene. The building was small, a single room with a toilet at the most, useless as a base of operations when backup arrived. The cameras mounted to the top of the station were coated in an impenetrable layer of ice, recording nothing, not even the white hills that glittered and dipped into the horizon.

I stared at the wrecked semi.

This was my ticket, my get-out-of-disciplinary-action-free card. The resources I'd wasted at the airport would become a distant memory when I delivered this bust. I should've been doing victory laps, but all the pills in the state didn't tell me what happened to Jonah and Eve. They didn't bring back Celina or explain why Alexis Dwyer's life had ended in a bathtub. As soon as Russell Ash and his load of narcotics were brought in, I'd be out. I'd file my report and watch the DEA whisk the entire case away, the fertilizer truck all over again. If I was lucky, the next time I'd see Russell Ash would be from the witness stand, where I'd flash my sling at the jury and give my properly grave two cents. If I wasn't lucky, he'd strike a deal, and I'd spend my life sifting through half-truths and speculations.

Dispatch confirmed state patrol was on the way. With the current conditions, they couldn't give an ETA.

"Copy that." I didn't take my eyes from the semi. "I'm going to make sure our guest is comfortable."

Earl tugged on my arm. Trying to stop me, I assumed, but he jabbed out a message on his notepad app. Find out what happened to Eve.

His grass-green eyes had filled with angry, unshed tears. Not Matthew. He wasn't asking about his flesh and blood. He needed to know what happened to his family.

I squeezed his bad hand with my good one and skated back across the ice. Climbing up to the driver's door, I lowered myself inside.

"Well, Russell, where should we start? Drug trafficking or murder?"

He didn't give me much, and what he did say were obvious lies. Kara Johnson killed Celina. Some geriatric farmer was in charge of the whole operation and he kept his network so hidden even the people who worked for him didn't know each other. He claimed he'd never heard of Jonah Kendrick or Eve Roth, that he didn't know anything about a hijacked airplane. I wanted to step on his arm again, to twist my boot until he whimpered the truth.

"Alexis Dwyer."

"I don't know who that is."

"I've got you on camera with her immediately before her death and a witness who heard you fighting."

That shut him up.

"Was she upset the operation was shutting down? That she wasn't going to get her three-grand-a-month storage fee anymore?"

"Lex was depressed. Talked about suicide a lot. Guess she went through with it." His eyes were flat and black in the strange half-light of the cab.

"There's one problem with the suicide theory." I leaned down, waiting, daring him to ask. "There was no syringe in the apartment. The piece of shit who ended her life took it with him."

A muscle jumped in his jaw. I smiled.

"We swabbed her fingernails. How much do you want to bet we'll find your dumbass DNA on her hands?"

Russell Ash glared at me with pure hatred and I knew: I had him.

Everything in me ached. I was running out of adrenaline. The wound in my shoulder sent pain through the whole left side of my body, to the point where I wasn't sure I could haul myself out of this cab again. But I was ready. I could leave Russell Ash behind and focus on what was important—finding Jonah, reuniting Earl Moore with his daughter-in-law. I wanted to go home and feel Shelley's arms wrap around me, to tell her I wasn't fine, that she should worry, that I needed help and I had no idea how to ask for it.

I stepped on the console and pulled myself through the door with my right arm, which almost gave out. Lurching to the side, I hit my hip against the doorjamb before managing to leverage my weight up and out of the cab.

On the ground, I leaned against the frame of the truck, holding the rearview mirror until my heart rate slowed. The sun glared off the windshield and from the shadows behind it Russell Ash stared at me, a wild animal finally caged. I was bruised, exhausted, and bleeding, but the hunt was over. I could finally breathe again.

Without taking his eyes off me, Russell lifted his head as high as he could, raising it to an awkward angle from his prone position on the side of the cab. He held the position for a beat, absorbing my confusion before bashing the back of his head against the shattered passenger window. I jerked up. He did it again. Swearing, I scrambled up the side of the cab one-handed, pulling my Glock out of the holster with the slick of blood and sweat coating my palm. By the time I climbed back up to the driver's door, the window was in pieces and Russell Ash fisted a long shard of glass in his bad hand.

"Put it down." My hands shook. The barrel of the gun wavered from his arm to his face to the smashed window behind him.

He smiled, teeth flashing white and sharp, before plunging it into his throat.

Jonah

"We all make decisions. Every day there's a choice. Most of us never know which one will be the last, the final thing we decide, knowing it'll be the thing that decides us."

Belgrave—the real Belgrave—stood over Matthew Moore, pressing his boot hard enough to Matthew's chest that air squealed high and thin out of his mouth. The barn had closed in around Matthew's screams, shrinking to the size and weight of a death throe, but the old man had taken a break from the boiling water in the thermos. He was here and not here, torturing his surrogate son and removed from it at the same time. I didn't know how long the wall around his mind would hold or the pits it would suck me into if it broke. He stepped harder onto Matthew's chest, and the supporting beam beneath the dying man shook.

"You get to know, Eve. It's a wonderful thing, a gift, to know this is going to be your last choice. Your moment. You can stand up in front of the Almighty and look him square in the eye, knowing you did the right thing, you protected the person you vowed to love, honor, and keep until death. It's up to you how long this death is going to take."

So far, Eve hadn't told him anything. She was in agony, watching as her husband flopped and writhed, but the faces of the people she loved burned in her head. A woman with hair like a river. Earl, strong and healthy, walking through apple trees covered in blossoms. Even Max's face was there, and Kara. The people she wouldn't sacrifice to Belgrave. She held them, the pieces her bruised brain could gather, quivering and tight.

"I told you the truth."

"Maybe part of it, but I know you, Doc. Better than you think. I'll find out what you know one way or the other. You get to choose how painful it's going to be"—he glanced at me—"for everyone."

I focused on the other people in the room, trying to separate the strands of energy around me. The bodyguard, a man almost as tall and wide as Belgrave but twenty years younger, had moved to the door. He was flat, stoic, ready to clean up whatever mess his boss made.

The black-eyed grunt holding me—Trick—reeked of obedience, too. His mind was dull and greedy, a pile of needs and animal instincts that would cow to the biggest alpha in the room.

I was least sure of Kara. She held Eve in place, her energy fractured with so many emotions I couldn't be sure if any of them were real or who they belonged to. Celina's face swirled in front of me in whorls of grief and anger and fear—Kara's or mine? I didn't know. She wouldn't look at me. She hadn't made eye contact since they'd come back in force, but her gaze jerked up as Belgrave kept talking.

"That girl made a better choice than you're making, Doc. She told me which DEA office she worked for and how she'd gotten close enough to my Kara to sniff out the fertilizer truck route."

I froze. Celina hadn't worked for the DEA. She was a waitress at an all-night diner. Didn't Belgrave know that? Or did he think that job was some kind of cover? I stared at Kara as a muscle in her jaw worked.

"We cut our losses to a minimum. Dropped that route and everyone associated with it. The DEA got a single dead-end bust for their trouble. I didn't fault the girl. She was doing a job, and in return for her good choice, I made it quick. No pain. She was a brave thing, too. Only made one last request, asked me to spare Kara. And I did."

Kara's fingers went white on Eve's arms. Celina's face became clearer, blinking alive then dead, then alive again, the vision of her filling the entire barn. The hole in the barn floor became a mouth, swallowing the last moments of her too-short life, twisting her memory out of the mind of her murderer.

"I wish I could've spared you too, Eve. I'm not like the god-damn cartels killing entire families and towns. That was never what we wanted to build." Belgrave eased up enough so Matthew could gasp, and a string of spit clung to his mouth. His head knocked from side to side, as though only vaguely aware it was attached to a body. His skin was blotched, a horror quilt of burns and bruises.

"Last chance, Eve. Tell me what you found."

Tears streamed down Eve's face. "I found a psychic who dreams of lost people." She turned to me. "And wakes to find them."

Belgrave unscrewed the thermos. Matthew screamed as another stream of scalding water hit him, this time in the face. The walls shuddered. Matthew tried to claw away, but the old man wasn't having it. He had at least a hundred pounds on his partner and he used every one of them to his advantage. He smashed his boot into Matthew's chest, and without warning I was sucked into his head. A flash of puppies stuffed in a sack. The mother hit by a passing car, the pups not yet weaned—he couldn't save them. Again the boot came down. Heel to sternum, to the lumps shifting under burlap. I didn't know where I was or who was dying. The pups whimpered, too small to even yip. He didn't like hurting them, didn't have a choice. More stomps, sickening liquid crunches. A board cracking.

Someone shoved me forward. I hit the floor, grateful for the pain that snapped me back into my own skin. Someone cinched my wrists with plastic. Zip ties. They didn't trust duct tape anymore. Eve appeared, inches away, as Kara bound her hands, too. And then it wasn't Eve. The form next to me became a bag of puppies, limp and buzzing with flies. I was free-falling through memories, tripping over racing hearts, sucked from image to image without any control or awareness of whose mind I was in. A cold torso hugged tight to someone's chest. An open grave and pile of clotted dirt, waiting, miles from anywhere. A spray of bullets. A woman crying. The bag of puppies moved, gasping back to life, and turned into Celina, lying facedown on the rotting floor, head turned toward me. She smiled through her tears, and her mouth moved, forming a silent thank you. For what, I tried to say, but she changed again, from a young woman into a ponytailed ten-year-old girl. The girl curled her bloodstained hand inside mine.

The steady drip of water surrounded us, seeping through the floorboards into the darkness below. The drainpipe was here, ready to swallow us as easily as rocks dropped into stagnant water.

I squeezed Celina's hand. I was ready.

Eve

Next to me, Kendrick's entire body shuddered. His eyes were glassy and unfocused, and a thin line of drool leaked out of his mouth. It was like the first time I'd seen him in the Iowa City police station. It might be the last way I saw him, too.

"What the fuck?" Trick stepped out of the way, as though Kendrick's panic attack could infect him.

"Seizure?" the bodyguard said from somewhere above my head. Matthew had stopped screaming. I didn't want to know why.

"Finish tying them up," Sam ordered, and Kara squatted over me. It felt like she was kneeling on my back. She pulled my hands behind me, making the welts around my wrists scream. A hard band circled my wrists, but instead of being cinched tight, the ends of the plastic were tucked inside my palms along with something else—a long, ridged handle with an edge of notched metal. The hand over mine dug into my skin, hard and insistent. Telling me something my fractured brain struggled to process. A new variable.

Someone walked across the barn. The motion moved through the floorboards and trembled underneath my cheek. I clutched the thing Kara had slipped into my hand. Energy. Everything distilled into energy, waves colliding, amplifying or destroying each other. The only trick was knowing which direction the energy wanted to move.

Like the barn.

It appeared in my head, the supporting beam of the barn we hadn't crawled across, the one that felt ready to snap underneath our weight. My heart, which had been pounding with terror and grief as Sam tortured my husband, slowed to a steady, determined thud. There were two groups of people in the barn, one on either side of the bad beam. I had to believe in the energy, to trust the knowledge that lived inside me and connected me to everything in the universe, whether my brain worked or not. But I couldn't do it alone. I needed more force.

"Kendrick."

He didn't hear me. His eyes stared vacantly, water seeping into freezing tracks across his gaunt face. He shook less now, but I didn't know if that was a good sign.

Sam spoke to someone, giving orders.

"Kendrick," I whispered as loud as I dared. He didn't respond. The clump of boots shook the floor and made the boards groan.

Before I could say anything else, Kara hauled me up to sitting. Sam was talking to the bodyguard, who handed him a long stick with a handle on one end and two prongs on the other. A cattle prod.

"I'm sorry you chose this, Doc." Sam—or Belgrave, the thing that was wearing Sam—turned to me. "Not the way I would've wanted for you, but I can't leave loose ends."

He took a step toward the bad beam, adding stress on the joist that held up that section of floor. I looked at Kendrick, willing him to get up, to move, to somehow register that he was still here with me and I needed him. Kara pulled me to stand, facing Sam as he closed the space between us. He lifted the cattle prod. I gripped the object in my hand.

Kara squeezed my upper arms. "Get ready to party."

Trick smirked, and that's when everything shifted. Kara lunged at him, grabbing his gun.

Sam and the bodyguard started. I dove to the floor, flipped open the switchblade Kara had smuggled to me, and cut the plastic tie binding Kendrick's hands. Energy exploded around us. Someone shouted. Shots blasted in the air, more than one. I dropped, flattening myself on top of Kendrick in time to see a body fall next to us. It was Trick, his mouth gaping open.

Kara charged the gap in the barn, straight for Sam and the bodyguard, who fired at her.

The noise echoed off the walls, an explosion of sound, and Kara stumbled over the crest of the bad beam. Sam intercepted her and shoved the cattle prod into her side. Kara fell. The bodyguard rushed forward. All three of them were on the beam. The wood buckled and moved like an earthquake.

Someone took the knife out of my hand. Kendrick. He was back. Rolling up, we met each other's eyes. Fractured wood filled my head, and in that split second, I knew he understood. He'd heard my thought. Two particles connected across space. I spun and he spun, too. Together we sprinted toward Kara, Sam, and the bodyguard, jumping at the same time, hurling ourselves as hard as we could on top of the beam.

The floor pitched, breaking underneath us. The bodyguard lost his balance, firing wildly.

Sam collided with Kendrick and the knife. His eyes blazed with fury and shock, the weathered cords of his neck bunched and straining. Then the world caved in.

Jonah

I hit the ground almost before I knew I was falling. Boards and bodies crushed together, breaking in snaps and screams. I tried to roll away, to get clear of the debris as more floorboards rained down and two more bodies tumbled over the edge—Trick and Matthew. The barn had swallowed us all.

Shadows. Gasps. A whorl of pain, bristling bursts of it everywhere, but none of it could compete with my leg, which felt three times bigger than it should, seizing white hot with every twitch of movement. I must've been shot.

"Eve!"

No answer.

A shaft of light from the broken roof illuminated the bodyguard, who panned his striker and sent a spray of fire in my direction. Blasts of light and noise turned me blind and deaf. I dove for the floor, reaching for Eve with my mind, trying to find her in the chaos.

Save her. I can save her.

I didn't know if it was my voice or Celina's anymore, or whether it mattered, if anyone was escaping this place. A bullet hit a board in front of me, grazing my arm.

The gunfire ceased and a strangled noise echoed in my skull. I lifted my head enough to see Kara in front of the bodyguard. He clutched his face, blood seeping around the gun and through his fingers. Kara lifted a two-by-four over her head. The board caught the light. It was dark and splintered, but it still had at least six nails driven through it, their rusted points jutting out from the end.

She slammed the board down onto the bodyguard's head. It crunched on impact, and when he fell, the board ripped out of Kara's hands to fall with him.

Something touched my arm and I whipped around, pain shooting through my leg as I braced for more horror, but it was Eve. She was covered in gashes, scrapes, and dirt. The throbbing in her head felt like something clawing and furious, but she was alive. She pulled me to a sitting position.

Kara picked her way through the shafts of weak sunlight. A trail of blood seeped from her shoulder, but I couldn't sense the injury at all. She didn't feel it. There was no pain in her. She didn't even favor the wounded arm as she bent over a body on the floor, checking for a pulse.

"Dead." She stood up, tracking the shadows. "Where's Sam?"

We found him next to Matthew, his eyes open and unseeing. The switchblade I'd buried in his chest was still lodged there. He had one hand closed over the handle, like he was waiting for us to turn around so he could pull it out and return the favor. I listened for any sense of the rage or righteousness that had poured out of him like bile. The puppies, even, whimpering in their burlap sack. I heard nothing.

Somehow, Matthew still had a faint pulse. Kara pulled a jacket off one of the dead men and draped it over him. She dropped to her knees next to Eve, handing her a few scarves.

"Can you wrap his leg and my shoulder? I'll go for help."

Eve did, binding both gunshots as tightly as she could. A noise from above made us jerk, but it was only a crow, flapping through broken rafters. Kara tracked its flight until it disappeared.

"The others won't be back. Sam always kept his killings quiet. The fewer witnesses the better."

"Where is she?" I moved into the shadows, searching the ground.

Kara didn't pretend to misunderstand.

"She's not here. Sam let me bury her, on a hill facing south, where she could feel the sun." Then, in a choked whisper: "She loved the sunshine."

The place appeared, conjured from the depths of Kara's memories. A flash of grassy hill, soft earth made into a final bed. It was quiet, open land, with unbroken fields rolling in every direction.

I can save her.

The voice. I'd thought it was mine, that oneiros call, but I finally heard it clearly. Her voice, her determination. They'd been Celina's words all along. She'd repeated them over and over to herself, right here. It had nothing to do with me. Celina had been the one saving someone.

"She did it for you." Everything crystallized as Kara stood up, pressing the binding wrapped above her heart. "You were the one talking to the DEA. Not Celina."

Kara nodded once. Her jaw worked. She was here, but she was also standing alone at a hillside grave, the field drinking her tears.

"And when Belgrave found out, she took the fall."

"It should have been me," Kara whispered. "Sometimes I hate her for it. I don't know why I'm here and she's not." Droplets of blood fell from her fingers. She didn't notice. We stared at each other, the seeing and the saved, the ones Celina had left behind.

Eve shrugged her coat off and added it to the one already draped over Matthew's body. "We need an ambulance."

Kara walked past me and disappeared into the shadows. Cracks ripped through the air, the sound of wood shrieking. She was beating down the cellar door, our only way out. The jagged mouth of the ceiling shook with every pound. Either the door would open or the barn would cave in on us. Maybe both.

"Danica Chase. Angela Garcia." My leg was a bolt of lightning attached to my body. "Kit Freeman. George Marcus Morrow." I crawled back toward Eve, over the pile of boards and bodies, my voice breaking on the last name. "Celina Kendrick."

The pounding turned to splintering. Dust rained down on our heads. Together, we faced the direction where the light would come.

One Week Later

Everything is theoretically impossible, until it is done.

—Robert Heinlein

Eve

A knock at the door. The force of clenched knuckles vibrated molecules of aluminum, sending sound waves pinging to my ears. My breath caught. I looked up from the box I'd been packing. At the table, Earl dropped his thermos of tea with a clatter.

It was late. We weren't expecting anyone.

Picking up the baseball bat I carried everywhere now, I went to the front of the house. I'd sprained my ankle in the barn collapse, and the brace clumped against the floor with every step. Part of me wanted to throw the door open, storm onto the porch, and meet whoever was out there head-on. The other part wanted to turn all the lights out, run upstairs, and hide.

"Who is it?"

"Investigator Summerlin." He lifted his badge on the other side of the peephole. I let out the breath I'd been holding, set the bat down, and unlocked the door.

"I'm sorry to disturb you." He was bundled up in a parka and stamping snow off his boots. A high formation of stratus clouds had brought snow yesterday, blanketing the city with an illusion of softness, but the ice hadn't melted. Doused with salt, covered in sand, and torn up in jagged chunks by the plows, it lay beneath the drifts, as dangerous as ever.

"Working late?"

"I'm off duty." Summerlin lowered his hood. One of his sleeves hung limp and empty, and the top of a sling shone white above the coat. "Can I come in?"

I locked the door and ushered him into the back. Summerlin looked around, taking in the sea of cardboard boxes, Bubble Wrap, and tape.

"Fixing to move?"

"We can't stay here." It broke my heart to give up the house, my weather station in the cupola, and the widow's walk. But living in the Victorian was untenable now that I knew what had paid for it. Natalia's plane landed tomorrow morning and she'd insisted Earl and I stay with her until we found a new place. I was counting the hours until she arrived.

"I hope you're not going far."

"I don't know. We'll have to see where we end up." Earl brought a bottle of water from the kitchen for our guest. He made a noise of inquiry, nodding to Summerlin's newly bandaged arm.

"It's fine. Same side as before, and the bullet didn't hit anything important this time."

The three of us were a sight: Summerlin's arm, the cuts and scrapes over Earl's face, my ankle brace. And we were the lucky ones. I glanced at the windows to make sure the curtains were shut. A month ago, it would have felt paranoid to think people were watching me. Now, I ruled out nothing.

We sat around the table. Summerlin scanned the pile of notes I'd begun collecting—a map of Iowa with pinpointed locations, a list of names and descriptions, the deconstructed elements of Matthew and Sam's pills—with a cop's cataloguing eye. "What's all this?"

"My other project."

I still needed to know how it had all happened, the forces that had destroyed our lives. Maybe I couldn't stop the monsters from coming, but I had to dissect them, to understand exactly how they worked.

It was more difficult than I would have imagined, not the work itself, but the bright, blooming ache behind my eyes when I concentrated on words for too long. The letters broke apart like a tornado had ripped across the page, forcing me to rest. I took breaks on my bed, closing my eyes to the skylights and breathing the concussion back. Everything this week had been about limits. How much I could pack before I was exhausted. How much I could research before my concussion throbbed. How many bites of food I could get Earl to eat before he wheeled himself to his room and locked the door.

"Did they get results on the samples yet?"

The local authorities searched Sam's entire property. Other than three dead men and an assortment of guns, they'd found nothing except fallow fields and equipment that had been winterized and put away for the season. No drugs. No trace of any illicit business. The camera in the barn had been set to a TV feed without recording any footage. They'd swabbed the wreckage for DNA, though, and taken samples of all the blood they could find.

"Nothing yet. It's in line, but it's a long line. Sometimes DNA results can take a year or more." I made a noise of disbelief, and Summerlin cleared his throat. "Seems they got an offer from the university to assist in speeding things up."

"I heard that, too." The entire department had rallied around me. Beside their eagerness to help test DNA, they'd handled all my final exams, grading, and student inquiries over the last week. Pawan hand delivered the results of the scorch mark samples, confirming the calcium carbide residue, and Natalia's biochemistry group threw themselves into full-blown research of Matthew's chemistry notes.

"I talked to Matthew."

"You did?"

Matthew was in the hospital for neurological rehabilitation. He'd gone into cardiac arrest in the ambulance, but the doctors in Des Moines had been able to revive him. They were treating his hands for frostbite and warned they might have to amputate if the tissue couldn't be saved.

We visited once. Earl sat at Matthew's bedside while I stood outside the room, watching as his chest rose and fell under layers of thin hospital blankets. After everything I'd done to find him, I couldn't bring myself to take those last few steps. I wanted to leave the ward, find Kendrick's room, and ask him what I should do. I wanted to consult a psychic.

Matthew hadn't been awake during our visit, but Summerlin said he'd spent several hours with him today. Earl and I leaned into the table, bracing ourselves.

"According to him," Summerlin prefaced, "he was shocked by Celina's murder and told Sam he wanted out. Sam was already paranoid about the DEA bust and responded by cutting Matthew off completely. That's when Matthew's cryptocurrency payments stopped coming.

"When Jonah and I showed up at Belgrave Properties not long after, Sam decided it was one too many close calls. He started liquidating the whole operation, emptying his stockpiles. He aimed to get out before he got caught. He moved the RVs, the inventory, the cash, everything, and told almost no one. Matthew and Kara worked against the clock to gather evidence before it was gone. They used Matthew's university access to run samples through the mass spectrometers, calling it prayer time when they arranged to meet there, and looked for trace contaminants that would help them track down his new storage facilities and identify suppliers. They wanted enough evidence to take down the whole operation."

They had all those drugs at the farm. Why didn't they turn Sam in with that? Earl asked.

"That would only point to Matthew. My guess is Sam knew that, which is why he left them there, for leverage. He didn't need to clean that out until Matthew's disappearance brought more police attention."

"Was Matthew telling the truth about Ryerson's Woods?"

Summerlin looked at the map of Iowa, the red point marking Iowa City. "He told me the same story he gave you, that he made plans to meet Sam and get him to admit to Celina's murder. Even with all they had on the drug operation, they knew it would've been hard to tie Sam to it as the head. Matthew wanted something more concrete to bring him down. We sent his burnt cell phone to a data recovery specialist to see if anything he recorded can be salvaged, but that takes a while. Overall, the story adds up. The diversion of the car fire. The location. Matthew said he chose that park because he knew the woods. He thought he could get away if he needed to, but it didn't go down like he'd planned. You know the rest."

It didn't feel like it. It didn't feel like I knew anything anymore. "Gail. The air traffic controller."

Summerlin shook his head. "The manager of the airport confirmed she'd worked there for over twenty years, never took a sick day or vacation. We believe she was getting paid to help coordinate airplane drops, transfers of product. After she diverted you to the other airfield, she punched out and never came back. We haven't caught up with her yet."

"And there's still no trace of Kara either?"

No young woman ever turned up at an area hospital or clinic to treat a gunshot wound. She'd vanished from her job and life in Iowa City as though—other than her university records, her haunted bird drawings, and the anonymous call she'd placed with 911 after the barn collapse—she had never existed.

"We've got a BOLO out on her. Hopefully someone's seen something."

Earl asked about Kendrick. We'd tried to see him after we visited Matthew, but the nurses said he was on a restricted ward and wouldn't let us in.

I toyed with the handle of my mug. "How is he?"

Summerlin leaned back in the chair. "That's exactly what he wanted me to find out about you. How you are."

"Doesn't he know?"

Summerlin smiled. "You got to know each other pretty well, didn't you?"

"We became . . . entangled."

It was ridiculous, impossible—but the past two weeks had reshaped my definition of impossible. Jonah Kendrick and I experienced the universe in completely different ways, but neither way was right or wrong. Both of our paradigms had limits and biases and in the end they'd brought us to the same place. We'd uncovered the dark truths in our worlds and survived them, together.

The investigator sighed. "Look, I understand what it's like to become part of Jonah's life, the possibilities that open up when you accept someone like him exists." He paused, pinning me with a look. "You need to stay out of this, both of you. Sam Olson, Belgrave, whatever his name was, he's dead, but his network is still out there, and we don't know how far it reaches. A beast without a head is still dangerous, maybe even more dangerous than it was before. A physicist and a retired farmer aren't going to slay this beast. I need you to promise you're going to step back and leave the case to me."

"How are you planning to protect Kendrick?" The hole in his leg had kept him—so far—from being charged with Sam's murder, but the local authorities found pills stuffed down his socks. He must've taken them from the plane for evidence. When the police took my statement, though, they'd talked about him like he was some unhinged drug addict.

"Jonah's different. He's gotten on the wrong side of the police and it's going to take a little more time to clear him. But I'm working on it. I've gotten him a private room at the hospital, away from other patients. It's the best I can do right now."

"Is it?" It didn't feel like enough.

"I know we don't know each other, but I'm asking you to trust me." He stood and pointed at the marked-up map and the list of drug traffickers who'd upended our lives in a matter of hours. "Get rid of this. All of it. And focus on this instead." He pointed at the boxes littering the floor.

"I can't just let it go."

"You won't. Believe me, when we get a case together, you'll be a key witness. Now, I've taken enough of your time. My wife's waiting for me."

As he left, Summerlin handed me a piece of paper.

Locking the door and picking up the baseball bat, I stared at the paper. I unfolded it gingerly, as though whatever was inside might vanish or combust. The handwriting was still new to me, but I recognized it.

Never seen anyone catch a tornado before.
What are you going to chase down next?

And farther down, at the bottom of the page:

Stop thinking so hard. You're giving me a headache.

The letters didn't break apart on the page. The words held together, their message clear for the entire distance of the light refracting into my eyes, the signals they sent to my brain, and the reaction transmitting along my entire nervous system.

I read it again, tracing the ink, and breathed. Earl sat with his thermos in the kitchen, staring at the map of Iowa, the home he thought he'd known. I set Kendrick's note down on top of the map. The next tornado on my list.

Acknowledgments

You wouldn't be holding this book if not for Stephanie Cabot. Stephanie, my dream agent, you are human-shaped magic and my life has never been the same since you came into it. Thank you for everything. All the books happen because of you. Thank you to Morgan Entrekin, Joe Brosnan, Sara Vitale, Zoe Harris, and the whole fabulous team at Grove Atlantic. I'm absolutely over the moon to be a Grove Atlantic author. Thank you to Claire Miller for being the best critique partner I could ask for, and for your delightful shock and horror at my murdery stories. Thank you to Helen O'Hare, for giving me truly transformative feedback on Eve and Jonah's story and helping to shape it into what it is today. Thank you to Nick and Melonie Lavely, who gave me a room to write in during the height of the pandemic and also corrected several errors in proofreading. No writer could ask for better friends.

I'm not a scientist—or a psychic, to be clear—and my knowledge of physics is on par with your average fourteen-year-old. My deepest thanks to authors Carl Sagan, Michio Kaku, Carlo Rovelli, Barbara Goldsmith, Neil DeGrasse Tyson, and Stephen Hawking, who wrote the popular science books and biographies I relied on for research. Any and all butchering of scientific theories, principles, or laws in this book is entirely my own. Thank you to the Wine and Crime gals—Kenyon, Lucy, and Amanda—who inspired the idea of Jonah with their true crime comedy podcast. (Episode 50, *Crimes Solved by Psychics*. Check it out!)

I am so grateful for my Saturday morning writing squad: Meredith Doench, Sharon Michalove, Geoff Herbach, Rebecca Brittenham, Margaret Dwyer, Sharon P. Lynn, and Kristen Gibson. You help me start every weekend right. Thank you to my family, my parents, my sisters (you too, Sean), nieces, nephews, and the most wonderful chaos demons any mom could ask for. Logan and Rory, you are my heart.

And, finally, thank you to readers everywhere. Your messages and posts give me life. The last 3+ years have been so hard in so many ways and while we don't know what's coming next, we will always have stories. Thank you for reading and sharing the literary love and for inviting these characters into your lives.